D1527066

Travis I. Sivart

Ætheric Elements:

The Rise of a Steampunk Reality

Travis I. Sivart

Travis I. Sivart

Ætheric Elements: The Rise of a Steampunk Reality

ISBN: 149124500X
ISBN-13: 978-1491245002

Talk of the Tavern Publishing Group

Want a free ebook?

Go to
http://www.TravisISivart.com/FreeBook

Travis I. Sivart

Contents

Dedication

For Ron, who made a bet with me over a pool table, I am finally paying up. For my brother Jay, for too much to mention and because I am still jumping. And for my son Aidan, who is my inspiration, support, and has taught me about love, life, and laughter.

Acknowledgments

Thanks goes to my editor and friend, Wendy L. Callahan, who is a formidable author in her own right. Without you, I would have been lost in many ways. Thanks to Chris Bartholomew of Static Movement for publishing my first story, which also appears in this anthology, and to Rebecca Snow who helped me get started and sent me the first submission request. A special thanks to my fellow author and trouble-maker, Tonia Brown, for all of her patient help during the middle of night, hers or mine.

Travis I. Sivart

Author's Note

This is a collection of my works which appeared in various anthologies and four original stories. When many of these stories were submitted, the editors often wanted something that took place in this world's history, and I complied. I have reedited them for this book to reflect my own world, including places, money, calendar, and other minor details. Some of the titles have been changed and the content double checked and cleaned up.

I decided to list the stories in the historic chronological order in which they happened in my world, except for the very first tale which is more of a prologue to set the mood. Discovery shows that this world has had visitors from other places, and they left traces behind. Final Entry shows the downfall of a long forgotten human society. PuppetMaster takes place approximately five hundred years before the stories which follow it and shows a bit of why the medieval world entered the Dark Ages, and is an excerpt from my medieval fantasy series, The Downfall. At this point I think it is worth mentioning that The Big Picture is also an excerpt, but from my Steampunk novel.

The remaining stories lead you deeper into this Steampunk reality, showing you the races, places, wonders, and terrors in the world. Each story gives hints and information relating to events in the larger world, and all of them tie together in some form, as well as being linked to my upcoming full length novel set in the same world. I hope you enjoy.

Travis I. Sivart

July 31st, 2013

Travis I. Sivart

"The right word can mean the world."

Travis I. Sivart

Travis I. Sivart

What is New is Old Again

I had thought to take the railplane. It was new, but it was a singular idea of modern technology. It was like the train I was currently a passenger aboard, powered by steam and rode on rails. Except it was suspended from a rail above the ground and had a huge propeller that made it two or three times faster than my current transportation. I had to settle for this more prevalent mode of transport because I was traveling the whole length of the country, across the northern territories and states, from Van Tinsvelete to New Philton. I was much more accustomed to traveling in a less public manner, but this time was too far to rely on horse or carriage, and my regular form of travel was very exhausting and much easier to get lost. A zeppelin would go the whole trip, but was not as fast, and cost much more. Also, I did not want to deal with the society elitists that tended to prefer them.

I stowed my pistol and other unneeded items in my private compartment. I ventured out, not liking the confines of a small room when traveling through such open country. I wore my wrist bracer with its dials, a thermometer, a time piece, and a compass in its own pocket. My red-brown sleeveless leather duster was open, leaving the brass buckles and straps hanging. My favorite hat was tilted back with the brim dipping to cover my eyes. I found the style in Southern Gallix two years ago in 6524. It was worn by a woman in a play called Fedora. In Teurone they teased me about wearing a woman's hat, but here in the North Mirron no one knew the difference. But to each their own; after all I mocked the current fad of goggles, except when they were worn at proper times such as flying, driving, or in hostile environments like deserts or the artic. To see an adventurer wearing them brought a smile to my face and made me want to buy the bearer a drink for a good story. To see a Bolton nobleman wear those on his top hat made me want to ask why - if they needed them for something other than fashion.

We were stopping in a station in Shy Falls, in the Dasism Territory, to let more passengers aboard. It had become much more populated since they discovered gold here a little more than ten years ago. I knew it would be divided up and given statehood one day. I watched as the ladies in bustles squeezed into the wooden benches of the coach class. Men sat sweating in their coats and top hats, crammed in beside prospectors and homesteaders heading back east for various reasons.

Claiming my satchel from beside me, I stood and offered my seat to an elderly lady and what appeared to be her grandson. She smiled her thanks with a small sigh as I tipped my hat. I made my way to the dining car, pushing past the crowd of new passengers. It was late and most would be settling down for the night. A nice brandy and maybe a pipe would be excellent at this hour. The dining car was a fine affair. Mahogany wood paneling covered the walls, tables and bar; highlighted with polished brass rails and crystal glass tulips over the electric lights. The new trains were amazing. The electric lights were actually a self-generated power gathered by turbines linked to the wheels. So the faster the train went, the more energy it had to distribute. It even had storage cells for when it wasn't moving. The steam discharge was also used and recaptured to help heat the water for hot showers. Moveable panels had been installed in the upper corners of the train cars. These panels would open on one side when it was cold and the steam coursing through the tubes that ran from car to car would heat the interior, or open on the other side to vent the heat out and let cool, fresh air inside during the hot days. Simple modifications made such a difference.

I sat at a table, not liking the 'center-stage' feel of a bar. This also allowed me to look out the window and not have to interact much with the other passengers. I drew my pipe pouch from my satchel and rubbed the well-worn leather with my thumb for a moment, deep in thought. Filling my pipe was routine, and I paid little mind to what I did. Dusting the tobacco off the table, I sprinkled it on top of the packed pipe to make for an easier lighting. Looking around, I drew a contraption from my pocket that wasn't well known and lit my pipe. The flame shot a few centimeters above my cupped hand each time I puffed. I could have asked the man with the handlebar mustache and apron behind the bar for a fag from the small stove, but I preferred not to start an obligatory conversation. I don't know how long I sat enjoying the rhythm of the tracks, when a faint shadow stopped at my side. A hand came into my field of vision, pointing at the other chair.

"Mind if I join you?" asked a man with a faint Midwestern accent. I looked up at him for a brief moment, and then glanced at the other dozen empty tables lining the wall. "You are smoking," he said, "I plan to smoke also. There is something about the 'Brotherhood of the Leaf' that makes me want to sit with someone that also enjoys the pleasures of a nice smoke. Besides, I know you won't complain about the smoke, and others are less likely to complain if we are both smoking," he said with a shrug.

I gestured to the other chair, gave a similar shrug, and puffed on my pipe as he set down a sketch pad and charcoal pencil and settled into his seat. I studied the man sitting across from me. The first thing I noticed was his wild hair. It had a loose curl and was neither slicked back nor trimmed short, but free. It was salt and pepper and I knew it would turn a wonderful white in time. His moustache followed suit and was a bushy affair that grew below the sides of his mouth, though the rest of his face was clean shaven. That face was lined with character that spoke of a life that had been lived to the fullest and I could see creases from frequent smiles as well as worry. He was about ten years older than me. From the pocket of his white jacket that was not neatly pressed, though not too worn either, he drew a cigar and lit it from the short candle in the crystal glass on the table. He leaned back and blew out a long stream of dirty grey smoke. We sat in silence and I returned to watching the shadowy landscape.

"It is a mystery of life," he said breaking my cogitation. I looked at him, eyebrow raised. He had a good voice, the kind that told good stories and made me want to listen, at least for a little while. "Can one man change the world?"

"Well, it depends how you mean that." My brow crinkled as I attempted to reason where his question had come from. I had done many things and had opinions on his exact question. I did not assume he knew me or where I had been, but I have a weakness for the great questions of life, and when someone opens a conversation with something close to one, I cannot resist but to explore their thoughts.

"Forgive me, my name is Samuel" he said extending his hand, his drawl very pronounced at that moment.

"Jack," I said, accepting his hand. His grip was warm and friendly, and lingered for a moment of rare human contact. It spoke of a man looking for answers.

"I just lost a dear friend and am returning home to Quarry Farm in the Empire from his funeral. And as such events will do, it has left me contemplative," he continued. I nodded, waiting for him to go on. "I think about the deeds of my friend and the people he left behind, and it is only natural, as humans are selfish creatures, that thoughts turn to my own mortality."

"I am sorry to hear of your loss," I uttered the common courtesy of sympathy, unable to think of anything better to say. After a moment added, "Tell me about your friend?"

"He was a man, like any other. He faced his challenges in life, perhaps better than most. We are very different men. He had his adventures when he was young; I had mine when I was a bit older. He wasn't much older than me though, a mere decade. We did have some things in common, we are both family men. My third daughter just turned four this summer, in Surem. His children are all grown and he is enjoying his grandchildren."

"You said he passed? You speak as if he is still alive."

"Isn't he?" He drew from his cigar, looking for a moment at the ash at the end. Waving the waiter to the table, he ordered a whiskey. "I will explain. He lives on in his deeds, his actions, and his legacy. Don't we all? Some men strive for greatness and become notable men in history, and we live in an era where history is being formed as we speak. Now, I don't think my friend will ever grace a history book, but I don't doubt his mark has been left. He was a forward thinking man and educated. He attended some University and had a military career. But I think he was best educated through his own efforts. But I do not think that is what makes a man." He drew on his cigar again and sipped at his drink, which had just arrived. "Do you believe in time travel?"

His question surprised me and it must have shown on my face. I fancy myself to have a good poker face, but some things slip past.

"Pardon me?" I asked.

"The ability to travel, not just through space, but also through time. Science has made many great leaps in the past few decades, and I think this is possible. And I think you do also. I noticed your fancy gadgets, also the odd colored mud that dried on those boots. That is not from anywhere near here, and I doubt it would stay on you for long enough for you to have traveled from someplace that has such soil."

"A bit of mud and a few brass trinkets do not a time traveler make," I said as I fumbled with my lighter, lighting my pipe again which had gone out.

"Oh, I agree. But your accent, your mode of speech, your mannerisms, and your singular reaction to my question makes me think there is more to you than you let on. Not to mention that unique tool with which you light your pipe."

"I am thunderstruck, sir."

"I think you are, but your eyes say I am not completely incorrect either. You see I have traveled three continents, piloted riverboats, and met many people. But none like you. That is why I sat here. Now, do not be querulous. I have no intention of exposing you, and perhaps I only want to believe it because of my current state of introspection. But I will have you know I am a Freemason, a member of the secret society Scroll and Key, and a member of the recently formed Society of Psychical Research. I even foresaw my own brother's death in a steamboat explosion a month before the event occurred."

He said all this louder than the rest of our conversation and I looked around to see if anyone had overheard. The room had grown quiet. As I looked around everyone began speaking again, and quite purposefully not looking in our direction. He laughed kindly.

"You see?" he asked. "They look away. They will not bother us. We are two eccentrics having a discussion in our cups. But I think perhaps you may have answers for me. I have a friend, Nikola, who does wonderful research. He made electric lights and many other tools available through his works, and he and I often discuss the very real possibility of time travel. He even works on a machine to make it possible." I stared at him and tamped my pipe, puffing to make sure it didn't go out. I sipped my brandy and sized him up.

"I don't believe time exists except in the mind," I said, thinking I would shock him. He nodded and leaned back in his seat, waiting. "Time, like any measurement was made by humans to explain our world, our surroundings, so we could better understand them. But when you define things you limit them, and that allows the impossible to exist. Without such definitions nothing would be impossible. And scientists that ignore such parameters are the ones that prove that the impossible does not exist, it is merely the undiscovered."

"Radical thinking. I am a very forward thinker also. I believe everyone should be allowed to have an education and an opinion. I support Women's Suffrage, Abolition, and Emancipation. But these are mundane conflicts compared to what you suggest." He paused. "I am still trying to fathom the full implications of what you are suggesting. If these things do not exist, except in our minds, what does that say for the rest of the physical world? Even our own bodies?"

"They are a form of definition also."

"So what is real?"

"Our minds. Perhaps our spirits, our souls."

"Do you believe in God, sir?" he asked, his eyes piercing me and I knew this question was a test.

"He is a measurement also. And by defining something like God, we limit it. Don't you think?"

He drew from his cigar and stared out the window for long minutes. His face went calm and the lines upon it went smooth. I could see him savoring the thought like the whiskey and cigar he held in his hands, considering it. He threw back the last of his drink and waved for another drink for both of us. We sat in silence as the waiter brought us our drinks and left.

"Perhaps Jack, but if we do not believe in God and the rewards and punishment that comes with that faith, would we not turn to evil ways?" he asked.

"Did you attend a college?" I asked and he shook his head.

"I educated myself in public libraries and through life."

"Yet you still learned without an institution. Religion is a fine institution, but it is not the only way to learn how to be good and moral. It is a way for others to control what you learn though, and how you think."

"I must agree. I often speak of how many evils have come from religious efforts: wars, theft, killing of whole peoples, and destruction of whole civilizations over a disagreement of the definition of gods!" His eyes went wide, "Jiminy Whiskers! There is that word again, definition. You have made me use it, enforcing your point. Well done," he laughed. It was a laugh from deep inside and heartfelt. He then asked a question, almost of himself, "What are you saying though? How does this relate to my original topic of my friend?"

"I don't know. I don't even know if this relates at all."

"Of course it does! That is why I was drawn to you. If time does not exist, except as a human concept, then he lives on. Forever, if you believe in time outside of time in the mind. Things come around again and again," he went on, now becoming passionate. "DaVinci thought of many things including submersible crafts and of flight, and now we have zeppelins and are developing flying machines, or so I have heard. My friend was part of the Air Corps you see, and my other friend Nikola says that with steam and electric we should be able to create machines that fly without a balloon attached. So what is old is new again. It is reborn with the spirit and defined by the mind."

We talked for many hours, about many things that night. I think he realized that no one is ever truly lost to us even if we no longer have them in our life. We all have a legacy; some are just more public than others. We all touch many lives and a simple touch is enough to change the world. He spoke of a world, places, and people I had not been a part of in a long time, but made me miss it and want to return for a visit. I don't know how he arrived on that train, but I am grateful he did. We never met again, but as we shook hands to part ways he left me with a parting thought.

"Perhaps I will write about you one day. A man that comes to a different place, a different time, with different ideas. And we will both have a legacy that others remember."

Discovery

Do you have any idea how long an octopus can live? Never mind, I will get to that. Allow me to submit my report for this expedition. It may read more like history in some places, because I don't know who will find this once I am gone, and I feel the need to be as complete as possible.

Our society was in a new age of science and discovery. The world was a shining object of hope and every country reaped the benefit of the advances in technology. Food was abundant and the energy was clean and no longer polluted our environment, as it had in the ages before. The wars and clashes which the different races once fought had also disappeared as it became clear we no longer needed to compete for anything. Steam, sun, water, and magnetics were the primary power sources now, which were renewable and clean, and only gave off natural byproducts that were absorbed into the environment with ease.

We flew through the skies in machines powered by our new resources. We began exploring the places which we could never reach before. We considered building machines that could escape the planet's atmosphere. Then we learned what happened when you mixed magnetics with harmonics. Portals. We had discovered how to journey to anywhere in the world by natural means in just seconds. Miniature holes in space which we could travel through, and they dissipated as easily and as cleanly as the steam that powered the ships and trains that traveled along the surface of the sea and land. We wanted more though, we wanted to go further. So we sought to extend our reach. Some wanted to travel to the moon, or even other planets. I was brought on as an explorer, scientist, and archeologist in the most far reaching of the programs. I would travel through time and space. This was different from traveling to planets, because these were places that normal telescopes could not see, though they did invent ways to peek into these other places.

The program had been active for a dozen years before we found other atmospheres compatible to what we need to survive, and I was chosen to be a member of the crew for the first exploration of a new world. Being the first to explore a whole new ecosphere was exciting. The scientific expedition consisted of three dozen others and me. We had the most advanced gear designed, much of it developed for this mission. Equipment to record the solar, magnetic, and other energy radiations, and body suits to help us fly short distances and survive harsh climates. Depending on the level of the threat we had magnetic guns that interacted with the nervous system that could stun creatures by disrupting the electricity within a body, or light guns which dispersed molecules and disintegrated organic material.

The portal would not stay open long because of the natural disturbance it created. We also would not be able to communicate directly with our home. They could check on us using their dimension-scope, and would open the portal so we could return when we gave the signal to do so. When they opened the dimensional doorway and we began our adventure, our gear was deposited in huge containers at the landing site. We followed and began setting up our permanent base. The containers became our shelters as we dispersed the gear inside, building our vehicles and sending out sensors. Natural resources were found as we traveled and we expanded our research stations when possible.

This place had much briefer solar cycles than ours, five-eighths times shorter. The seasons here were incredibly intense, and many areas on the planet were so inhospitable with ice that we decided not to even attempt going there at this point. We traveled on the oceans most often, enjoying the freedom they allowed us for travel. Traveling on land was restrictive due to forests, mountains, deserts, and other obstacles. At least with water we could go deep in a storm, or float on top for study. Either method was fine for travel though.

Life was abundant here. We found thousands of species in the first few weeks, including what appeared to be ancestors of the terrors of our own oceans, sharks. Just like the beasts that we had hunted to extinction on our own planet, these were mindless destructive beasts which only lived to eat. Within a month we also found mammals in the ocean, whales and dolphins. Each species were of varying intelligence, but we attempted to open communication with each of them. The dolphins were the most positive responses. Like similar species on our own world, they had not formed more than the most rudimentary of societies because of not having any way to manipulate tools besides their mouths. This is the one thing that made my species the superior animal to all others. We even found species that were so close to ourselves, we could only conclude that somehow our two worlds had some sort of connection that had been lost far in the past.

It wasn't long before we encountered a somewhat intelligent land dwelling native species. It was a primitive simian-like creature. We could see it had begun farming, using tools, building boats, wagons, structures, and using other animals for beasts of burden. There was much debate whether we should make contact, knowing the violent nature of primates in general. But the choice was taken from us. Our sensors went off moments before the rogue wave hit our research station. Not a real issue, our ship was built to handle such things. It rolled across the concentric circular walls and the drainage holes took care of the excess. Our gardens got a bit extra watering, which was fine because we only grew plants that were engineered to process the salty waters which we traveled, whether it was under or on top of the water.

When the wave subsided and the water drained we found a boat had been deposited in the third octrant of our vessel. We had no choice, except to help the creatures. We stayed in our exploration suits, feeling that would protect us if they suddenly turned violent. They were amazed and fascinated by us. They almost worshiped us. We moved their ship to the canals that were like spokes of the wheels of our vessel. Soon, they were on their way again. And that was the biggest mistake we ever made.

It was about a single cycle of this world when we next encountered these creatures again. It was a single ship, and it flew the same colors as we had seen on the previous ship we had rescued. We allowed them to come alongside us, and that was when they attacked. We were totally unprepared. They swarmed over us, and their purpose became apparent. They meant to disable our station. Dozens of other ships appeared, filling the horizon. They were like the horrid insects you found on land, distantly related to crustaceans such as lobsters and crabs, but with a hive-mind and swarm tendency.

In the creatures' ignorance they triggered our defense systems. Without an objective being set, our automatic security targeted the beasts attacking us, and fired upon our own vessel. Explosions rocked us as more filthy primitive creatures joined the fray. We didn't have enough time to do much except pull the plug. It was easy enough to sink our whole craft; it was part of the design and these creatures would drown. We floated to the bottom in a swaying manner, like a leaf falling from a tree. We took stock of the damage over the next few days. It was incredible how much destruction those ignorant savages wrought in such a short amount of time! Our ship was ruined. We had no navigation, propulsion, weapons, or power. Even the magnetic and solar reserves had been damaged and released, damaging our navigational and communication equipment and destroying them.

We had no choice; we had to leave with only what we could carry. We split up to cover more territory. We had to find our original landing site, deep on the ocean floor. Maybe we could send the signal and return home.

That was a long time ago. I have not seen many of my people, though I have seen their offspring. They must have mated with the native species which we hypothesized we are related to, because I can communicate with them. They have a similar pheromone dialect, as well as the innate electric pulse code which my species uses. Our descendants are not as intelligent or curious as we were, which may be a good thing. Our species is not what it was, living drastically shorter lives due to the atmosphere here - it doesn't nurture these mix breed offspring the way our home world nurtured us. I see the hatred and fear for the surface species has been passed down also. Some of the races grow to huge sizes and I have heard tales of them attacking ships on the ocean surface. Most of us just avoid them when we can. Other than that, our age old war with sharks continues. My larger cousins will still attack them on occasion.

In closing, I have lived for centuries of this world's time and I have watched the savage surface simians grow in power and technology. I have seen them imitate our technology in art and science. They now explore the ocean depths freely, and I am concerned that they will soon find the home portal and gain the ability to travel as my species once did. I pray that they do not find my world, though it may be inevitable. As I said before, the two places seem to be connected in some way. I never did find our base camp, but I hope another did and made sure that the link was closed so that these monsters can never use our own portal against us.

Final Entry

One way or another, this will be the final entry in a journal of humanity's fall. From the beginning I have chronicled the events since we found the actual Fountain of Youth. I shall now close this chapter in human history.

In the beginning it was an amazing thing. It had astounding restorative and regenerative abilities. The men who found it hid it well, even sending out missions to continue to search for it centuries after it was found. Lesser wells were found, but none like this. It would be many centuries after the Fountain was found before science would finally discover the properties of this God Water. It could not heal the sick - merely enhance your current state and put it in stasis of sorts. The health had to be supported though, and the ways some made sure they kept their youth created myths and stories that lasted millennium.

For hundreds of years they protected it, and as they continued to live they amassed wealth and power. They could not die and literally had all the time in the world. The way mortal men would play chess on a board, these men and women would play with the world as their plaything. They formed what became known as the Illuminati. They formed governments; they toppled kingdoms, all from the whim of men bored from centuries of time.

They could not get sick or be injured severely enough to kill them. Hunger would pain them, thirst would make their throat crack and bleed, but it was easy enough to bypass all that. They each found different ways. It seems that your nature decides how to replenish your body. I saw some men with dark souls, if I can even believe in souls any longer, which would feed on blood from the lesser species of man. I saw good men that replenished themselves with meditation and music.

In the thirteen hundreds a faction broke away, wanting to gift this to the whole world. They sought to share the source with everyone, but were blocked by the men in power of the site. Instead they turned to science and magic of the era, alchemy. They attempted to duplicate the God Water. It was a disaster and created the pandemic now known as the Black Death.

They brought new people into the fold over time, expanding their secret society. They brought in the elite, the beautiful, the rich, and the artistic. Some of the new, younger initiates did not agree with the established rules, and rebelled. They ran. And they were hunted. It was called the Inquisition. It was during this period they realized they had no way to reverse it or remove people from eternal life.

When science began catching up in the late 1900's and after, they began to uncover what it was that allowed them to live forever. They found it was a virus of sorts, but different than any other. It was joined between each of them and linked them, but had mutated into a new and unique strain in each person. It wasn't until quantum physics came into play they realized the full extent of this symbiotic life within them. It spanned worlds and realities. Some called it the God Virus and wanted to replicate it. They could not.

It started small, minor diseases which grew quickly out of control, until the virus would destroy other people's immune systems and deliver that health to the men that began the research. It was like a worldwide vampire system, with home delivery by carrier pigeon made of microscopic creatures. Once again they realized their folly too late.

It wasn't until the group split again, as it had done many times before, that things took a turn for the worse. The two groups bickered over who should have access to the Fountain of Youth. With the technology available, weapons were no longer personal though, and wars were fought from afar now. This one would not be any different. Politics, propaganda, and then the attack. It was a new weapon, it was not meant to hurt the huge protective structure, but instead vaporize the God Water source. And it did what it was meant to do, with unexpected results. The cloud that escaped from the ventilation system mutated again with the new radioactive elements introduced to it.

It traveled across the land, unseen and untrackable. It interacted with rain and electric storms. It was ingested by animals, plants, people, and machines. The machines became infected by the electricity in the air. Soon, life was changing. Humans became like animals, and vice versa. It was then that the governments began preemptive strikes and the machines rewrote their commands to suit their own newly born ideas.

I don't know if humanity will survive, but the men that started it all did. Hours ago I threw the last shovelful of dirt on their metal casket at the foot of the unstable volcano. One large metal container the size of a back-yard shed and made from a reinforced trailer. All forty-two in one container, in the dark, forever. I leave them to their well-earned fate. And I will cross this broken, blasted, and diseased land hoping to find a new start for humanity. Or my final rest, though that may not be possible, because I once had a taste of forbidden fruit also and may now be doomed to wander forever, unable to die of thirst, hunger, or exposure. I shall live in this hell I helped create.

Anonymous

Puppetmaster

He was almost always hidden from mortal eyes, but not this time. Many eyes sought him. He had many enemies; he reveled in that, delighting in the challenge. He thrived on the contest, and rose to face any obstacle. It made him feel alive. He cherished anyone he drove to rage, despair, or best of all, over the edge of sanity. Nomed loved what he did, which was why he was the best at manipulating and controlling people - his puppets.

The string quartet filled the room with the music of a dancing tune, light and airy under the domed ceiling that housed a dozen crystal chandeliers. Scented oils in the censers made the room smell like spring, even though autumn approached. Black and white clad servants carried silver trays laden with wines and brandies, food from all corners of the continent covered in savory sauces, and sweets swimming in syrups. The crowd spun to the music, graceful riots of color and jewels.

Always a flair for the dramatic, Nomed swirled his short cape, and spun away from a maiden he had lured to the dance floor at the grandest ball of the season in the Kingdom of Humbrey. All thirteen noble houses attended, as well as every small-time hopeful in the realms. All eyes

25

watched his graceful actions -- some with envy, others with desire; the movements he did without thinking were more than any other could do. The men watched with jealousy, and the women watched with lust. The charming man, who danced with the movements that could not quite be explained, was dressed simply compared to most of the men in the room. His cape was a basic black; his breeches, tucked into polished black knee boots, were a dark brown with gold buttons. A brown doublet over a cream-colored blouse – untied -- showed more chest than appropriate in a cultured gathering. Dancing without care, his pearly smile glinted in the thousand candles that lit the hall, his dark hair almost indigo and his eyes the deep blue of a stormy ocean. He smiled at man or woman, bowed to all, and startled, charmed, or confused everyone he touched.

Nomed knew what he did to people, and it made his grin grow, though he was careful that it did not become wolfish. He loved what he did, and no one could do it better. He moved from woman to woman, and stopped to kiss the hand of an effeminate nobleman. The man's face blushed under his powder as he fanned himself to keep from fainting. The aristocrat noticed a plain-sheathed dagger peeking from under the dashing man's cloak as he spun away to dance with another woman. Men openly wore daggers, swords, and other showpieces, often covered with gems and jewels, but Nomed's – with its utter lack of decoration -- appeared sinister and dangerous.

Plucking a glass of wine from a tray, and a spiced shrimp from another, Nomed moved into the night air, gliding onto a balcony with a rhythmic gait. Even his walk was a dance, and every movement drew people's stares. Popping the shrimp into his mouth, he leaned against the wide marble railing, sipped his wine, and watched the crowd. He spotted a man in a small knot of the upper crust's finest patrons. It was an older man, slightly round and graying at the temples, who carried a jeweled walking stick, the type men his age preferred rather than a rapier or other weapon. The noble stood talking with three others. Nomed grinned as he decided how to break into the conversation. He approached the group.

"Jaeken, I need to speak to you about matters of great urgency, the fate of the land is at stake," Nomed interrupted the discussion of the day: the comet in the sky, the Talisman.

Jaeken paled, staring at the man who had appeared from the night shadows. The other men looked back and forth between Jaeken and the stranger. They shuffled and looked towards the well-lit ballroom.

Nomed stared at Jaeken, and reached out to run a finger across a line of pearls sewn onto the doublet of one of the other men. He turned his head to look at the nervous fop as the man jerked away. The dandy's eyes locked on Nomed's hand in a mix of fear and excitement.

"Dandelos, you should return to your manor to check on your wife, Myrian, who was not feeling well this eve," Nomed's sly grin hinted of forbidden knowledge.

The man turn and fled the balcony.

Nomed turned to another of the men. "Candol, perhaps you should go with him to protect your son, Kinvin's, life when your friend finds him with his wife?"

With a cursory bow to the two remaining men, Candol also took his leave.

The third man began to excuse himself when Nomed interrupted, "Perhaps you should stay, Alixin. This concerns the church of Jonath also, and the horrors you bring upon others."

The two remaining men were taken aback. This unknown man, who had appeared from nowhere and spouted information each of them thought to be private, now insulted the church. Neither noble was a stranger to confrontation. They drew a breath, stood up straight, and steeled themselves for the encounter.

Nomed smiled, knowing what was about to come next.

"Lord Jaeken, do you know this man?" The second man was dressed in a long gray robe and wore the symbol of

Jonath the God of Justice,.

"No, Lord Father Alixin, I do not, but I do not like what he has implied of the church," Lord Jaeken replied.

The men puffed up and tried to comfort each other with their own importance and indignation. Humans were predictable. But then again, so were plays, yet Nomed kept going to see them. The men began the inevitable barrage of questions.

"Who are you, and why have you come?" Lord Jaeken asked, turning to face Nomed.

"That's really not important to you, Jaeken." Nomed left the insult of the lack of the man's title hanging in the air. "Something comes this way, and are you prepared?" Inserting himself between the two men, he took Jaeken and the priest by their elbows and guided them towards the railing. Both men, talking at the same time, sputtered the expected responses to deny what Nomed suggested.

"Gentlemen, stop," Nomed said in a quiet but strong voice, pausing by the edge of the balcony overlooking the city and gesturing at the night sky. "Humbrey has stood for centuries as the gleaming example of knighthood and all things associated with it. Now, it is rotting from within. You both have seen it. Jaeken, you have two sons, Cyril and Cyrus, who were closer to one another than your own testicles are to each other, and now they have split. The lads that is, not your testicles. Dire times indeed. I would watch your testicles just to be safe."

The Lord jerked as if slapped when his sons were mentioned.

"Alixin, you have been a priest for decades," Nomed ignored the priest's title also. "You have hidden your affairs with married women, never been caught siring children with those women, and now you have used your God's blessed gifts to do something horrible. You have created divisions between fathers and sons, and made brothers' love and trust become a weapon to tear them apart." Nomed watched the implication sink into Jaeken's thoughts. Nomed knew part of

28

what he insinuated was true, but often learned more by watching others mull over his intimations. It was fun watching others play with the thoughts in their heads, like watching a dog given a treat that tastes bad, but won't spit it out.

"This Kingdom is in danger," Nomed continued, "it is on the brink of destruction. The Talisman foreshadows many things to come, but some things can be stopped. I think you both have to consider the larger picture."

"What is it you are getting at?" Lord Father Alixin jerked away from Nomed's grasp.

"Alixin. Never has the church created such an atrocity as the monster you helped create from a loyal servant of Jonath, and the corruption that took seed from this abomination will lead to devastation across the land, great houses changing hands, and more than a few pregnant housemaids. Giving one man so much power is often dangerous, don't you think? And think what would happen if certain people discovered what you had done."

Nomed held the priest's gaze before pointedly turning to the other man.

"Jaeken, you have sat back and let petty politics keep your lesser fighting over scraps, and in turn this has made you impotent," Nomed smirked, "well, not in all ways, but politically it has stopped you from moving forward with plans that would have protected your allies from losing valuable assets. How would they know that your aloofness and concern for minor nobles gain made them fall from grace, and even fall prey to the schemes of the same men? What if someone heard about such things and let it slip to the right, I mean, wrong people."

This time Nomed held the Lord's eyes before turning back to Alixin with raised eyebrows. The two men stared at the interloper, then glanced at one another, dropping their gaze when it met.

"But the two of you together, that would be a force to be reckoned with. You would cover all sides and contingencies, forcing others to follow just so they weren't left behind. Your combined strength could move castles and counties.

"I know my craft well, and I love what I do. There is no one better at any craft, than someone who loves the work they do. And as you see, I love what I am doing here, which is bringing the two of you together, to help the greater good and save each of you, this country, and even the whole continent a whole lot of trouble."

"That's enough," Alixin said, his face clenched as if he had just suckled a lemon," I think we see your point."

"Yes," Jaeken fiddled with his belt, straightening his gloves and jeweled dagger, "what would you suggest we do?"

"Jaeken, use your influence. Rouse the knights of each of the thirteen great houses. Look to the south. Alixin, rouse the church. What happened may not have been your, or the church's fault. Much magic lies in Malvor, the city just south of Humbrey's lands. It has been secretive for far too long. It is time it spills some of its secrets." Nomed stopped and looked at each man. "Go now, no more arguments. It is urgent that this begins now, and the Changing Wheel will need time to grind out what it must."

The men turned and left; Lord Father Alixin with haste and worry in his steps, Lord Jaeken much slower but with a steady determination. Nomed almost felt pity for him, but knew the sins of the father were the sins of the sons. Soon Jaeken would be able to worry about only one, either his sons or his sins, but not both. Nomed smiled, the shadows enveloping him so that people no longer noticed him, instead walking around where he stood without realizing they did so.

The celebration sparkled and spun in its drunken haze as the night went on. Chill night air enveloped Nomed as the scent of sweat and sour wine wafted from inside. He was considering reentering the fray of a festivity, when he felt another presence in the darkness; it stole his smile from him. It returned a moment later, as he thought of the fun he would have if he could manipulate the man behind him.

Nomed turned and offered a wolfish grin.

"Duke Malvornick, how nice to see you again. It has been, what, twenty-five years or more since we have spoken, hasn't it?" Nomed asked.

Duke Malvornick stepped forward, the shadows touching him, wavering. Sometimes they flowed to meet him, other times they emanated from him in waves. The Duke was powerfully built, decked out in the finest silks and jewels; his brown hair was in a meticulous wave, shining in the dim light. Other men moved in the curtain of shadows around the Duke, but Nomed saw through the façade that hid their true forms. The beings behind Duke Malvornick were akin to demonic jackals in human form, and they were hungry.

The Duke circled Nomed, forcing him to either turn to follow him, or allow him access to his back. Nomed grinned wider at the juvenile tactic and stood still, focusing instead on one of the entourage trailing after its master. The beast stopped and leaned against a pillar, confused but not wanting to show it. Nomed watched it, letting his smile fade into a tight-lipped glare. The beast shrunk back behind the pillar as Duke Malvornick completed his circuit of Nomed and stopped, blocking his view of the creature. Nomed stared through Malvornick, in the direction of his quarry.

"Ah, it is good to see that you know not to look into the eyes of your betters," Duke Malvornick said, picking a non-existent piece of lint from his gem-studded doublet.

Nomed looked up into Duke Malvornick's eyes, as if he had not noticed him before. In a tone of stating a simple fact, Nomed said, "I do not notice rats, curs, or whores whose services I do not plan to purchase either. When one's ego precedes him, much as yours does, it is unnecessary to bother to see if you are preening or not. I was just thinking of you, and much like an upset stomach predicts stinking gas, here you are. How may I be of service to you, Your Worshipfulness?" He imitated and mocked the Duke's superior tone.

"I see you are watching my pet. Do you desire it? Perhaps

you miss the taste of the flesh that helped birth you?" Malvornick asked, as if Nomed had not spoken at all. "You remember what happened when you last crossed me, just a year ago, half-breed? All the people you were dealing with died. You wouldn't want that again, would you?"

"My dearest Duke, I do recall that. But you wound me. They died at my hand. How many city blocks did I bring to an end for the sake of destroying your fun? How much of your time and resources were lost in that endeavor in the city of Everyway?" Nomed chuckled. "Those lives meant nothing to me; they were well worth the price to watch you choke on it, and yes, I did watch. Right from the little courtyard and assembly you keep, with your drug-bought sycophants and power-hungry lapdogs. I sat amongst them and even rubbed the belly of a few of your favorites, and now they roll over for me upon command."

"Yes, you did destroy it, but I rebuilt it, and thanks to your actions, it is better hidden than I ever could have done myself. Once again, you were my pawn." Malvornick smirked.

"Until someone informed the brave city guards who discovered it. Now Grenedal Dragonblood was born and Hue Blueaxe was reborn, and I have again shut down your plans to bring more vermin into this world. Now, we can go back and forth on this for hours, days even, but I do not have the time nor interest in wasting time on offal such as you. If you have a point, please come to it; otherwise, please expire." Nomed turned and sauntered towards the pillar that hid his earlier quarry.

"You would be smart not to turn your back on me, half-breed!" Malvornick growled, his silk gauntlets turning a metallic silvery gold swirl of color, spikes growing from them. "I can destroy you whenever I feel the urge,"

"Then do so, Malvornick, or go away. I doubt you want to harm your image here in Humbrey though. You may be able to destroy many people, but could you handle the whole righteous Kingdom at once?" Nomed turned and considered at Malvornick with a bland stare.

"They would destroy you if they knew what you are. Without hesitation, they would end your miserable little existence," Malvornick said, turned on his heel, and began walking into the lit interior of the ballroom.

"Perhaps so, Duke, and perhaps one day it will happen, but today is not the day. Your plans would spoil if you moved to take action against me now. Ever wonder how much I know of those plans, Duke?" Nomed asked to the Duke's back as he left earshot.

The next morning, more than a dozen men, women, and children were found dead in the streets of the capital of Humbrey. They had been violated and torn apart, many found partially eaten by teeth that did not belong to any animal. The authorities could not find any witnesses or survivors. One death they did not discover was in the rooms of Duke Malvornick. One of his entourage was found dead of natural causes, odd for a creature that could not die in a natural way. The only mark was a smiley face traced on its left buttock with a grease pencil left planted in the creature's arse.

Three days later, and hundreds of kilometers south of Humbrey, Nomed waited underneath the city of Everyway for a man. He knew the man - if that is what you wanted to call him - would be coming. Nomed's spies and magics had warned him well in advance. The tunnels under the city were cool and humid from the runoff of rainwater. Odd echoes often led any unfortunate enough to get lost in the forgotten halls to their doom.

A rat scurried along the edge of the room, watching the large man on the gray stone dais. He was as still as the stone itself, but something emanated from him that made the scavenger keep its distance. The man stared down the long square hall in front of his seat, and watched it fill with the shadow of the one for whom he had been waiting to arrive.

Nomed leaned forward and looked closer at the man in front of him. The new arrival's skin was gray, a definite change since last time they had seen each other. The extra foot of height was even more defining. The man had shown surprising resourcefulness in finding Nomed, something even the most powerful people in Everyway could not do. The guest smelled of powerful magics, and of something more ancient and dangerous.

"Nomed, I didn't seek you out to banter or have some sort of competition of ego or wit," Grenedal Dragonblood said, striding into the room. He stopped three paces from the other man.

"Fair enough, I am in no mood for that anyway," the demon-kin said with a wave of his hand. "So where are your wings? I heard a rumor that you have wings now, and that you fly over fields and steal sheep for snacks. You aren't going to cough up some horrid bloody cotton ball, are you?" Nomed grinned.

"The priest named Cyril, which you sought," Grenedal said, ignoring the other man's taunting, "I have found him. He is going for his God's ultimate temple. I think others may know about this too."

Nomed cocked his head, his smile slipping into a look of boredom. "Why should I give a hairy nut's handy damn about some priest?" Nomed sighed. "The other-worldly blood in me veritably boils to think of any do-gooder priest."

"Don't play games, or if you must, at least wait until I have left to play with yourself. Great evil spills from the comet, Talisman. Unnatural things come to the lands, and though the people fight it, they need leaders to stop them from squabbling amongst themselves and powerful allies to help them in the coming war. No matter what happens, good or bad, it is guaranteed to change the face of the land."

"I know what it means. Is your tongue becoming forked too? I see your skin is etched; are those scales?" Nomed asked and the man, giving a frustrated sigh, turned to leave when Nomed spoke again. "Spend any more time strapped to huge machines that drain magic, Grenedal Dragonblood? You were just a man before that, weren't you? I am just curious if your change is accelerating on its own, or if you have had more of the treatment that activated your heritage in the first place. Your dragon heritage. It must have been a hell of a woodpile to hide that relative in it."

The visitor turned back to Nomed, his cloak rustling and bulging. Nomed smiled a charming grin; glad finally to get a rise from this man who could track him down when no one else could. Grenedal raised a clawed hand and pointed at Nomed.

"You know about that machine? What else do you know of it? What did you have to do with that?"

"Nothing. I know there are others like it in the city, hidden in sewers and basements. I had nothing to do with it, though, except being the cause of its existence. It was made by the Troöds to drain people of enough magic to draw demons to this plane and blend them with people, like bait in a rattrap. It is nice that you and your friends broke it; I really don't want my kin showing up and ruining my fun. It seems that the frisky little bastards who dreamed up this scheme are still out there though," Nomed said, leaning forward in his armchair.

"No," Grenedal sliced the air with one clawed hand, "I will not be distracted. I found you the same way I know how to find Hue Blueaxe, your balancing counterpart. We three are connected, but you two only through me. We need to be prepared to fight. I warn you, you will help, or you will perish."

Dragonblood turned and, in one movement, stepped to the end of the tunnel, a step that was more than a fifty meters. Nomed lurched forward, his eyes shifting to the spectrum of magic that would tell him more of his guest. A wide set of wings unfurl from beneath the man's cloak as Grenedal took flight upward and out of the well that served as entrance to this hidden place.

Grenedal Dragonblood, a man who had been changed by time and magics, watched. In the Kingdom of Humbrey to the north, was the Duchy of Velent. It was the southernmost noble house of thirteen. It was on a small stretch of land between the Lost Swamp and just north of the border of the Kingdom of Trysteria, and the Duchy of Malvor. Duke Malvornick was often seen in Velent, and was recognized to be a close friend of the Duke and Duchess. To the north of Velent was the County of Trism. The Count often appeared in Velent, also, but did not seem quite as friendly as the southern Kingdom's Duke did.

At that very moment, the Count was leaning close to the ambassador from Malvor and whispering. They both looked up, at the same time, at the man watching them.

Grenedal looked down, staring at his skin. The lines on it had become deeper and more pronounced in the past year. People thought it was hair that was on his arm, but if you looked closely, you could see that the lines were too close to the skin and too uniform. They resembled scales more than anything else. In the shadows of the evening festivities of the Autumnal Equinox and holy day of the Changing Wheel, few people noticed the oddities. People noted his height though, which was more than two meters tall.

Duke Malvornick had plans for this Kingdom, but Grenedal knew not what those plans were. The dragon-kin could not counter any of the Duke's intentions without that information. Grenedal was good at getting information, though, and had spread enough coins through the hands of others in the past few days to buy a fourteenth noble house in Humbrey. Soon, information would begin to trickle down to him. Once it did, he would piece it together and start to ask the questions that would uncover the well-hidden schemes of Malvornick.

Lord Jaeken stood by another noble. The aristocrat had

been making many visits to Velent lately. He had not been sending messengers or knights, but rather attending the meetings himself. Both of Lord Jaeken's sons had disappeared, and each of them had once been priests of Jonath with promising futures. The Lord spoke with great feeling, and the Earl listened to every word he said.

Grenedal turned to his companion. They had dressed for the celebration and wore matching finery in golds, browns, and yellows; his breeches and vest tight and creased, her gown full and flowing. A slim woman with exotic features, she sipped at the crystal chalice of wine, eyeing the men in the room with an almost predatory gaze.

She noticed him looking down at her, and raised her glass in toast. "Well, Lord Dragonblood, here is to the upper echelon living up to its exciting possibilities."

"I know what you mean; there is a reason I wasn't disappointed when I was disowned. You missed nothing by being raised on the streets."

"But you got it back easily enough."

Grenedal glared at her for a moment, and shrugged. "My whole family being murdered was not necessarily easy. At least, not for them, I would guess. Ironic though, if they had not sent me away, they would all still be alive."

"You sound like you had it done for the sake of revenge."

"You know where I was when it happened, strapped to a machine that killed most people in less than a week. You found me there, three months after you lost me."

"Yeah, but look what came of it." She snaked her arm around his body. "Tall, dark, and handsome. Not to mention the magic you now have. That machine brought out more, much more, than just your family's dragon blood."

"We don't have time for this. You have a job to do. Talk to the Earl; find out what Lord Jaeken has been doing. I will put a tail on Malvornick's envoy."

"Oh, you have a tail too now?" she asked, her hand slipping to his posterior.

"Go on, and don't use your real name, Kaht." He pulled himself free of her groping hands.

"Have I ever?" She sauntered into the crowd, every male head turning to watch her sinuous movements.

When Kaht returned, she told Grenedal dire tales of Malvornick's plans to overthrow each land in the north, and control all the people. Rumors of hordes of monstrous beasts and dead in the land added to the urgency of bringing leaders forward to guide the people. It was in Grenedal's dragon blood to plan for centuries, urging him to look beyond the lifespan of a single human. They would need to travel north to Trism, to find allies.

The County of Trism was the third most powerful house in the Kingdom of Humbrey. The House Trism had come to power more than three centuries ago after fending off a horde of reptilian men from the Lost Swamp to the west, raising the fifth noble house in the Kingdom. The Count of that time quickly opened trade with the city of wizards, Pantageas, to the southeast and allowed them access to the dammed Weird River. Five generations ago that Count helped establish the Duchy of Velent, seating the final noble house in the Kingdom, giving a crown prince his own lands and a debt of honor to Trism. The two noble houses had been allies since.

The latest Count of Trism, Yearl Marshlord, had opened trade agreements with the Kingdom of Trysteria to the south and east, including the Duchy of Malvor. His house had flourished under this trade agreement, and he had been knighted for his efforts. There was even talk of the marriage of his son and a royal princess, which would make Trism a Duchy. Count Marshlord was a moral man who always saw to his duties, and tended to his people and trade agreements without hesitation. He wanted to bring his house honor and glory without having to fight a war.

A light snow dusted the sprawling streets of Trism. The metropolis's stone buildings were a picture of serenity. The setting sun gave way to chill winds and moonlight reflections, making folks want to be inside with a mug of hot mulled cider and good company. Music and laughter spilled out onto the snow-sprinkled avenues from pubs and taverns, along with the amber light of oil lamps.

In an alley, an undernourished dog sniffed at the back door of a pub. The door opened and a sweaty man in a stained apron emptied a bucket of kitchen scraps across the cobblestones. Hands on his hips, the fat cook drew a deep breath of air that wasn't heavy with smoke, enjoying the crisp bite of autumn. The animal crouched, growling, as its hackles rose. The man looked down, seeing the dog for the first time. He shouted at the cur to scare it away. The mutt crept forward, showing its teeth through foam-flecked lips. The unnerved man retreated inside, and slammed the door.

Grenedal glanced down the alley as the dog began nosing through the scraps. The cur glanced his way, whimpered, and slunk behind a barrel as the man trudged through the slush, leaving shallow boot prints that would be covered soon enough. Dragonblood had been in Trism almost three weeks and had learned a lord was raising a resistance to stage a coup from within the court of Trism; that lord had gone missing; and the local criminal syndicate had been infiltrated and was under the control of an unknown crime lord. Grenedal knew who it was though; it was the same man that compromised the loyalty and honor of a kingdom legendary for those traits: Duke Malvornick.

Grenedal had never been good at digging up information, but Kaht had a way of digging up things that he couldn't. Whether by intimidation or by bribe, Grenedal always pushed too hard. He was an expert at putting information to work, though. He had sent his companion back to Everyway, tasked to find Hue Blueaxe and bring him here to Trism. The giant man would be more prone to get along with the men here than Grenedal. The dragonkin believed in being more flexible with the law and rules than the people who lived in this country. Hue would feel that the law was sacred, just as the locals did.

Grenedal walked along with his cloak pulled around his wings, sluching to hide them, still unused to them and not wanting to attract attention. His family name was Dragonblood, but he had never thought it was literal, until his 'awakening'. Since that moment, he had changed every day, not just physically, but in other ways also. He could feel the magical force lines that were tapped by wizards; he could use the magic of his own mind like the mages; and even the art of sorcerers and alchemists were not out of his grasp. He found himself sensing other things - communications flying through the air. It was as if someone was sending messages and he was receiving not only those, but the responses from the other party. He couldn't recognize the language, but it was familiar.

He made his way to the appointed place where he had instructed Kaht to send Hue. It was an hour after sunset and he was at the statue of the realm's greatest hero, Trism the Bold. It had been five days since he sent her. It was two hundred kilometers to Everyway and would take about twelve days to reach it on horseback, but Kaht had other ways to travel, and she may have made it in two days, then three days for Hue to travel back. Pantageas, the city of magic, was due south. The right amount of coin, and one can be transported almost anywhere, but the right amount was a lot. It should be possible that Hue was here; he also had other ways to travel.

Standing in the growing snowdrift in front of the statue, Grenedal watched stragglers hurry home. The sky lost its remaining light as the sun set, and dusk turned into night. He saw Blueaxe approaching from a distance. The man had an unmistakable stride, bold and confident, and the double bladed axe strapped to his back jutted out past his broad shoulders. He was a giant of a man and his pale blue skin glowed in the dim light.

Grenedal remembered when Hue had been a blind beggar man, nicknamed Smiles. The man had always been happy, even though he had been on the bottom rung of the social food chain. When the Talisman had appeared in the sky, abominations had crawled from unknown places. The dead rose up and walked the streets. The elderly and young caught outside were exposed to the magical emanations and transformed into mutated horrors, and Smiles had become one of them. Grenedal and Kaht had found him in a room of living dead, recognizing him as one of their street informers. They had slain the rotting monsters and brought Smiles back to a safe haven. Finding a sorcerer to help had not been easy, but Grenedal's sense of duty drove him. Drawing upon the energies of another realm, the sorcerer had healed Smiles. When the homeless man had awoken days later, he was changed. He was in his prime once again, and took a name from that time in his life when he had been a gladiator. Hue Blueaxe returned, but changed by the powers that touched him. Grenedal guessed that the Gods decided to help equip the world with people who would have a chance to face the Talisman and all it brought.

Hue smiled at Grenedal as he walked up. The blue-skinned man stood a few centimeters shorter than the dragonkin, but was more than a hand span wider. He wore a sleeveless tunic and wool pants. It was hard to find boots in his size, so the man had made a pair of simple sandals. The cold didn't seem to affect him.

"My friend," the blue skinned man said, "Kaht said it was urgent. What is it?"

The taller, thinner man explained in hushed whispers all he had learned, that there were men gathering to face Duke Malvornick and break his hidden hold on the Kingdom of Humbrey. He gave his axe-wielding friend the names and secret meeting places, and imparted the urgency to him.

"Gather allies; lead them north, warning of Malvornick and his plans. You have to organize them if we are to survive the darkness of the Talisman and the horrors it brings."

41

As they stood talking, their heads bent close for secrecy, the sounds of rapid hoof beats and a crier was heard approaching. He charged straight through the square, shouting his message, and kicking snow up behind his mount.

"Velent has fallen!" the crier yelled. "Demon bugs attacked from the Lost Swamp! Prepare! Beware! They come this way!"

Velent was a day ride south; less if you changed horses on the way. Magic could have been used to send the news quicker. It was a few hours east of the Lost Swamp, and Trism was about twice the distance. Hue and Grenedal looked at each other.

The mangy cur from the alley crept out of the shadows, hackles up, its snout twisted in a snarl. The two men turned to look at it. It stood on its hind legs, and began to warp and change. In a moment, Nomed stood where the beast had been. The demon half breed smiled.

"Gentlemen," Nomed said, nodding to each of them in turn, "did you plan a meeting of half breeds without including me, your brother in this odd triangle of fate?"

"Nomed," Grenedal muttered acknowledgement, "we don't have time for you and your games."

"Nomed!" Hue took a large stride towards the demon spawn, grabbed his hand in greeting, and pumped it up and down while slapping him on the shoulder with the other hand. Nomed stumbled under the power of the greeting. "You're always welcome if you come to help, my dark friend. Don't pay any mind to Grenedal, he forgets hope and happiness when he's under pressure. Always gets too serious and forgets the small things."

"Yes, good to see you also, Blueaxe," Nomed said, straightening his leather cape over his bare chest. "I am here to help, Dragonblood. Don't be so snotty. I can be of great help. I witnessed what happened in Velent, it wasn't pretty. And it is coming this way. In fact, it should be here in just a few minutes."

"Then we don't have time for the simple things, like idle conversation," Grenedal said to them both. Turning to Hue he continued, "Go to the people I told you about and gather them, I will check into this new menace. I will find you again."

"Godspeed, Grenedal, and be careful." Smiling, Hue slapped the taller man on the shoulder. Grenedal threw his cloak from his shoulders, and it settled down the middle of his back. His leathery wings unfurled and he launched himself into the cold night air.

Nomed grinned as the two disappeared into the night. As he turned, a dog stood where the man had been a moment before, and loped into an alley.

The people of the County of Trism were bewildered. The news of Velent's destruction stunned them. They gathered in the town squares, taverns, and inns, wanting to know more, to find out it was not true, to learn they were safe, and Velent alone was threatened. A mass of people congregated in the massive square in front of the city hall.

Count Trism was present, with High Lord Father Alixin of the Church of Jonath. They calmed the crowd, saying that the news was exaggerated and Trism was safe. Even if such a threat did exist, even if it did come this way, they were prepared for it, and would deal with it quickly and efficiently. They were still making speeches when the first swarm hit.

The temperature crept up and the weather changed from snow to a light rain. Yearl Marshlord rallied the people, calling for them to hold their places and defend as one. They ignored his pleas, and in a panic, pushed past him, knocking him aside, rushing to get into the solid stone building that housed the government. Clouds of minuscule biting gnats swarmed the crowd. As they descended on the people, they left barely perceivable traces of digestive acid wherever they bit. A woman was bit, and it left a red mark. Another bite left a small dimple. As thousands bit her, her skin became a pitted, burning landscape in a matter of moments. She slapped and crushed the bugs, but it did nothing more than release extra acid from the insects onto her skin.

The press of people jostled the Count, and he was heaved off the stairs, falling to the wet ground under the great statues that bracketed the marble steps. Relieved to be out of the throng of maddened people, he looked around for his guards. He spotted them, but they fell victim to the black clouds of insects. He saw the Lord High Father calling upon the power of Jonath, bringing protection from the insects for the mass of panicked townsfolk. He saw the priest's silver aura glisten in the falling rain as the he called upon the powers of the earth to destroy the invaders and save his flock.

The attack intensified. Mosquitoes the size of squirrels flew into the crowd, unaffected by the spells of the priest. Alixin called upon the power of his god once again. His prayers were ignored. Instead, all he received was the attention of the new wave of pestilence. The blood-sucking insects had already fed on dozens outside the building, and now turned their bloated hunger towards the being that slowed their feeding with his magic. The priest called upon Jonath again, screaming for the god to protect his most valuable priest, to save the one man who could allow the church to survive.

The result was astounding. A flash of light shook the square, magic shot upward and out from the priest, and died without a sound. The church of Jonath that stood across the way began to tremble and the keystone fell from the overhead archway that led into the temple. The god had spoken; as the magic faded from the cleric, the church collapsing, dust rising into the sky.

The Count stared in horror as the priest turned and began throwing people out of his way, forcing his way into the safe haven offered by the building. He rose up to tell the Lord High Father to stop, and to help the people. As

Marshlord stood, the ground opened up, and hard-shelled black beetles swarmed over him.

Fog formed and rose from the cold cobblestones of the streets as the warmer water fell. From the murky haze, came more bugs. Rising from the sewers and crawling from rotted wood throughout the city, they came. Silverfish longer than a man's arm swarmed across plazas, snapping at people with their thin mandibles. Cockroaches the size of cats flew from rooftops and landed on people's heads and backs, biting and chewing, their rancid stench surrounding them as hundreds covered a city block.

The mutated insects of the Talisman arrived next. Long thin flying insects that radiated heat and crackled with energy flew overhead, alighting on buildings. They pressed their abdomens to the wooden shingles and the thatch of roofs. Steam rose, and the wood and straw dried smoldered then ignited. The wind fanned the flames as another horror slithered across the cobbles. Centipede-like creatures glistening black in the fire's glow glided by, leaving a slick trail of what appeared to be mucus. Anyone who crossed the path of one was attacked. The beast would wind its way up their body, a thousand tickling legs clinging to flesh, then sink its cruel barbed maxilla into softer tissue of its victim's throat and neck.

The sparks from the flames on the rooftops rained down on the slick trails left by the giant centipedes, igniting them. The rain flowed through the gutters, carrying the gelled flaming liquid to alleys where trash lay. Soon the city was ablaze. The guards trying to fight the insect invasion now were needed to man bucket brigades to douse the growing inferno. Townsfolk abandoned their homes, carrying children and their most prized possessions, only to be brought down by the man-eating insects.

It was into this chaos that a rider from the east rode, to deliver his news of the approaching undead army that had claimed the Earldom of General the day before. The city would have to face two armies that could not be routed or demoralized. Two behemoths of unstoppable death were about to meet.

The undead horde shuffled into the city on cats' feet. Silent in the moist night air, their fetid stench announced their arrival. The zombies trundled through the streets, dragging down anything warm blooded and moving. Swift predatory shapes leapt from rooftop to rooftop and slid down darkened alleys, pulling out humans who tried to hide and devouring them, ripping into flesh to satiate their unquenchable hunger, and savoring their victim's struggles. Their appetite never ended, but they only ate until their prey no longer moved. They preferred a warm meal, and death only brought cold.

Rondarius's generals moved through the crowds, picking and choosing their victims from the strongest. The hero who stood in the mouth of an alley with a line of archers behind him soon fell, as Omega took possession of an archer behind him and fired arrows into his back. The Wizard who burned the undead and insect armies with flames turned to find the cold lips of Choulidiat waiting to drain his very soul. Lord Emite swept through the city with his three progeny as shadows that rose up to kill, feeding as they went.

The necromancer sat just outside the city, finding the dead inside of it that had the seed of magic and raising them to join his army. He cackled from his divan, then screamed and beat at Vicktor, "You filthy dog eater! Why does it always rain when I destroy a civilization?" He immediately laughed again and sent forth the command to his legions to save the pretty girls for him. Winter was the time for warm bodies to share his bed, not cold ones.

Hue met a group of mounted, armed, and armored men at the edge of the city. The commander was preparing them to charge into the city and fight the monstrosities that had arrived. The officer saw Blueaxe, and nodded in recognition.

"We are yours to command, my lord," the captain said. "Shall we form ranks and enter the city?"

"No, my friend," Hue said, hanging his head in sadness, "we have a greater duty today. We ride north and west. We gather all the men we can, tell people to abandon their homes, cities, keeps, and castles. There is no stopping what's happening. We would all just die in the attempt. We will bring what people we can into the frozen north, and try to survive. We will entreat the barbarian chieftains to join us, or at least shelter us through the winter. The dead and insects won't be able to survive in the cold tundra during winter, and we will have months to gather our forces and plan our return. This land is lost though, and I grieve to say it."

The two score of knights and soldiers looked stricken at the news, but the grim-faced commander, a man of many battles, nodded in understanding. Issuing sharp orders, the captain lined his men up in ranks of four and spoke to them, explaining the chain of command. Hue Blueaxe was their general until this war was past; Lord Jaeken of the resistance and his compatriot, Grenedal Dragonblood, commanded this. They would ride swift through the night, sending five men to each city or castle they passed to gather more troops and civilians. Sometimes a hero had to run, and live so they may fight another day. This would be the hardest battle they ever faced, the one they had to run from. It would be harder for good soldiers to live than to die.

They rode into the misting rain. Time slowed, the road and minutes counted by their horses' hoof beats. The men sweated in the chill night air, and their horses lathered. They ran, not just for their own lives, but the lives of those in the north. Hue ran beside them, easily keeping pace on foot. He didn't sweat or even breathe hard from the exertion.

The screech of a predator tore the night, and a man was torn from his horse by a dark shape that swooped down. Hue's axe was in his hand as he turned and leapt over the mounted troops heads. His axe connected with something, and a wet thud sounded as two bodies hit the ground.

"Keep riding!" Hue yelled, as the men began to turn their steeds. "I will catch up, but don't stop whatever you see or hear. If you stop, thousands will die because of it!"

The soldiers obeyed the command, righting themselves and their course, and disappeared into the light snow that replaced the misting rain. The three-quarter moon showed through the clouds, a milky disc behind swirls. Hue looked at the two forms on the ground in front of him. The soldier lay twisted in a puddle of slush, and a second form rose to confront Blueaxe. Baring its pointed canines, the dark creature leapt towards Hue. With a swing of the axe, the monster's head flew from its shoulders, a look of surprise on its face. Hue squared off his stance, and waited for anyone else that may be following.

Two more forms appeared a moment before striking the large man, tearing at him with clawed hands and trying to sink their teeth into his neck and shoulders. Hue tumbled across the ground, axe flying from his grip. Rolling head over heels, Hue gained his feet, grabbing one of the creatures in each hand and pulling them to an arm's length. One bit into Hue's forearm, and a stream of bluish light burst forth from the wound, burning the monster's face and melting its features. Hue bashed at the attacker with the body of his other foe, and heard the neck of the second assailant snap.

Dropping the second one, he reached out and tore the head from the first. Black liquid gushed out of the neck of the limp form that remained, covering Hue with a slimy liquid that burned his skin. Before he had time to do more than drop the broken form of his enemy, he was set upon by his remaining adversary.

The monster's head lolled to one side, bouncing as it tried to claw at Hue's eyes and throat. Hue snapped his elbow back, connecting with the face that limply hung from the neck, tearing the skin with his powerful blow. Grabbing the creature by an arm and keeping it at arm's length, Hue dragged the gnashing beast towards where his axe had fallen. Snatching up his weapon, the blue-skinned man finished off his foe, its head making a wet noise as it rolled across the ground.

"You have taken out my apprentices," a deep, calm voice said in the dark, "but they were pups. I am the master, and I do not think you will fare as well with me."

"I don't fear you, any more than I feared your filthy offspring." Hue answered, standing straight and focusing on the dark where the voice seemed to come from.

"Then, though brave, you are a fool."

The snow fell heavier and stuck to Hue like ash. It smelled of fetid rot, and the clouds overhead had taken on a green tint. Something clicked repeatedly outside of Hue's range of sight.

"Join me now," said the voice, "and you can be a man of power in a new order. You can command thousands and live in luxury for the rest of your days. Women will throw themselves at you and men will worship you."

"You offer me this because you fear me," Hue replied, gripping his axe with both hands, ready to defend himself. "You saw what I am, and what happened to your children. Come now, let's finish this. Your final death awaits you."

"Shame, but only one death awaits, and it is yours."

The darkness split as dozens of crawling forms clicked forward on the cobblestone highway. Centipedes as long as a man is tall writhed towards Hue, their mandibles clicking along with their hundreds of feet. The first to get close rose up, its segmented body supported by dozens of legs. Hue cut it in half, and a half dozen of the monsters swarmed their dying companion, tearing chunks from its armored body. The rest swarmed towards Hue. The man swung with precision, slicing through three before the others could wrap themselves around his body.

Curling themselves around his legs and crawling up his body, their pincers sliced into him. Dark blood welled from a dozen wounds as Hue fell underneath them. His axe did him no good this close, and he dropped it and began tearing into their armored forms. Heads flew, legs were ripped from their bodies, and ichor coated the man and the ground around him. Hue struggled to his feet, fighting his way from under the press of insects almost as large as he was. Kicking and punching, he crushed the bugs as they ripped at his flesh.

A dark form flew past him and he was tossed a dozen feet away. The remaining centipedes crawled towards him, clicking as they did. The mist moved around him, thickening until he couldn't breathe. Blows rained down from his unseen assailant as the bugs once again began slicing into his legs.

Hue's head swam and his vision blurred as the shadow form pummeled him and the monsters slipped their venom into his wounds. Acid from their ichor etched his skin, blistering and bubbling along his body. He stumbled under the onslaught. Falling to one knee, he gasped in the thick air, trying to gain a breath.

Closing his eyes, he called upon the energies that had brought him back from death and restored him once before. His skin glowed, his wounds and blood shone like moonlight. The clouds parted and the moon cast light, eerie and yellow, across the road. With a roar, Hue released the energy and the centipedes flew away from him in a blast of magical energy.

Everything was silent as Hue struggled to his feet. A finely dressed man lay on the ground a few meters away, just an arm-length from Hue's axe.

"Lord Emite, I presume?" Hue asked, his voice weary and his breath coming in gasps. "The same man, if I can call you that, that brought forth the evil from Aborgas centuries ago? You were the one who called down the werewolves on Red City and made it what it is today?"

"Yes," the dark figure said, rising to his feet without using his hands or body to do so. "I am the one who conquered a land, and I am the one who helped bring about the birth of Nomed. And though you don't know it, I am the one who will command that demon half breed once more. I have manipulated him for centuries, even from my prison.

Now, you will die by your own weapon for bringing me such pain."

The vampire bent and retrieved the fallen double-bladed axe. He stopped and stared as Hue began to laugh. A laugh that started as a chuckle, and rose to a maniacal level. Hue gasped a breath, forcing the laughter down. Lord Emite cocked his head, looking at the man with a quizzical look.

"What you don't understand," Hue said, chortling, "is that axe would no more hurt me than my own hand would."

With a gesture, the axe twisted in Lord Emite's hand and swung towards the vampire. The dark lord threw up his other hand to stop the blade that approached his throat in a blur. Fingers and part of his hand flew into the air before the weapon lodged in his neck. Hue was there in a flash, ripping the axe from the vampire's throat, and then swinging again. The lord tried to obfuscate, but his head left his shoulders before he could. His severed head landed on the wet ground, rolling face down into an icy puddle.

Hue bent and picked up the man's head by the hair in one hand, and the axe in the other. The eyes blinked and the mouth worked, trying to say something, before falling slack.

Exhausted and wounded, Hue looked over the scene of carnage around him. He hoped the rising sun would finish what he started, but couldn't spend any more time here. He turned and ran. The future was in his hands. The head he carried would have to be proof enough for arrogant lords and overconfident soldiers. He had to get thousands of people into motion, and travel to the north where they at least had a chance of survival. A chance until spring, when the monsters would come.

Grenedal had flown over the city for hours, diving in to protect those he could. The town was almost overcome by the first line of the insect horde advance from the Lost Swamp in the west. Just as the people halted the attackers, the pale undead line crept in from the east. He felt Hue in the north, moving away. He saw the column of fifty or more horsemen that marked his friend's retreat.

Three of the twelve cities of Humbrey had fallen in less than twenty-four hours, the two invading forces growing with each conquest. The cities to the north would be cut off from any reinforcements from the south, if Duke Malvornick would even allow his Puppet-King of Trysteria to assist them.

Grenedal felt another presence, one he should be able to track and find as he had before, as he could Hue Blueaxe. He could not pinpoint Nomed now, though he was below in Trism somewhere, but it was only a vague feeling. The demon half-breed could now hide somewhat from Grenedal. Dragonblood never was sure why he could track these two beings, what connection tied the three of them together, or why the other two could not feel each other. Like a seesaw, it was Grenedal that balanced Hue and Nomed. Three hybrids from different stock, and they all influenced the world.

Unsure what to do; he rode the air currents effortlessly, circling the carnage like a huge carrion bird. Deciding that these people must be saved from the terrors that ravaged below, he tucked his wings tight to his sides and dove. Magic welled inside him, along with hunger, and magical electricity burst forth as he leveled his flight off.

People screamed all around Nomed. The voracious insects gave no quarter as they made their way deeper into the city. The undead lurched through the night. He watched as what could be called the sergeants and lieutenants of the corpse horde dashed here and there. Wholesale slaughter was the order of the night. Before joining them, Nomed had watched Grenedal meet with the blue man and learned his theory was right. Simple magics could make him undetectable to Grenedal if the other man was close.

Malvornick would not hold Humbrey now. Nomed had succeeded in breaking the man's plans. The Duke's puppets were dying by the hundreds. No armies from the north would dance to his tune; no kings or nobles would answer his call. Events were in place and moving. Grenedal had helped bring the last bastion of hope out of these condemned lands. They headed north on a tide of death, led by a man reborn. Now the observer had other things to do. Business in the south required his attention. There was a matter of a demon, Kez'et-dual, who wanted him dead.

A thin, bony dog skulked out of the alley, and in the swirl of a short cape a man stood where a dog had walked a moment earlier, and stepped over the forms of the fallen humans. He crushed the head of a zombie rising for the first time.

Grenedal had been roused; even now, the dragonkin swooped down, bringing death to the hordes of insects and undead, rallying the humans of Trism. Death was in that one's future. Even a dragon could have strings attached, and be taught to dance upon command. Nomed loved what he did, and no one was better at it than he.

Nothing but a Dog: A Trio of Travelers Tale

"Our children are being slaughtered!" Grigor shouted in his rough baritone, as the gathering of villagers yelled and argued. The room quieted to a murmur, which allowed him to speak at a reasonable volume. His thick beard quivered as he said, "Three of our children have been killed, ripped apart and mauled by an unholy beast. We need to take action, not sit here, hiding like scared children."

"I know this is horrible," Jaroslav said, Grigor's unofficial rival as leader of the community. "We all love and cherish our children. But the three that are missing wandered off when it was dark." He scanned the room with his clear blue eyes and ran a hand through his trimmed beard, "It has been a lean harvest and the snows are coming. The beasts are on the hunt because they know this."

The crowd muttered.

"No!" Grigor interrupted. "Marko was fourteen, practically a man, and had already joined the woodcutters and was betrothed to pretty Dariya," A young blonde girl in braids hid her face in her hands and gave a shuddered sob as Grigor pointed at her. "Beasts would drag the body away. These were only partially eaten. Do I need to remind you? They were torn apart. Their stomachs torn out and only the tender organs eaten by the monster that did this! The trees around were painted with the blood of our children! And these children knew to not wander away. Why? Why did they go so far from their houses after dark?"

Jaroslav sighed. Always the more level headed of the two, he didn't want panic and fear running through the village, or to scare the women with the details. "We can avoid anymore tragedies by staying inside after dark. There is nothing to fear if we keep our heads. This is nothing more than the work of a pack of hungry wild dogs; they know people and the children may have thought they were friendly animals."

"I do not think so Jaroslav," interrupted Grigor. "This is the work of a demon. Fedir told us what he saw. Do you need to hear it again? I think you do. Fedir, tell us again what you found at the stream."

A large man stood slowly, towering over his friends. A matted fur cloak hung over his shoulders, a trophy from a wolf that had attacked him in his youth. He was not smart but he knew the woods better than most men. The day the children had gone missing he had led the team of woodcutters as they went the woods.

"This ain't about the children, but three weeks ago," Fedir said in his halting manner as he held up four fingers, "I went to the stream, to fill the skins, before we were to be coming back to the village. I saw the bones first. Lots of them. Then I saw the carcasses. I think they were deer. I think. Lots. Many." He held up his hands, flashing his fingers, showing the count of fifteen. "They all were missing their bellies, and they were missing their throats too. And they were laid out, all neat like. The water was red with blood." Looking down, the big man shuddered, not meeting the eyes of the other villagers. Women made the sign to ward off the evil eye as he continued. "I, I didn't know what to do. I didn't tell anyone. I didn't know what to do."

His brother, Oleksander, put a comforting hand on Fedir's shoulder, always protective of his older, but slower, brother. A cold breeze whistled between the cracks of the wooden log walls of the inn and community hall, making the goat fat candles gutter. Thick, black smoke swirled and danced, and no one spoke for a moment.

A wiry youth named Luka leapt to his feet. "I say we slay the fiend!" The lad had been to the city once and thought he was worldly. Since returning he was always shouting about the next cause. "It doesn't attack grown men, and together we can kill it! Lord Talon may even reward us for it. He rewards people who take initiative." The crowd took up his cry to pursue what hunted villagers in the woods.

"Confound it, Luka," a white haired man, Zenon the Elder, said with a wheeze. The room quieted to a murmur as the man rose onto his good leg using the table as support. He leaned on a wooden crutch, "The beast is a smart and tricky thing. It would not show itself. As for Lord Talon, you do not know everything. Perhaps he would not be so pleased if we decided to do as you suggest."

The door banged open and cold air swirled through the room, causing the candlelight to dance. Petro, the night watchman, was silhouetted in the doorway, his eyes wild, hair tousled, and fur cap missing. "Something this way comes!" he said. "A horrible beast, as big as a wood shed. I saw its glowing eyes in the light of the moon. It will be upon us in moments!" He stumbled in and slammed the door behind him. Going to the cask, he grabbed a tankard, filled it with the dark frothy brew, and drank. All eyes turned to Zenon. The old man held up his hands to calm the crowd when a noise cut through the night.

A deep growl came from the distance, as if a great beast were on the prowl. The guttural noise was rhythmic and unnatural. The villagers could hear it coming closer as it climbed the hill which led to their homes. A high pitched whistling screamed, shaking the shutters and doors, and the tankards hanging on the wall clanked together. People crowded to the back of the hall, but Grigor and Jaroslav rushed to the window to see what approached. The sounds slowed. The ground shook with footfalls of the encroacher.

"I see it," Jaroslav said so the others could hear, "it is as tall as a hut, with four legs, and its breath steams in the night."

"Our doom has come then," Grigor said. He turned to the wall, and took down the blunderbuss from above the cask of ale. Packing it with skill and speed, he readied the weapon with shot and steel, tamped down the cotton, and prepared to defend his people and family.

"Jiminy whiskers! Someone is coming out of the side of the monster. It looks like a woman!" Jaroslav said as he moved towards the door.

"The witch, Baba Yaga?" asked Hanna, the local midwife and gossip, "I heard she has been seen in the woods not far from a village to the south. She has a walking hut with legs of a chicken. She surrounds it with a fence made of human bones, and skulls top each of the posts, with always one missing so she can put her next victim on top of it! She lures children away and eats them."

An unseen caller watched from the above, hidden in the shadows of the rafters. The dark presence loomed over the villagers and drank in their dread, the way a mortal man would drink wine. The being was intoxicated with the ambrosia of the murky fear of the people. It could feel their panic pulsing in the air. This was just one way it fed from these people. It had many reasons to tend a flock, even if it was a flock that belonged to another. For now.

A soft knock at the door stopped any further talk and the room went silent. All eyes turned to look as the door slowly creaked open; the biting cold whipped in and tore the cloak of warmth from the superstitious folk. The being above watched, as the tension rose. Three shadows stood in the door, silhouetted by the watch fires of the village square behind them. Two of the figures moved into the room, as the tallest turned to look outside before following.

They came into the light as the third of the three shut the door. The wear of travel showed on the newcomers as clear as the distrust showed on the faces of the residents of the hamlet. The first to enter was a woman with dark hair in a tight bun. Her dress was a proper blue walking dress, with buttons that went up to her throat and lace at the cuff of the sleeves. She carried a lace parasol and rings sparkled on her fingers. She was no mythical hag that peasants should fear.

The second was small man, hooded and dressed in a long cloak that covered a purplish gown underneath that resembled priestly garments. The last was a tall, wiry man with short, dark hair. A plain, curved sword was at his side, and a holstered pistol hung from the opposite hip. His outfit was more leather than cloth, and gleamed a reddish brown in the dim light. Grigor raised his gun.

"I did portend these travelers," Evdokiya, the wise woman, said and glared around the room. She tossed a half dozen bones on the table from the wooden bowl in her hand. They clattered as the village waited for her soothsaying. "They will help us," she continued as she pointed at the bones. "I see more than a beast hunting. I see that dark clouds have gathered, and evil is upon us." Cries of distress and panicked discussion rose from the crowd. "Shush, you squawking geese! The watch fires are lit, and the gods watch over us. The danger may not take us if we offer the sacrifice they want." The room quieted.

"Pray, I am Elizabeth," the woman with the strangers said. "We mean no ill, nor fright. My companions are Suykimo and Zachary. We seek a place to rest for the night. We have traveled far."

"What is that armored, screaming beast outside?" Grigor asked, his weapon still held at the ready.

"It is no beast, good sir, tis a machine. Like a steam locomotive, but using legs and roads instead of wheels and rails. It makes for a noisy and bumpy ride, but it is as adequate as a horse and carriage. It eats wood and makes steam, rather than eating oats and producing fertilizer."

"It growls and shrieks like a monster though!"

"It is a machine, and that is the sound of its engine and

the steam being released, just as a train does."

"Grigor," Zenon said, "pray, lower the gun. Evdokiya said they are here to help. This is her realm. Do I make myself clear?"

The man lowered the gun. The trio of travelers exchanged worried glances. Suykimo looked up, staring into the rafters, his hood falling away from his face to reveal slanted eyes.

Grigor's gun rose again to point at him. "He is a demon. See his eyes?"

"No," Zachary spoke with the crisp tone of authority, "he is foreign born, from faraway lands, and no more a threat to you than anything else in this room."

"Something watches from above. No one ever looks up," Suykimo said in a quiet voice. An icy wind cut through the room, and the candles flickered then brightened. "It's gone now." The villagers looked around, and many made a sign to ward off the evil eye.

Evdokiya spoke again. "They are not demons, and they are flesh and blood like us. Quite so, they hunt demons, even now I can feel that evil has fled upon their entry. Come, sit with us, you are welcome here."

Elizabeth smiled at the people, a gentle and reassuring smile, as she sat with the wise woman. "We shall help you."

"I don't like that Elizabeth stayed with them," Zachary said to Suykimo, as the vehicle lumbered along the road, swaying side to side with each step.

"It was necessary," Suykimo assured him again. "Women do not hunt, and if the villagers have her with them, they know we will do as we say."

Zachary looked at him with sharp blue eyes. "She is being used. She is a hostage."

"She is a guest, and she will keep them calm with her gifts. She was a nanny, and knows how to soothe people.

Now, as the wise woman suggested, we go south to find this Baba Yaga and hope the witch's reputation is exaggerated."

"I am not worried about her reputation. Why do you think she is not the source of the village's problems?"

"She is a symptom, but we must explore the symptoms to cure the illness."

They traveled for hours, and Suykimo navigated in ways Zachary did not understand. The younger man was not a tracker, but he knew how to find his way by the compass on his bracer, along with the timepiece and weather dials. What he did not have an instinct for doing, he had the tools to assist him instead.

Just before sunset their vehicle stood in front of a cottage. It stood three times the height of a man on chicken-like legs made of rusted metal, which gave the look of dried blood in the waning light. The feet were clawed monstrosities that had clumps of mud in the gears and wires. The hut was a ramshackle affair with cracked timbers jutting out. A plume of black smoke rose from a short brick chimney. A rickety door made of sticks faced them. Orange light filtered through the slats of the door, as the chill autumn wind whistled, and dead leaves danced through the barren trees of the forest. The sun was concealed by storm clouds, and in the distance an owl hooted as it began its hunt.

Like the village gossip woman said, a bone fence surrounded it and skulls decorated every post except one. Bits of dried meat still showed on most of the bones, and they were lashed together with sinew. The whole area had the stench of decay.

Suykimo took the lead and Zachary followed, hand on sword. The two men circled the cabin, trying to find an entrance. No windows or doors could be seen. The smaller man led the way through the gate, which swung shut with an eerie groan behind them.

"Hut, O Hut," Suykimo intoned, "turn your back to the forest, your front to me."

Zachary didn't question the man's knowledge of such things, trusting him to know his business. The hut began to move, turning and squatting, till it came to rest a half meter off the ground. Zachary stepped protectively between Suykimo and the hut, moving forward to knock. The door creaked open before they could reach it. The younger man grasped his sword.

"Stay your hand Zachary, we are being invited in as guests. Be wary, but let us not be hasty."

"Though you may be tasty," said a voice from inside that sounded like leather scraping over a stone. "Come in and share my fire. You have no reason to fear me; you have not invoked my ire."

Zachary looked to his elder who had advised and trained him since he was a boy. Suykimo stepped forward, drawing back his hood, and entered the small dwelling.

The interior space of the chicken-legged hut defied the confines of the exterior. It had the feel of a large hunting lodge that had been blended with a clockmaker's workshop, if clock makers worked in foundries. The ceiling was hidden in shadows far above, the light that danced across the walls was cast by flickering gas lamps, and a huge open hearth made of copper plates welded together in an oven shape. A bellows stood at the mouth of the oven, and an iron arm which held a pot was swung away from it. Smoke crept over the edge of the kettle onto the floor, slithering to shadowed corners. The walls had mounted trophies decorating it. Some were animal heads, others were dried flowers, a beetle the size of a man's chest, and various limbs of unidentified creatures. A ladder led to what appeared to be a sleeping loft in the rear of the room.

Four long tables were in two rows, with half of their surfaces covered by various beakers and burners, which were bubbling and popping. One table had dried animal parts laid out in distinct patterns. The last had a sparse dinner for four laid out on it. Dark bread, dried fruits, unidentifiable meats, and wine waited. A wrinkled figure in a rocking chair sat at the head of this table. She was wrapped in a shawl, many sizes too large for her rotund frame, and smoking a long stemmed pipe. Her eyes were dark hollows, and her nose was a crooked jag. She smiled and showed a handful of teeth that matched the rest of her appearance, weathered and contorted.

"Come in," the figure said. "Join me for supper and tea. I have been expecting you three."

"Baba Yaga, I presume," Suykimo said as he stepped inside. Zachary stepped inside and the door shut with a click and whirr, assisted by gear works.

"That is what you assume. You are missing one?" the woman moaned. "Three. You should be three riders, red for the sun, white for the day, and black for the night. Where is the white rider of light?"

"Is she mad?" Zachary whispered.

"No," Suykimo answered with a shake of his head, and then spoke to the woman, "Elizabeth could not join us. She was otherwise detained."

"A woman?" She cackled. "Of course, why not a woman? A man of mysticism, and a fighter I see," she petted a ragged squirrel, the size of a dog, on her lap. It did not move and appeared to be long dead but well preserved. "So the night speaks for the riders three?"

Suykimo nodded as he took a seat on the bench, leaving space between the hag and himself. He reached out and broke some bread from the rough loaf and placed it on the wooden trencher in front of him. He added fruit and poured a bit of wine into a crystal chalice from the cracked clay urn on the table. He smiled at her, as he sprinkled herbs from a small packet he had drawn from his satchel.

"I would not poison my guests or any such fuss, though it is a surprise that a fellow alchemist sits at my table. Will the red rider join us?" she asked, pointing at Zachary with her wart covered chin.

"I will stand." Zachary said, as he watched the shadows at the edge of the room move with a purpose of their own.

"My friend is cautious. Usually that is my role, but this time I am the bold one. Do you know the purpose of us seeking you out?" Suykimo asked and Baba Yaga nodded, but said nothing. "The villagers are of the mind that you may be causing mischief."

She hooted. "They know nothing. They are sheep for the slaughter and jump at shadows in the brush when they should be looking to the sky," Suykimo raised an eyebrow as the woman continued, "and you know this, I think. You are not like the others. You are much less, human, and much less likely to die."

"I am what I am, nothing more," the foreigner answered, "but I am curious, what troubles the people we agreed to help?"

"There is a singular price for knowledge, always a cost. Are you willing to pay that price for what I have lost?"

"What is the price?" Zachary interrupted. The woman looked at the warrior as she drew on her pipe and stroked the animal on her lap. It moved, with jerking motions, to a more comfortable position. She blew smoke outward and it formed a shadow beast, which lunged across the table and dissipated.

"Why, just a few flowers, nothing sinister. Women love flowers. We have a weakness for them. They renew us and work magic with our souls. I like roses, blue roses and their powers."

"We can find those for you," Suykimo said, and looked at Zachary with a meaningful glance, "and you will tell us what haunts the people that sent us?"

"I think when you discover one, you shall discover the other. What fun!"

"How do we find your rose?" Zachary asked.

"With blood and knowledge. One of you shall pay former; the other shall pay the latter with prose."

"We agree to the price," Suykimo said.

"You must both agree!" The woman stood. The animal in her lap fell to the floor and disappeared under the table without a sound. She reached for her gnarled walking stick. "Do you also agree Zachary?"

"How did you know my name?" the warrior asked, his hand on the hilt of his sword.

"I know what I need to know," she said, as she came towards him. "Tell me you agree and we shall begin the show." Once beside him, she looked up into his face. Her breath reeked of decay. She smiled.

"I agree."

"I see. Then let us seal our accord." She held out a twisted hand to him. He reached for it, and she screeched and scratched him, drawing blood. Cackling madly, she moved with a speed that belayed her form to another table. Zachary began to draw his sword, but stopped at a shake of Suykimo's head.

"I have been around for many years," she said, in a sing-song voice, "and seen many things. I know what you ask. I saw the fall of ancient cities, witnessed sermons that changed the world and became legend, and I have cheered at the death of martyrs that have changed the world. This is a simple task."

She lifted a glass beaker from a gas burner, her hand sizzled as she hung a clawed nail over the opening, and a single drop of Zachary's blood fell into the vessel with a hiss. Swirling the liquid, she moved to a parchment. With the utmost care she poured the viscous potion onto the leathery skin. As she did, words and images began to appear.

"It's a map," Zachary muttered.

She cackled. "Yes, a map to your fortune, or your doom. As it is always in these cases, I also give a caveat: you must seek it alone in the dark and gloom."

Zachary was alone. The moon was full and gave a small amount of light when the clouds did not cover it. The machine was behind him, and Suykimo was still at the witch's hut. The older man would pay his price with knowledge, and the younger man would collect the flowers and any blood he came across.

He hunted now. To the east of the village was a mountain, a forbidden place that was owned by the lord of the region to whom the village paid tithe. On these lands Zachary would find what he sought. The witch had told him to take what he needed to protect himself from unnatural things, things that would hunt him for sport.

He lowered his goggles, which he wore only at specific times to keep dust from his eyes when riding, in cold and snow to protect his tears from freezing his eyes shut, and their third function was to allow him to see at night. Special green glass lit his vision with an eerie tint, not allowing him to see color, but allowing him to see into the shadows almost as clear as day.

He was not the only one that could see in the shadows though. The hunting owl, the small animals that foraged in the dark, and the predators that hunted at night could also see. One such predator had caught his scent; a taste of blood, the smell of oil and man. It followed the trail. It skulked closer, creeping silently, waiting for the perfect time to beset its quarry.

This was the ultimate hunter. The arsenal of weaponry both natural and crafted was at its disposal. The best money and nature could provide. Tracking by scent, sight, sound, and taste, it always ran its victim to ground. It never lost its prey. It patiently followed this new interloper in its territory. Sighting its game, it leapt to a higher ridge to stalk the man.

Zachary twitched. The hairs on the back of his neck stood up, and he was sure they would do the same on his arms if his leather and brass bracers didn't cover them. Something was wrong. Stopping, he peered into the darkness. His breathing slowed and he allowed his senses to blanket the area. Staying still for many minutes, he waited. The leaves rustled across the deer track up the side of the mountain, following the path of the trailing clouds across the sky. Sweat cooled on his skin as he waited. He trusted his training and instincts.

Zachary knew whatever it was he sensed was not going to make a move until it was ready, so he moved on and continued his search. In less than an hour, he found roses. Kneeling, he brought his torch forward, a small device powered with electric, to light his prize. He lifted his goggles as the beam showed him the color of the flowers. Blue. He drew a knife from his boot and cut the stems, making a pile of as many of the blooms as he could find.

The only warning Zachary had before the attack, was a slight growl then he was knocked over from behind. He tucked his body into a roll as claws tore at his back. His leather protected him, but he felt it tear. He came up in a defensive crouch, knife at ready. Blinking, he turned off his light and tossed it on the roses and let his eyes adjust, trying to size up his foe.

The moon came out from behind the clouds and Zachary saw his attacker was a full head and shoulders taller than him. Lupine in appearance, it stood upright and wore some clothing. The enemy had the hind legs of a wolf, bent backwards as if ready to spring, and each thigh had a weapon strapped to it. The right had a large pistol of brass and glass, and blue current danced inside of it. The left had a long black steel baton with a thick handle with switches and a single dial. Each hung from wide twin leather belts that crisscrossed the beast's waist. A long coat, with gold braids on the shoulder, was worn open, and showed it was a male of its species. The man-wolf's forearms had leather and black steel bracers that came down to cover the back of his steel tipped, clawed hands, each ending in brass knuckles made to be part of the defensive covering. The metal that ran the length of each side of the bracers gleamed with a razor sharp edge. The attacker had a contorted face, more beast than man. It showed large mutton chops on its cheeks that stood out further than the brown fur that covered its mushed visage and the rest of the body. The nose was wide and flat and gleamed with wetness, though the eyes were very human, glaring blue at him with hunger and hatred. Tufted ears swept back from the head, and the monster's lips curled back showing spittle and a red froth.

Zachary scanned his surroundings. He was on a small cleared ridge no more than five paces in either direction. The beast had jumped from another, thinner ledge, above him. Below was a straight drop off to the rocky canyon, filled with rubble and scrub trees, not a soft landing if either took a spill in that direction.

The werewolf lunged towards him, trying to come between the cliff wall and the warrior, testing the other's reflexes. Zachary quickly side stepped towards better footing and drew his sabre in the same breath, now holding his knife in one hand and the ancient weapon in the other. The blade was given to him by his mentor and it was a unique weapon. The steel had been folded many times, strengthening the blade. It was also imbued with blessings of priests and alchemists to enhance the alloy and allowing it an edge like no other. The handle was smooth in his gloved hand, and became an extension of his arm. Zachary made himself a smaller target by balancing on the balls of his feet in a partial crouch. The beast would have to pass two blades to reach him.

Zachary stepped forward, leading with his left foot and his knife, and slashed. His enemy dodged with unnatural speed, and its black steel tipped claws shredded the armor on the man's ribs as easily as a child would tear through cheesecloth. Leaping with ease, it bounded to the upper ledge, four meters above, and let out a hyena laugh that echoed off the cliff walls. Distant thunder boomed as the monster toyed with its prey.

Zachary spun to face his foe as the werewolf jumped down again, falling onto its back and sliding on its haunches below the expected sword swing, and sliced deep into the warrior's calf with the deadly edge of the blade on the bracer. The man-wolf rose to standing as it passed the man, and with incredible speed rained down a flurry of claws and punches at Zachary's face. Blood flew as contact was made and the warrior stumbled back three steps, holding his weapons in front of him to ward off any more damage.

Breathing deep, Zachary found his balance physically and mentally. Reaching up with his knife hand, he placed the night goggles back over his eyes, as much for protection as to improve his vision. The world turned bright green and his pulse slowed into a steady rhythm as he became what he was born to be, a singular force and combatant. Stepping forward, he feinted with the knife in his left hand and brought his right foot and the weight of his body forward for a full swing with his longer blade.

The werewolf blocked it with a deft movement, and it clanged on the same bracer that had torn the man's face open moments ago. Expecting this, Zachary brought the knife in low and the weapon tore deep into the gut of the monster. The warrior pulled to the side, and then up, hoping to disembowel his enemy. Both clawed hands shoved Zachary away, towards the cliff. He stopped centimeters from going over the edge.

The monster looked down at his midsection and both watched as the gash closed, healing itself in less time than it took to cause the wound. The werewolf gave a rictus smile, its lips drawing back in a sneer as it sniffed the air, testing it for the scent of fear. The hyena laugh came again, and it raised its head and howled.

Zachary did not let the opportunity go to waste. He threw the knife at the beast, and as it was knocked aside midflight, the warrior closed the distance between them. The sword flashed as he attacked his unnatural opponent with a combination of blows to the shoulder and chest, jabs that came in straight, aiming for the heart. The werewolf blocked with a bracer, but the tip of the sword slid into the meaty bicep. Sparks flew with that cut, and a gleam lit the surface of the sword. This cut did not close.

The werewolf's angry howl shook the valley, as it

reverberated through the chest and throat of the killer. Zachary did not let up on his attack. The werewolf blocked strike after strike. In the midst of the attack the monster slashed with his bracer, cutting deep into Zachary's chest. Blood flew with the strike, and the warrior staggered backwards.

"I am Lord of this land," the werewolf growled, in a deep baritone that was almost unintelligible, "and some whelp shall not best me!" The beast of noble birth reached down and pulled the metal baton free of its thigh, and with a movement of a bent thumb, it crackled with yellow electricity.

Charging forward, relying on its size and strength, the monster battered Zachary. The warrior blocked each blow with his sabre, and electric current traveled up the blade, numbing his arm and fingers. Within seconds the blade fell from his hand, and his foe kicked at the sword. The ancient weapon caromed over the side into the deep canyon below. The baton flickered as it used the last of its power, but it had already served its purpose. The beast charged, weapon upraised, to either force the man over the side of the cliff of crush his head with the steel club.

Zachary grabbed the forearms of his foe, who was stronger, and fell to his back. He kicked upward with his legs, throwing the beast over his head and the edge of the precipice. The warrior rose into a crouch, spinning to face the cliff. Edging towards it, blood and sweat dripping from his face, he wiped the distraction away. His chest throbbed, and a piece of flesh hung loose, along with the shreds of his armor.

He approached the ledge with caution, and was not surprised at what he saw. The beast hung by its claws, and leered up at him. The Lord flung himself upward with ease, bowled the battered man onto his back, and landed by the wall, leaving the wounded man by the drop-off.

The werewolf reached for its last weapon with a slow and casual move, smiling through the bloody froth around its jowls, a low rumbling laugh issuing from its throat. "This will not kill you," it explained. "Merely make you unable to move so I may enjoy your flesh while you still live." The weapon was clear of its holster, and the fiend flicked a switch on it. Zachary could see the glass light up with energy as the weapon charged for the shot that would incapacitate him. The warrior watched as the beast took aim.

As the energy burst forth, Zachary rolled to the side, drawing his own gun as he did. A loud explosion echoed as the cliff face lit up from the energy pistol, dirt spraying. Another explosion sounded as Zachary fired his own pistol.

The beast stared at him with wide eyes, its clawed hand going to the center of its own chest. Blood trickled through its fingers, and it slowly slid to its knees. Blood crept from between its canine lips and it spit on the ground.

"I hate these things," Zachary explained, holding the gun up for inspection, "no style. But they have their place, especially when I have silver bullets and am facing a beast like you." He fired twice more into the skull of his adversary.

Zachary watched as the man-beast twitched and convulsed its final death throes. Looking around he saw the flowers, and his knife. His calf, chest, and face pounded with each heartbeat. He looked into the chasm with a sigh; he would have to go down there to get his sword. Though it would have to wait until after he gathered his gear, and field dressed his wounds. It began to rain.

"This one was not like any other. For he was not made, but rather had a mother," Baba Yaga said, as she stroked the roses Zachary had brought like a bride at her wedding. "He was neither beast nor man. Five generations of dog, wolf and man, and in a few minutes you destroyed God's plan." She cackled. "He worked long for what he had gained, all according to plan. The moon waxed full and his power was at its peak, but your weapons made his blood leak. Be wary of the effects his blood has on your own body, for you are in danger. Not just from it, but from a much more dangerous stranger. Oh yes, there is another that covets these lands and herd. Now my pact with that dark being neither has to be seen nor heard!"

Suykimo and Zachary stood in the clearing where the hut had been, dazed and blinking. The woman and her chicken-legged cottage had disappeared. They had nothing left to do except to return to the village with the news of the Lord's demise. The villagers were free of his reign.

The men mounted their walking carriage. Suykimo took the controls so Zachary could check and clean his wounds again, resetting the field dress he had done in haste after the fight. They rode in silence.

They reached the village just before dawn, relieved to see that the watch fires were still burning. They were greeted by Oleksander and Fedir, who welcomed them with smiles and hearty cheers. When they saw Zachary, they called to the women to help the warrior, and Elizabeth took charge of the activity. The men demanded to hear the tale and listened, spellbound, to the encounter with the witch and the werewolf.

A dark shadow roosted on the peak of the hall, watching as the villagers rejoiced. The heroes would leave as soon as they had rested, and then the village would be ready to feed upon. In a swirl of mist the creature flew into the remaining night, returning to its nest before the sun rose. Tomorrow, a new era would begin.

The Case of Dark Disappearances: A Croaker Norge Case File

It crept further into the shadows, watching and waiting. Hidden from the sight of any passerby, it stalked the prey. It had chosen well this time and knew the Master would be pleased. The quarry was barely more than a child, but enough of a woman that she would fit the needs of the man that commanded the monster. She left the warehouse with the other workers and moved at a brisk pace, her plain woolen dress and long coat swishing as she walked. Her hair was hidden by a bonnet but yellow curls peeked out. She carried a bundle of brown paper tied with twine under one arm as if it were precious and watched for anyone coming close to her with the caution that a lone woman has at night. The foot traffic thinned as people went into the entryways of apartments in the district. She lived in rooms above a tavern with her mother and four sisters.

It had followed her every night for the past week and watched her and her family from its position crouched in the shadows of the second story veranda outside their rooms. The girl smelled of sweat and must from the bolts of cloth in the factory.

She crossed the street, stopping for a moment to let a horse drawn trolley pass in front of her. Darting past stacks of crates in the unseasonably warm February night, it kept its quarry in sight. The gas lamps of New Sylians flickered, casting orange and yellow light, making the gloom jump and dance to their fiery beat. A fog settled as the night deepened, making the shadows bleed grey and roll like the ocean surf when someone passed nearby.

Two more blocks and she would be home, safe in the stinking crowds of drunken men, hidden from its ability to smell her in the haze of smoke of a parlor. The cacophonous noise of the player piano and rowdy calls at the burlesque dancers was enough to keep it away; combined with the other elements of humankind it could no more enter that place than the Master could enter the dark portal.

It leapt with cat-like grace atop a wagon full of boxes covered with a tarp and sprang across the street onto a green and white striped awning that extended over the sidewalk. It saw the girl behind it and, moving forward, it dropped silently into an alley ahead of her.

As she passed the alleyway, Alisa turned to see a fine dressed gentleman leaning heavily against the wall. His coat had been torn and his face showed marks where he had been beaten. He stumbled and almost fell.

"Help me," he moaned.

"What happened?" she asked.

"I had just returned from seeing all the electric lights at the World Cotton Centennial when three men approached me. They beat me and took it all. My walking stick, my top hat, my wallet, but they missed my watch. You can have it if you help me into that tavern where I can call for a constable," he said in a southern Gallix accent. He held out a gold pocket watch that was missing a chain and she moved forward. He put an arm around her to steady himself and they both flew backwards into the fog-laden darkness of the side street. Her muffled scream was never heard over the noise of the revelry from inside the building.

The sun rose over New Sylians as the lamplighters made their rounds to turn the gas off at each post. Morning traffic woke with the light of day and the click of horses' hooves on cobblestones began to fill the air. The whistle of the train could be heard competing with the steamboat's clarion call as more guests arrived for the 6524 World's Fair, as well as the Day of Torgoth, a yearly festival of debauchery. It was three days until Big Bestuf, the day before the holy celebration, and the whole city was ramping up for it. Two men stood in the dawning light at a hotel, two blocks from last night's incident. As different as night and day, the older one in wrinkled brown tweed and the younger in pressed black silk.

"I would rather stab you in the face!" Croaker Norge said, turning to the younger man.

"Come on, just try it." Phoebus Buckroe held out brass spectacles with various lenses jutting from the frame.

"No, blast you. I have my magnifying glass; it has worked just fine for thirty years, I don't need some bloody contraption you found at a junk dealer. You are always looking for an easy way out. Some things just require hard work!" the older man said, taking a swig of whiskey from his flask and wiping a dribble from the stubble on his chin with a sleeve.

"Lord Remington wants this done quickly and I think this is the right tool for the job."

"I have all the tools I need right here." Croaker patted the hard leather pouch under his jacket with his bare hand. "And his daughter is not the only one that has disappeared. I've been asking around. At least four others have disappeared in the same area in the past month - one just last night, not two streets from here."

Phoebus smiled as he straightened the fingers on his white gloves, checking his reflection in the silver cap of his walking stick.

"Well, young Miss Remington is the only one that

matters, as she is the one we are being paid to find," he said, without looking at his companion. "And I told him you were the best around."

"You did no such thing, you blasted liar. You told him you were the best around and called me your bleeding manservant."

"I wouldn't have to call you such a thing if you would bathe, shave, and dress properly. You look like a chimney sweep. And besides, I was the one that found us this job. You could try to be grateful. Before I decided to take pity on you, you were scrambling to find two bit jobs, and you could barely cobble together enough coin for a haircut, let alone to pay rent. You were a beggar, hoping someone would have enough to pay you."

"I did an honest day's work for honest folk," Norge grumbled as he inspected the hotel room with his looking glass.

"You should at least buy a proper coat and hat when we finish this case. It's indecent to not have your head covered and besides, you need something to tip when a lady walks past."

"Oh, you and the ladies. If you spent half as much time on the case as you spend preening and smiling for the women, you might actually be of some use."

Phoebus sniffed at the older man and looked out the window. Staring into the crowd bustling in the street below, he noticed something.

"Master Norge."

"Yes, your Lordship?"

"Come, look at this."

"I already know about 'that'."

"The footprints? Outside on the roof of the porch?"

"Yes. I also noticed the odd three toed gouge marks in the shingles."

"Oh? It has... of course it does. What sort of beast has claws and three toes?" Phoebus asked, pressing his head to the window to look closer.

"No beast that walks on two legs." Croaker swatted at the man's shoulder. "Stop marking up my window with your greasy forehead and breath."

"Don't you think this is important? Perhaps our most important clue?"

"Yes, it's important. No, it is not the most important clue. The fact that she met with a young man here is more important. The fact that the window was not forced is more important. The fact that the claw marks outside go to the roof is more important."

"You saw all that? But you haven't even opened the window. How could you know such things?"

"Because I have eyes and I look beyond my nose. There is a snuff box under the bed - a silver one with the initials 'CTR' on it. Her hanky on the dresser has traces of snuff on it, showing her suitor used it to clean himself after taking a snort. Two champagne glasses and only one has her lip rouge on it, the other just has slobber. The window itself was closed by the maid this morning, see the curtain still stuck in it? Look at the window frame; you can see distinctive scratches, showing the intruder went up to make its escape."

"How do you know it didn't climb down from the roof?"

"Because of the marks from the claws at the edge of the porch, showing where it leapt up to get in the window."

"Why would it be able to jump to the porch roof, but not the roof above?"

"Because it had the girl, you dolt! And see the hand print at the top of the window, on the outside? Those are the slim fingers of a young woman. Don't you see anything?"

"Fine work, Master Norge!" Phoebus said, slapping the older man on the shoulder. "We will have this case closed in no time."

"Stop touching me," the older man growled as his companion wiped his hand on the drapes to rid himself of whatever imaginary dust he had picked up in their brief contact. "And stop touching things. You are disturbing the scene of the crime!"

"I think I shall go speak to young Master Roosevelt," Buckroe said, as he slipped his high tech spectacles into his coat pocket.

"Who?"

"Christopher Thaddeus Roosevelt, the young man that owns the snuff box. He is an eligible bachelor and has been courting young Miss Remington. If you kept up on the social papers, you would know this. May I have it?" Phoebus held out his hand.

"What?"

"The snuff box, it is part of our investigation and I may need it when I call upon the gentleman."

The older man handed the silver tin to his cohort, grumbling that it would be a waste of time to talk to a society dandy.

"Perhaps, but we must explore all the leads. Why don't you do what you do, and scurry along and try and track this thing while I deal with the civilized folk?"

It was a small meeting but all included were important men. The Mayor, the Honorable Joseph V. Guillotte, State Treasurer Edward Burke, Alternate NEM Exposition Commission and acting Master of Ceremonies the Honorable W.I. Hodgson and Phoebus Buckroe of the Bufton Buckroes all gathered in the sitting room of the gentleman's club known for its high quality service and its ability to not overhear conversations, The Velvet Conundrum.

Drinks and cigars had been brought in and left on the silver serving trolley for the men, the rail-like servant with thinning grey hair and pointed nose closing the doors behind him as he left the room. The men poured either brandy from crystal decanters into oversized snifters or deep maroon wine in crystal glasses and sat in large wingback chairs, the leather creaking under their silk trousers as they settled. The

Mayor turned to the Master of Ceremonies of the World's Fair and spoke.

"Hodgson, why has this delay happened? Edward tells me you have some knowledge of a conspiracy."

"No, Your Honor," the chubby man muttered, glaring at the thin man who ran the state treasury. "I have concerns about money that has disappeared. I have young ladies checking the numbers a third time now to make sure that I shall not accuse anyone except for the guilty parties."

"Women?" asked Burke, his pinched face becoming even more distorted and his voice rising to a shrill nasal tone. "Why would you have women working with figures? We all know that their soft brains do not work as well when it comes to the sciences like mathematics. You may as well bring some of the Rokairn freedmen in to do it. Why would you ever choose something so inferior to do such an important job?"

"Because no one would suspect them and they cannot be bought by petty bribes," the heavy man huffed, wiping his sweaty brow with a kerchief. "I have brought in a new girl, a well-educated one from a good house. It seems the one I had working on it before has disappeared. She left the workhouse one night and was never seen again. I would give a pretty coin to find out what happened to her. Not even her family knows where she went."

"Was it young Miss Remington you brought in?" Phoebus asked as he held his brandy to the light and swirled it around the glass, coating the sides with the amber liquid.

"Yes, how would you know that?" the Master of Ceremonies asked.

"Because, I just returned from speaking to Master Christopher Roosevelt about his missing sweetheart. It seems she was kidnapped last night. He mentioned some bookkeeping work she was doing, said she was all aflutter about something she found."

"Kidnapped?" The Mayor asked, sputtering on his wine.

"Probably ran off; you know how flighty women can be,"

Burke said with a dismissive tone.

"Another one?" Hodgson cried.

"Yes. I will accept your coin to investigate this and Mayor, if I may be so bold, this may be something to which you would like to add a reward. If I find out where this young woman has been taken I would deserve something extra."

"Indeed, you would. I will match what Hodgson shall pay. This is quite the scandal! The Telestic Krewe is already breathing down my neck about the upcoming parade. They are the oldest Society in the festivities and are very concerned about this investigation the Commissioner has begun."

"We should worry about the planning," Burke chimed in, "and not some women who wander off."

"Yes, perhaps you have the right of it Edward," said Joseph.

"Oh yes, I couldn't agree more." Phoebus smiled. "I will do all the work, quietly and discreetly. No one shall know except the four of us and my serving man that assists me. I will begin immediately, if I could just have some money for expenses from you gentlemen and I will submit my bill for the remainder after this task is complete."

Buckroe looked at the Mayor and Master of Ceremonies as he stood. They hesitated for a moment before reaching into their coats and drew out money.

"Very good, and you wouldn't mind if I took a few of these excellent cigars to help me with my investigation, would you?"

Croaker and Phoebus met in the gaming parlor the younger man preferred, to discuss what they had found. It was an upscale establishment and had fine quartz tulip shades around the silver gas chandeliers above each table. Mirrors made the room appear larger than it actually was.

The green velvet of the table tops matched the thick carpet and drapes, the dark wood of the wainscot and tables offsetting the white pillars. Music tinkled from Professor Nightingale's Magical Musical Mechanical Clavichord. Similar to the player pianos, this musical monstrosity also simulated a string quartet and percussion, creating a small symphony in a box.

It was early and the evening business had not yet arrived. Four other tables had clientele, playing dominos, cards, and drinking from fine crystal snifters and wine glasses. Smoke wafted on the evening breeze as the waiters with their ankle length aprons, bow ties, and greased hair served appetizers to the upper crust of society.

Phoebus set down his gin and drew a cigar from the monogrammed case he kept inside his jacket. He was dressed in the height of fashion. Dove grey gloves matched his top hat. His coat and vest was balanced by straight cut white slacks and shirt. He sniffed as Croaker took a shot of whiskey and chased it with his beer.

The older man wore the same clothes he had worn that morning, but had added a leather vest. He had removed his jacket and hung it on the back of the chair to the chagrin of his companion. He rolled up the sleeves of his shirt and tucked them under arm garters. He leaned back and packed a pipe from a leather pouch, wiping the spilled tobacco from his trousers onto the floor.

"Sewers," Croaker said.

"Why must you be so common?" Phoebus asked.

"Because I speak plainly and it is where we needed to go. You already made it clear your trip was a waste of time, as I thought it would be."

"It was not a waste of time. The young man is paying us well to search for his intended. And before you object again, there is nothing wrong more than one person paying us to complete a job."

"You would go to the Mayor, Honorable J. V. Guillotte himself, to get more money if you thought the city would pay us for finding the cause of this rash of disappearances."

Phoebus's face lit up with amusement at the suggestion and he turned his eyes to the ceiling as he gestured towards the older man. "Now you are beginning to think! I knew there was hope for you."

Croaker sighed and continued. "This thing came from the sewers and it brought the women, or at least Miss Remington, to the Fair grounds. We need to search there."

"The World's Fair? I went there and saw the Eighth Dasism Calvary Band. They played a beautiful rendition of Tagler's overture and grand march from Thredbeir. There must have been more than ten thousand people there." Phoebus leaned back, smiled and drew on his cigar, blowing the smoke out in rings. "The fair is almost two-hundred acres."

"Two hundred and forty-nine acres from the St. Charles Street to the Whiting River, to be precise. The main building is three-three acres by itself and is the largest roofed structure in the world."

"Where would we even start?"

Croaker smiled back and he puffed a cloud of blue smoke from his pipe. Raising his glass, he toasted his friend. "I have a hunch. How do you feel about horticulture and electric elevators?"

The two men walked through the Fair grounds. They had both been there since it opened in the month of Witen, but now they looked at it with new eyes. It had over five thousand lights, more than ten times the amount in the city. The overcast night was chill and their breath puffed in front of them. Croaker wore a long brown duster in addition to his usual clothes and had his collar turned up against the cold. Phoebus had changed again and wore his long black wool coat and blue waistcoat, accented with a cravat with a diamond pin that matched his ring. His silver handled walking stick clicked with each step.

Couples strolled arm in arm and looked upon the wonders of the modern world. It was as bright as day and the men stepped to one side as the experimental electric streetcar rolled past, crowded with people experiencing the future of transportation. The men made their way to the Horticultural Hall, wandering past the observation tower and its electric elevators.

Croaker slowed his steps and wandered in a circle around the structure, staring at the ground. He bent and touched an area at the base, running his fingers over an indent in the cobblestones.

"Scorched," he said.

"What does that mean?" Buckroe asked.

"It means we wait here and once the people are gone, we take a ride."

They waited. Phoebus tipped his top hat to a group of ladies and smiled. The women tittered and dipped their parasols as he complimented them and offered a calling card and the rose from his lapel to the one he liked best. Norge grumbled as the younger man picked another rose from the display of flowers to replace the one he had given away.

In time the crowd thinned and Croaker pulled his companion into the shadows behind the elevator to avoid the patrols that made sure the grounds were empty as the Fair closed for the night.

Rounding the structure, the older man opened his coat and drew various tools from inside pockets. A small crowbar, a rubber mallet and various pliers all went into a pile beside the girder structure.

"You have all that in your coat?" Phoebus gawked.

"Yes, what do you carry in your jacket?"

"You know, snuff, money, falsified documents. The usual."

Croaker looked up at his companion with amusement as he drew out a box with dials, meters, and vacuum tubes. Prying the elevator's power box open, he attached two clamps from the small device onto the wires of the control system. His gizmo whirred to life, he studied it and proceeded to poke it. The tower purred as it woke from its mechanical slumber.

"Don't you think this may attract some attention?"

"Yes, that is why, right now, the three urchins I paid are on the other side of the horticulture exhibit, creating enough ruckus that we will go unnoticed."

"You think of everything, don't you?" the younger man said with admiration.

Croaker snorted and detached his machine. Prying open the maintenance panel with his steel bar, he winked at his friend. "Yes, now follow me."

After gathering the tools, they crawled into the small space which led to the open shaft of the elevator, as Phoebus grumbled about getting his trousers dirty. Rungs led downward into the depths of the earth, lit by electric lights every six meters. They descended.

The hooded men gathered in the large room, twenty of them in total. The room was lit by gaslight from sconces in the walls. It was warm compared to the chill Frear air above ground; the men had doffed their outer coats and replaced them with black robes.

The room was dank and smelled of must and mildew. It was a forgotten storeroom that had been used for various purposes over the years. Most recently, it had been earmarked as the maintenance room for the discarded underground train system. Before that, it was used to hide runaway rokairn slaves and its original purpose had been for workers when they had built the sewage system.

A dark wood table dominated the center of the room. It had symbols carved into its face and the floor around it. Metal manacles had been attached to the four corners of the makeshift altar and straps attached to the center. The surface was stained darker than the rest with remnants of previous rituals.

One man stepped forward. He was broad shouldered and his presence brought a hush to the assembly, he was physically imposing and the way he moved was sanguine, radiating power and mystery.

"Tonight we usher in a new era. We call upon long forgotten forces to come do our bidding. In this age of wonders, of gas and steam bowing to the new lord of electricity, we shall summon servants from another realm that have long waited to return to our world. But this time man shall not be the servant, we shall be the masters!"

One of the men began to clap, disturbing the leader's speech. All heads turned to the interloper and his clapping slowed then stopped, his head bowed in awkward silence. The speaker ignored him and began to speak again.

"Power, my friends, is the key. We used to fear and worship fire. Now we have harnessed lightning and it dances at our command, and so shall the dark forces that once enslaved humanity with our own childish terror. Knowledge and our driving curiosity have made us the Lords now, and the universe shall bow to our whim! Bring in the sacrifice."

A hiss sounded from one of the many corridors that led to the room, and a figure entered carrying a limp form in its arms. The new arrival moved with a reptilian grace, sliding side to side with each step. It wore no hood or robe and each man saw something different than the others.

Some saw a well-dressed man in finery, others saw a mechanical monster that whirred with cogs and gears, and one man saw its true form. He shuddered, backed away, eyes wide and vomited on the floor by the wall. The speaker knew the true form of the creature and smiled an oily smile as it laid its burden on the table, a woman clad in nothing more than her white undergarments. Men darted forward to clamp each of the limbs of the girl and strap down her midsection with the restraints.

"Now we begin and the Telesic Krewe shall rise to its

rightful place of power, as leaders of this city of New Sylians!"

"Why are you down here?" Phoebus grumbled as his foot slapped in a puddle.

"Hush," Croaker hissed, dodging the plethora of webs that hung from the low ceiling to the floor. "We're almost there."

"Almost where? The electric lights ended ten minutes ago and where did you get that contraption?" Buckroe asked, gesturing at the humming electric lamp the older man carried. It was the size of two bricks and looked to weigh about as much. A flexible metal conduit ran under Croaker's coat to a power pack concealed on his back. Strange metal nozzles jutted upward from it on a pivot so they could point forward when needed.

"I made it. I told you I always have the necessary tools. Now hush, we don't want to be overheard before I'm ready."

"And you didn't want to use my glasses?" Phoebus muttered.

Soon they saw dim light ahead issuing from a doorway. They could hear a deep baritone voice speaking. Croaker switched off the electric lantern and proceeded forward without the light, Phoebus trailing behind. They crept forward to the doorway and peered around it, Norge kneeling and Buckroe looking over him.

They took in the scene with a glance. Two circles of men, twelve at the clock points in the outer circle closest to the wall. The inner circle had eight men at the compass points. A large man stood at the head of the altar, one hand clenched in the young woman's hair that lay on the table. A malformed and blurred figure hunched at the foot, caressing the prisoner's ankles with anticipation.

"By design of destiny and the hand of the elders of the

Telestic Krewe we have brought this sacrifice so the powers beyond the cloak of darkness and past the meager sight of mortal men may come forth once again and be reborn into this new world of wonders and harnessed energy. The tenth sacrifice comes this night!"

The tinny sound of dripping water echoed as the man paused, raising the wavy bladed kris above the heaving breast of the girl strapped to the table. A rat scurried past the two hidden men in the door and let out a squeal as Croaker pierced it with a dagger. The older man pulled himself back from the doorway as the men in the room turned at the noise. Phoebus watched as twenty-two pairs of eyes turned to stare at him. He felt a hand on his back shove him into the doorway and heard Norge whisper, "Make 'em chase you," as he stumbled forward into the room.

"Hello there, chaps!" Phoebus said in an amicable tone. "Am I late? You see, Smith didn't get me the invitation until just this evening. Oh, it seems I'm underdressed. Perhaps I should go find my favorite moth-eaten rag of a robe so I will blend in better with the rest of you."

There was a moment of silence before a sibilant whisper cut through the air. "Kill him!"

The outer circle of twelve men surged towards the door as Phoebus turned and ran around the corner, in the opposite direction of Croaker. He pressed flat to the wall three strides down the hall. His dark clothing mixed with the shadows, making him almost invisible.

Croaker drew an "L" shaped device from his pocket. He pressed a button and the pneumatic pressure shot a dart with a thin metal wire across the doorway. It embedded itself in the stone of the arch. He slid a button to activate the second chamber and slammed the short end of the device into the wall beside him. It bit in with a hiss and click. The men had no chance to see the trip wire before five of them went down in a pile. The wet thud of a head on stone and the click of teeth shattering and sliding across the floor were heard for a moment before the shouting began.

The remaining seven men looked down and leapt the fallen cultists, stumbling and tripping into the open part of the hall, waiting for their eyes to adjust to the dim lighting. They didn't see the shadow of Buckroe slide forward, walking stick at the ready, as the master of Bartitsu began the simple exercise of engaging more than a half dozen men and removing them as a threat.

An elegant dance began, sharp and crisp like the snap of a tango. The young man extended his arm, hitting one man in the throat with the handle of his makeshift weapon, then popped it sideways to hear the satisfying crunch of the nose of the next man. Those two men fell at his feet and he stepped forward, one foot landing on each of their hands, breaking fingers as he went to his toes and spun.

His arm was stiff as he turned in a full circle. The metal handle of the cane connected with the temple of another charging man and spun him to the ground, then continued to the jaw of the next assailant. That man's head snapped back and the sound of bone shattering was audible as he crumpled to the floor.

Phoebus smiled as he crouched and took a huge step forward past the four fallen foes, while still staying low and out of the adjusting vision of the remaining men. Three still stood and two more were struggling to regain their feet from the pile in front of the tripwire. Buckroe dropped his weight onto his hands behind him and kicked forward, destroying the knee of one man, then hooked his leg around and caught a second man behind his knee, causing him to collapse backwards on top of the two men that were attempting to stand.

Phoebus, still crouched, shot forward, walking stick extended and rammed it into the groin of the last man standing. As the man doubled over, he was struck three more times by the Bartitsu master, once in the solar plexus, making him bend further, then on the side of the neck, snapping his head sideways and one last blow on the back of his head, rendering him unconscious.

Buckroe stood with the grace of a gymnast and, taking a stride forward, stepped on the still bent knee of the man that had fallen on the others, and heard the crackle as cartilage and tendons tore and broke. The two men underneath only had a moment before the weapon met their respective temples and darkness fell over them also.

The three remaining men of the twelve that had charged into the hall and fallen over the wire lay still. Phoebus could see small darts in the back of their necks, still quivering.

Moments before, Norge had seen none of the fight yet, as he jabbed three of the fallen men with small needles and, feeling them go limp, rolled over the pile and into the room before his friend had touched the first man in the hall. An odd pistol was in his right hand and the knife in his left still held the impaled rodent. Atop the long barrel of the firearm was a copper cylinder the size of a small loaf of bread, a rectangular clip dropped down in front of the trigger and two smaller copper cylinders in front of that had a tube that fed into the clip.

Croaker's hand was steady as he pulled the trigger a half dozen times, a soft pop and hiss issuing each time. He moved the gun a bare centimeter as he fired and six of the men clutched their throats where darts appeared, falling to the floor seconds afterwards, their eyes rolling backwards.

Standing he dropped the gun and drew out his electrical light from its place on his right hip. Twisting dials and lowering the metal tube on top to point at one of the remaining two men from the inner ring, he pressed a button and a blue electric arc reached across the room and gripped the man in its tingling embrace. The man twitched and danced for a handful of seconds before collapsing to the ground.

The last man closed the distance and batted the contraption from the older man's hand, snapping the leather strap that held it to Croaker's side. The cultist pummeled the detective, slamming his fist into the older man's stomach, chin, and face, forcing him to collapse to the floor.

Norge was no stranger to a fight. He did not have the grace and style of his younger friend, but he had his share of bar fights and scrapes and was not defenseless. He snapped his right wrist and a pair of rubber coated brass knuckles shot from his sleeve, held in place by two metal rods. He slipped his fingers into the waiting circles and the only metal not coated shone in the dim light.

The man continued to pound on Croaker as the older man pressed a button on his knuckle weapon and a humming noise began. The robed figure swung a fist and it connected with Croaker's own hand. A spark and crackle sounded as the two met. Electrical current ran through the assailant's body and he did a small jig before falling unconscious to the ground.

Croaker stood and wiped blood from his nose and mouth as Phoebus stepped into the room behind him.

"You ok?" The younger man asked.

"I've had worse," Norge answered, looking at the two figures that remained. The leader of the cult barked a command in a language that twisted in the men's ears and the monstrous creature at the foot of the sacrificial table lunged forward. Phoebus shoved Croaker aside and ran to meet the inhuman beast.

"No!" the older man shouted as his younger friend fell into a fighting stance, feet wide for balance, and swung his walking stick. The creature caught it in one hand and snapped it. Punching into Phoebus's midsection with the other, the beast propelled him backwards across the room and slammed him into the wall beside the doorway.

A deep laugh came from the man at the head of the table as he raised his blade to finish the ritual. Croaker's left hand blurred and the rat laden knife flew across the room, burying itself in the man's armpit. The cult leader's arms dropped as tendons were severed, the curved dagger striking the table beside the girl's head. Blood welled from the wound and the beast stopped in its tracks, turned and sniffed the air. It cleared the space between itself and the hooded man in two strides and tore into the man with claws that hadn't been there moments before.

Croaker Norge watched as the force of the attack carried both to the ground and the creature began to feed. It had devoured half of the screaming man's chest before it slowed, then stopped. Convulsing, it vomited blood and chunks of flesh onto the dying man. It raised its head and howled a monstrous keening noise that rattled the fixtures in the room. It scrambled towards one of other exits from the room, clutching at its chest, and disappeared into the dark tunnels.

"What the hell just happened?" Phoebus asked, standing on unsteady legs, touching the back of his head and looking at the blood on his hand.

"Simple deduction. They needed pure victims. I gave them one. The rat," Croaker answered as he drew a metal stick wrapped in copper wire from inside his coat. He flipped another switch and the small magnet hummed to life. He held it to the first lock that held the restraint on the girl's ankle closed. It popped open as he brought it close. He continued to the next lock.

"You have a gizmo that opens locks, too?"

"A simple electro magnet, super powerful. It interacts with the mechanism and rolls the tumblers, unlocking the padlocks."

"Well done, old man! Now, why did that thing run off instead of killing us?"

"Again, you weren't paying attention. The rat finally died when the knife completely filled its body as it entered the man's armpit, and it became the sacrifice. The cult leader dropped his arm, stopping the beast from getting to the sacrifice it needed to devour and instead it ate him. He was not pure, so the ritual was unable to be completed."

"A rat? Why didn't they just kill animals the whole time if that would have worked?"

"I don't know it would have worked. I don't think they have enough psychic energy to do the job, even if all animals are pure in the sense they needed. Now, we need to find the constable and bring them down here."

"I'll go get them."

"No need. They have already gathered at the elevator because of the sparking that would have started about fifteen minutes ago. I set the machine up to malfunction and draw their attention. They will see the forced maintenance door and find my marks on the walls that will lead them here."

"You, you brought the police here, already?"

"Yes, if I am correct they should be here…" holding up a hand for silence, they could both hear shouts of men from the direction they had come, "in just a few minutes."

Croaker Norge and Phoebus Buckroe stood in the Mayor's foyer surrounded by police as Guillotte came down the wide staircase in a dressing gown and nightcap, rubbing his eyes.

"What is the meaning of this, Chief Johnson?" his Honor asked.

"Forgive the late intrusion, sir," the Chief of Police, who had also been woken, said. "We found these men in the old tunnels committing atrocities in a horrible midnight ritual."

"We didn't do any such thing, you incompetent bastard," Croaker muttered, loud enough to be heard by everyone. One of the duty officers hit him from behind with a billy club, dropping him to his knees.

"Ah, good officer, that will not be necessary. My manservant is just a bit rough and overzealous in his opinions, no matter if they hold truth or not," Phoebus said as he took a step forward, holding his manacled hands out in a peaceful manner. The Chief looked confused as he attempted to determine if he had just been insulted.

"Buckroe!" The Mayor said, "Explain the meaning of this!"

"He said he was working for you, your Honor," the Chief

explained.

"And I am. And I have single handedly uncovered a plot so foul that it will shake the very foundations of this city," Phoebus said.

"Do not be dramatic; just tell me what is going on," the Mayor said.

"It seems the Telestic Krewe was up to dark deeds, but I have put a stop to it and rescued young Miss Remington from certain death and worse. The head of the Krewe was leading the rituals personally to summon things from the unknown."

"You put a stop to it?" Croaker asked as he stood. "Perhaps you should tell them how one of the men was no other than Edward Burke, State Treasurer?"

The Mayor looked aghast and he turned to the Chief of police with a questioning look. Johnson nodded, showing that the man spoke the truth.

"Of course, Norge. They knew that. They arrested him with the other men."

"Did they also know that he had been pilfering funds from the World's Fair? That with forgery and fraud he had already embezzled more than one million, seven hundred thousand bites of Federation currency?" The room went silent. "Just a little something I found during my investigation. Oh, excuse me, your Lordship, your investigation. Was I remiss in mentioning the detail that I had searched his house when you were in your meeting with the Mayor, gaining his financial and political support in this matter?"

Phoebus's mouth opened and closed as he tried to speak. Croaker stared at him with a smug smile.

"It was simple to see, if you are observant. I merely followed a trail of paper, instead of blood and mud. Perhaps we could be released and discuss this tomorrow after his Honor and the good Constable had a chance to finish their investigation?"

Travis I. Sivart

The Warm Glow of Companionship

And here I sit with you gentleman. Thank you Wadsworth, the cognac and cigar is all I require. Please, see yourself out for a while.

I can tell you, my friends, I am happy to have returned to the fine city of St. Lucas. Now, as I tell you this tale I must insist on absolutely no questions. Allow it to unfold before you in all its glory, mystery, and dark secrets. I shall reveal all to you by the end, as it was revealed to me. Lord Cross, you feel you shamed poor Henry Cabot with your tale of the vile religion in the Talic Islands of men brought back from the dead as slaves? Well, I mean no disrespect sir, but your tale could be told in a nursery by the nanny when held against the truth I am about to tell to you.

As you both know, I had journeyed to South Mirron, the country of Zatchu. Many men do this for adventure of the wilds, the mountains, or hunting the exotic beasts, but most do it for the glittering siren call of the gold from the ancient Dasism. I went in search of none of those. Rather I sought knowledge of a more ancient people, the Naveribe. These people and their civilization were once as great as any in this world's history. They left great lines behind, only discovered last year when men of science flew a zeppelin over the area for the first time.

I had flown over them myself, a week before the expedition. They were breath-taking. Many said they could not have been made by primitive men. Some said that other technology had to be used to make these great lines. I would search for that, the source of these ancient mysteries. If I could prove that great civilizations existed five millennia and a half before our time, it would change the world.

We began the excursion in early Axara with the usual contingency of scientists, soldiers, local guides, and men to set up our camp and carry our expedition's supplies - about thirty in all. We traveled south from Tiflur on foot with llamas for pack animals. These beasts smell less than camels, but they spit just as their Drungian cousinsdo. There was boundless camaraderie. We all knew great things waited for discovery and we would be famous. At night we gathered around roaring fires and the porters sang their native songs. The scientists gathered in small groups with their notebooks, comparing their knowledge. The Dasism joked with each other in their crude language and laughed, and the hunting men enjoyed the sport they could find as we traveled.

We had made it to the great lines, though we couldn't discern what they were from the ground. When we arrived, about half of us came down with a debilitating fever. We decided to press on, but it wasn't long before we had to stop. I also became afflicted, and I spent many days shivering in my tent. My fever was like none I had experienced before, and everything was a haze and fog for me. People's voices were swollen and almost undecipherable. My hands were red and puffy, making it difficult to hold a tin cup of water, let alone a glass of whiskey.

A storm came upon us at this time. It was a horrible squall that arose in the west. We thought it was a hurricane that broke on the mountains and the remainder drenched us for days. This was supposed to be the dry season. The winds tore at our tents, bringing them down upon us. Our chief guide, a stout Dasism named Kenzet'tua, told us we must head west for shelter in the mountains. The land ran in great valleys in a northeast to southwest direction. We were forced to follow these, as we could not scale them in the weather with half of our men sick and barely able to walk. We lost over a dozen men to accidents and sickness. The porters began to desert us, even though we had already paid them. They would just disappear, leaving behind their gear and duty. These primitives had no sense of honor, and were terrified of the simplest things. I soon learned that their fears may be more real than I gave credit.

When we reached a sheltered area there was only a half dozen of us left: myself, the big game hunter Kyle Johnson, Kenzet'tua, a porter named Philip, and two archeologists - Marcus and Wendell Carrington (of the New Philton Carringtons). We only had four llamas remaining, and our guide recommended we sacrifice three of them to the Gods. I argued against it, but Mister Johnson sided with our guide, stating it would also give us food while we waited for the storm to subside, as well as put our two locals at ease. The archeologists were no help in this, as they were in the grips of panic.

That night the sky cleared and we saw the stars for the first time in three days. I am no navigator, but I pride myself on knowing enough to find my way. We were very much off course. The mountains loomed to the west, but from what I could tell in my feverish haze we were days south of where we should be. We slept in puddles of mud under tattered canvas and a rocky overhang. It was that night that things changed forever.

I woke with a start. Everything was quiet, and nothing seemed amiss. My fever had broken and my head was clear, but I was ravenous. I stumbled to the dying fire to have some of the llama that was still on the spit. I cut at it with my belt knife, devouring it as if I had not eaten in weeks. I could see the shadow of another, not too far away, also having a late night snack. He was hunched over his meal, his back to me, shoving it in his mouth with wet smacking noises.

As I began to feel sated, I looked around the camp. I could see the sleeping forms of Mister Johnson and one of the archeologists. Kenzet'tua was silhouetted on a hillock not far away, praying to whatever ancient powers he believed in, and I said a quick prayer to the patron saint of travelers. Philip was huddled at the far back of the recess, staring past me with wide eyes. I followed his gaze to my meal companion. It was then I saw the drag marks in the mud leading to the man. Confused, I stood to see what the other archeologist had dragged out of our shelter. I thought perhaps a blanket to keep warm, or to spread on the ground to keep the mud from his meal. He had made a mess though, archeology tools scattered between me and him.

I froze in mid-step as the moon revealed his meal. I could see the mutilated limbs, contorted unnaturally, on the ground under him. It was not beast he was dining on, it was human. My fellow diner turned to gaze upon me. Its eyes shone with a faint greenish glow, and its mouth was an open gaping maw. I could not tell details in that dim light, but I could see squirming things inside that ravenous craw. A dozen or more of the hideous vibrissa swayed, like serpents' tongues, tasting the air. Its arms had extra joints and were a third again the length of a man's. And its legs were jacked backwards like a cricket's.

It was then that Philip's scream split the night. I spun to look at him, and saw two more of these creatures scaling downward from above him. Mister Johnson and the one remaining archeologist sat bolt upright. Behind me I heard a shriek, not unlike a fox's, but much louder and angrier. The monsters were upon our porter in a flash. Their hands which had no fingers, but instead were three elongated jointed claws, tore out his throat in a moment. They fell upon their prey in an instant.

Mister Johnson was up and had his long gun leveled at the creatures. The muzzle flashed and the sound deafened me for a few moments. One creature flew backwards and crashed against the rocky face of the cliff. Relief washed over me, feeling I was saved. But it rose into a crouch and eyed the hunter.

Allow me to take a moment now for a drink of my cognac. The memory of this makes my hands shake, as you can see. Ah, the drink will help me steady my nerves, and my cigar has gone out. One moment while I relight it, then I shall continue. I see you sit as quietly as I have asked you to do, and for that I offer my gratitude. I think if you asked questions, I would lose my nerve at these memories, and seek the sweet smoky streets outside. The noise and clatter of the throngs of people offer quite a comfort now. You see the heads of the great beast on these walls; the lion, the rhinoceros, the crocodile, and even the massive elephant? The danger of hunting these in no way compare to what I saw and experienced that night, and the nights that followed. Very well, I see your anxiety, I shall continue with my tale.

Our big game hunter was well recommended, and his steel lent me courage at that moment. As the beast launched itself at the man, I dove for my bedroll for my own sidearm. I always carry a Teurone handgun. There is a reason that gun has become such a staple of certain armies. A shadow and breeze passed above me as I did this, and I realized that if I had not moved at the moment I did, I would have been disemboweled from behind. The creature that had been quietly dining had chosen that moment to join the fray. It sailed over me, landing on its feet three full paces beyond. Thinking about it now, that would mean it had leapt at least six meters with ease.

The remaining archeologist sat frozen. I do not even know which of the two brothers it was, but he sat as still as a statue. I reached out and shook him, and he seemed to wake as if from a dream. He leapt up and ran out of our shelter. I could not track him at that moment though, because the beast that had been eyeing Mister Johnson sprang at the hunter. That man was a rock, he did not flinch. He remained perfectly still except for the barrel of the gun that tracked his quarry with astounding skill. Another blast issued forth, this time catching the monster in its open maw. I insist its head melted when that shot, meant for taking down bull elephants, found its mark. It flipped backwards, and its boney legs fell centimeters short of the hunter. I will name my first son after that man, for without him that night I swear to the gods and all the saints that I would surely not be here to tell this tale. I had always teased him for sleeping with his gun and fully dressed, but now I see the reason. Thankfully, in order to stay warm, none of us had disrobed that night.

I heard three clicks and without me seeing it, the rifle was reloaded. He shouted at me to back up, but not run. I did as he said, my pistol held in front of me. Funny things happen to a man when faced with death and danger. When you do not have time to think, some freeze, some run, but others act. And that saved my life a dozen times that night. We backed out of our shelter and towards the fire. The archeologist was there, holding a flaming brand and a lantern. I think it was Marcus, but I am still not positive. That alone may allow you to guess his fate.

The next few moments became a blur. Our attackers bounded from our sleeping shelter, Mister Johnson snatched the lantern from the terrified scientist and threw it into the fire. The fire flared four meters into the air. The creatures screamed again, that eerie sound like a fox, a barking scream that women often swear is more an evil spirit than an animal. In this case, I think they would be spot on. Pardon me here for my informality, but after what he and I went through, I feel it is only acceptable for me to call Mister Johnson by his given name.

Kyle shouted for us to run, roughly shoving the stunned man in front of him. We ran. We went straight for Kenzet'tua. It was all very surreal, as if in a dream. We ran as if in molasses for the first score of steps. We could see the guide, and I am guessing he was also some sort of Shaman, for he was still on his knees praying. His arms were held wide, supplicating to the stars, and his voice had risen from a mumble to shouting. We bolted past him, calling for him to come with us. But we had no time to stop and drag him along. But it was not the last time we crossed paths with him.

We were the hunted then. I do not know how long it took these nightmare apparitions to recover from the flaring light of the fire, but soon we could hear their barking screams as they pursued us. We ran. The night had grown chill and our breath was short white puffs of air in front of us. We tried to run faster, to make those frozen wisps fall behind us, but they always stayed in front of us, as if we were standing still.

The scientist still led the way, though Kyle told him to follow rather than lead. I spotted the cave in the mountain-side as I ran and realized that was where the man was heading. The hunter tried to shout at him, telling him we were being corralled like sheep, trying to get the man to keep running and that all we had to do was survive until sunrise. The scientist did not listen. He ran straight into the cave, and we began to run past it when we saw five of the creatures in front of us. We followed our companion into the cave.

Kyle went to the back of the cave, which was only about a dozen paces deep, and knelt down, dropping his ammunition on the ground in front of him. He said we could make a stand there. The beasts could not enter all at once, and perhaps he could hold them off. I stood beside him, my weapon at the ready. He told me not to waste bullets, only fire when I knew I could hit them in an eye or their mouth. We waited. We could see the shadowy forms outside, mere steps from the entrance of the cave opening. My hand began to shake as the cold set in and chilled the sweat on our bodies. I know this is how hypothermia can set in, and I stamped my feet to keep my circulation going.

A half an hour had passed, if it was a minute, and the beasts still had not approached our position. They would not enter. This emboldened our archeologist friend, who still carried his stick from the fire, though it was no longer lit. He began laughing like a madman. He taunted the creatures, and no amount of advice or threats from myself or Mister Johnson would quiet him. He began dancing closer to the mouth of our hiding place, shouting insults at our enemies. Two of them crouched just outside, watching him with their small heads tilted as if listening to his gibbering. They were mere silhouettes with pin-point green spots that told us the location of their eyes.

It was inevitable I guess, but the man underestimated our foes. He stepped too close to the entrance, and apparently they had not come as close as they could. With lightening reflexes one snatched the man's charred club as he swung it towards them. It became a tug of war for the space of two heartbeats, but he refused to give up his weapon. Before we could react, they had dragged him outside. I saw the spray of his blood as they disemboweled him. Horrified, I stumbled backwards and hit the wall. I am ashamed to say it, but I could only stare at what transpired. Kyle was made of sterner stuff though, and he stood and marched forward firing his weapon. Two shots were fired. One of the beasts flew backwards, its head missing. The other was rocked by a glancing blow to its shoulder.

The man was still alive, and tried to drag himself back into our shelter. But it was too late. Three more monsters came into view and one grabbed him by his foot and dragged him outside, screaming. The archeologist was lost. His shrieks died away, much too slowly for my tastes. It seemed the beasts kept him alive as they did their ghastly deed.

We waited for the sun. I do not know how long it was, but to be honest I think we waited days before the sky finally began to show a hint of pink from sunrise. What happened next is not something from the year six thousand and thirty three. It is either technology from far beyond ours, or from legends of dark magic that we scoff at as we tell tales around the fireplace. The silhouettes of the creatures filled the doorway and they placed their malformed hands on the edge of the cave. A deep vibration came from the mountain as if it were growling, though I don't know if it were in warning or aggression. The beasts began screeching in answer. High pitched, irregular, and discordant. It scraped at our nerves and I found myself crouching with my hands covering my ears. I was like some terrified animal, hardly in control of my own actions. Kyle was behaving the same, having backed himself all the way to the rear of the cave, his eyes were wide and showing bloodshot whites, his pupils dilated.

An odd sound came from the front of our shelter, as if pudding were dropped from a great height. When I first looked for the source of the sound I only saw the monsters crowding the doorway, but soon saw what caused this new noise. The cave was melting. It was not hot, or at least it did not put off heat or glow as lava does. But the mouth of the cave was closing by melting. I could see pointed spikes growing downward, like teeth in a mouth. The scientific part of my mind realized this must be what it is like if you were to watch stalactites grow over a thousand years. Stalagmites also rose from the ground as pieces of the upper cavern dripped down like black drool, building the lower teeth of this alien maw.

I still do not know if what I saw was real. I had a jungle fever for days and that may have touched my mind. I snapped. I turned and ran for the rear of the cave, clawing and slapping at the walls. I do not know how long I did this for, but I know it was dark when I came to my senses. Where light should now be streaming into the mouth of the cave, there was no longer an entrance. As I felt along the wall I discovered an opening. It was not large, but I think we could fit through it. I could feel warm, moist air around me.

I called to Kyle, and heard a hoarse reply. In short order he had crafted a rough torch from his shirt wrapped around the barrel of his gun and doused in fine grain alcohol. The opening was larger than I had realized. It was almost to my shoulder in height, and wide enough that I barely had to turn to enter it. I had enough wits to recover my weapon before entering. We ducked around a smoothed stalactite we previously had not noticed and began our journey in the further unknown.

It was a horrible descent. If we had not been going down I would have thought we were going in circles, for the floor angled deeper the whole way. The walls were smooth and slightly curved, and the ground was similar except for rounded bumps that crossed from wall to wall every couple of steps. The air was thick and smelled of foul and fetid things, and it became hard to breathe as we traveled. The air grew warmer and I would swear to the gods and all the saints I could feel it moving around me. Our torch guttered and smoked. The fuel he used was pure and originally was a blue flame and should have continued to burn clean, but as we spiraled further into the bowels of the earth, the light became a sickly yellow color and the torch spewed thick black clouds, like an outdated coal foundry.

I cannot say how long we traveled, though in my mind it seemed to be more hours than we would have traveled if we were above ground and in open air with a full retinue for safari. It was endless and our minds were as lost as we were. From the corner of our eyes we began to see things shifting in the tight, enclosed spaces and shadows. Quick movements of small things and slow languid movements of much larger things. In the beginning when we stopped to look we only found rock, but later we found crystal. The oddest crystals I have ever witnessed. Sharp, like broken glass, but black as oil. They were small when we first noticed them, but they became larger as we descended further into the depths. They jutted up like bamboo grass, but they would not give way when we stepped on them. Instead our feet slid on them, and they raked our calves and legs. They left some residue on our skin, and I daresay in our cuts. Soon enough the walls were these same black crystals, as round as a horse's trunk and as long as a tropical palm is tall.

I must confess, my mind was no longer stable. I had just recently recovered from the fever, hunted by monsters for kilometers at a run, breathed the tainted air of that cavern, saw things that were not there, and taken some foreign chemical into my wounds from the crystals. Kyle's eyes were rimmed with thick red and surrounded by dark circles. With his torn shirt and tattered pants he looked like a prize fighter that had seen the king of demons himself. I can only imagine what he saw when he looked upon my face. I do not know if what I describe next is real or the fiction of my fatigued body and strained mind.

The world we knew had ended. We were in an utterly foreign realm. The crystal passages opened up into a huge cavern. The air was now hot and I could see red glowing rivers below the crystalline floor. A raised dais of polished obsidian dominated the open space. It had been carved with strange symbols and pictures that resembled the Naveribe lines I had seen from the air just weeks before. Kneeling upon that unholy altar was Kenzet'tua. He was painted with a dark liquid that I knew to be blood. It coagulated on his skin in places, and ran free in others. I saw some was his, from freshly made cuts, and the rest were from the hideous sacrifices that lay around him. I could see several dismembered torsos, each glittering in the hazy red light with runes carved into their flesh. As I stared in horror, he began chanting and I caught sight of other movements. These things no longer hid when I looked directly at them, but I could not focus on them either. They slithered and crawled everywhere, covering what was the ground. My mind would not accept their very existence and I have woken every night since then, with dreams of these things in my room, coming closer to me.

Johnson screamed and lowered his weapon, firing it twice, slapping it open and shoving more shells into the barrel. Snapping it closed he fired again and again. He dropped shells around him and they rolled off from where we stood to the glowing streams below, popping in small explosions as they did. I raised my eyes to where heaven should be and prayed. I prayed to the Changing Wheel, to

Jonath, to the Saints, to the Holy Promethene, to my own mother (May the gods protect her and give her soul rest), and anyone else of which I could think. I was babbling. As I did, a moment of clarity struck me… the smoke was rising, swirling, and being taken away up a passage.

I grabbed Kyle by his shoulder and shook him, intending to point this out to him. His eyes were mad and his mind was gone. He did not see me. He looked through me. He loaded his rifle again with instinct and skill blending into a smooth action, and lowered his gun at me. I slipped and fell at his feet as he fired where I had stood a heartbeat before. Kenzet'tua screamed for me to sacrifice the man, to join him with these gods that crawled all about me. My hand drew my belt knife without me realizing what I did, and I had cut the man's ankle tendon before I could stop myself. The hunter fell.

His eyes cleared and the insanity melted away. I grabbed him and shouted about the smoke, and a way up and possibly out. He shook his head and tears rolled down his dirt streaked face. He mouthed one word, run. Run. And I did. Firing my pistol at anything close to me, I clamored towards the ridge nearest to me. I left the man that had saved my life countless times, thinking only of escape. I could hear the cavern thrumming with a heartbeat of its own as I did. I followed the passage where the air currents led me. I was blinded from the toxic fumes and tears. I lashed out with my knife, cutting into things I could not see. And I ran. I do not know how long I ran. I only know I climbed upward. As I did the air became thinner and cleaner. The sounds faded behind me, though I swore I could hear pursuit.

I finally emerged into daylight. I walked towards a setting sun. I walked through the night. It may have been days, I am unsure, but I finally reached the ocean, the mountains towering behind me. I continued to wander for days before I was found by a fishing boat. From there I made way home. I later discovered I had traveled to the southernmost tip of the mountains. I was delirious for a week or more, and owe my life to those fishermen. And now here I sit, sharing my tale with you, and a warning. There are ancient, hidden things, long forgotten, that still lurk in dark places.

Now, if you will excuse me; I must return home to my lovely wife and young son, Waldorf.

The Tridington Birthright: Shadow Heritage

Machines hummed and whined as sparks flew as the generator exploded and steam filled the air. The atrium glass shattered and the building shook. As it rained down on Trudy as she tried to keep her feet and instead bounced across the floor. A fog descended as bright orange and yellow flashes lit the air, simulating the lightening Uncle Waldorf had tried to harness. A series of static electric arcs crackled and swirled in the mist near the center of the room. A weak sound, reminiscent of a death rattle, came from the area in which the Prime Machine had been with Uncle Waldorf at the controls. A final explosion was followed by a hollow boom, and Trudy was thrown backwards, head over petticoat, landing beyond the outer ring of machines.

Murky forms crept from the epicenter of the explosion, crawling and lurching away from the light that surrounded the wreckage. Leathery and hunched, skittering and crawling, they sought darkness. Low and close to the ground, four legged beasts left a trail of moisture as evidence of their passing. Lumbering, humanoid forms bemoaned their freedom as they covered their misshapen heads from the unaccustomed brightness.

The workshop was devastated. Many of the windows in

the hangar-sized building had been shattered. It was large enough to house a dirigible, but had felt cramped once Ol' Uncle Waldorf had piled his equipment inside. Spencer stood up, coughing and squinting through the yellow dust that hung in the acrid air. Glass crunched underfoot as he worked his way to where he had last seen his twin sister. He wandered past the twisted wreckage that had taken almost four years to build and calibrate, and was stunned by the extent of the destruction. The haze inside the building was clearing, being drawn up through the broken windows, and a cloud rose into the dawning sky. It would be seen for kilometers away.

Unseen, other things withdrew into the dark shadows at the edge of the room. Rats scurried out of their path, or their lives were ended with the snap of a hungry maw. The strange energy which had opened the doorway for these creatures had waited for an opportunity such as this. Plans of millennia had come to a head, and as the dust settled, dark strategies went into action.

Spencer stepped over the debris and called for his sister, not noticing a fleshy appendage slither away at his approach. Hearing her sputtered reply, he rushed forward. She was partially hidden by a fallen boiler. It was wedged against a copper plated workbench which was covered with scoring from acetylene torches and marks from the electricity. Splinters of wood littered her yellow skirts and her bonnet still smoked where an acidic mixture had landed. Spencer helped her up and they looked each other over, her with a critical eye and he with a worried look.

"What happened?" he asked. "Did Uncle mess up?"

"Spencer Theodore Matthew Tridington! You know perfectly well that Uncle Waldorf double and triple checked every machine, gear, cog, pulley, wire, whozit, whazzit, thingamabob, whirligig, and screw in this building! This was not an error on his part," she huffed in a single breath. "This was something else entirely. The laboratory is in shambles and the time machine is destroyed. This was sabotage!"

"What?"

"Oh, don't contradict me, young man," she said, even though he was only minutes younger than her, and even that was contested. Trudy chose to believe their Great-Aunt Gertie had the right of it. Trudy had been named after her, and followed in her footsteps as a strong and opinionated woman. Great-Aunt Gertie was Uncle Waldorf's mother, and a twin herself, though her brother had disappeared a decade before Trudy and Spencer were born, lost to the exploration of the wilds of the Dark Land. "It makes perfect sense. Uncle Waldorf is a genius, and methodical in every aspect of his work, barring his enthusiasm and not taking notes and not remembering where he put things," she muttered under her breath, "but that is what he has us for!"

She spun towards her brother, her face flushed. "Spence! We must think, think hard. You are perspicacious and you will be the key to this!"

"Trudy, I don't even know what that means," he replied with a droll tone. His attention was attracted by movement out of the corner of his eye and he turned to stare into the shadows.

"Don't be querulous, it doesn't matter. What is important now is that you put those skills to use," she continued as he returned his attention to her, rolled his eyes, and sighed. "I expostulate this was an act of malicious intent and a heinous deed with, with, with, very mean objectives. Maybe even criminal. Yes! I shant be magnanimous in this; I shall be assiduous in my endeavor to discover the varlet who would dare to bring an aubergine shade of despair to our house!"

"Trudy, stop it! You have tongue enough for two sets of teeth," Spencer interrupted her tirade. "You will call down the ghost of the great bard himself to smite you if you keep using all your big words."

"You are just upset because I am smarter, and older, than you."

"Not at all, you were being grandiloquent and sententious, and it was superfluous," he responded, mimicking her lofty tone as she glared at him, with hands on her hips and lips pursed in a moue. "Remember, my dear sister, we attended the same school. You just feel the need to use words people don't understand to make them uncomfortable. And before you go on about women's suffrage, let us focus on the task on hand," Spencer gestured to the spectacle in front of them, "and discern what precisely took place here, if it were not a grievous error on our crazy uncle's part. Now, we should start at the beginning, and as I recall that was almost four years ago when Uncle's friend visited …"

"They graduated at the top of their class," Uncle Waldorf bragged to his friend, his white moustaches wiggling as he nodded, "both of them. And they did it a year early too. We sent them to progressive schools, not just the haughty and tuft-hunter social grounds. And Spencer even has chosen a young lady to court, haven't you lad?"

Uncle Waldorf tugged the elbow length rubber gloves from his hands and set them on the marble hall table that Mrs. Gibbs kept stocked with fresh flowers. The plump housekeeper gasped and removed the offending hand protection, concerned that some chemicals may remain on them and score the furniture. It would not be the first time.

A cool spring breeze wafted through the house, and the scent of blooming flowers was in the air. Uncle Waldorf wore a white lab coat with a brown leather apron over it. His hair was a wild mass, resembling a wheat field crossed with an angry sheep. His goggles hung around his neck. He guided his friend to the parlor for tea. The guest was not a tall man, but neither was he short. And that description seemed to fit him in all aspects. Neither fat nor thin, neither dark haired nor light, and though not an imposing presence he did stand out for an unexplainable reason. His shirt sleeves were rolled up, and dust from traveling showed. He handed his low brimmed hat and ruddy leather duster with brass buckles to Mrs. Gibbs. He ran a hand though his short hair. It was unfashionable and did not have any pomade in it to keep it in place; instead it hung loose and wavy.

Trudy stared at him the same way she stared at the first mantis she ever found. Fascinated by its mystique, but cautious because it was strange, and all things that were strange could be dangerous. The girl wore an ankle-length white dress which she hated. She always looked upset when she was presented with a new dress, thinking of her brother's full length trousers, vest, striped shirt, and open collar with envy. She outright refused to wear a bustle, which she called 'a ridiculous spring loaded horse's posterior', though she would wear a hoop skirt on formal occasions.

Spencer's hair was parted in the middle and slicked down, as was the style. He could not yet grow a mustache at seventeen, but he did try. His Uncle insisted he shave it, citing that only men that earned it could wear facial stylings. Trudy thought Uncle was trying to save Spencer from embarrassing himself with a lip that appeared to have a shy caterpillar hiding under his nose.

The twins sat on a divan as the two gentlemen took seats on two leather wing-backed chairs. A small table stood between them with a brandy decanter, snifters, and cigars. Mrs. Gibbs entered with tea and biscuits, glaring at Spencer as the boy eyed the alcohol with the hope of youth, dreaming of being included in the adult pursuit. The maid left with an audible sniff of disapproval.

"Wally," the stranger began with a familiar tone, "I see you are still dabbling in chemistry. Or should I call a spade a spade and use the term alchemy?"

"Jack, my oldest friend," the uncle said, smoothing his glorious walrus-like moustache, "I believe science is ignoring what was discovered in the past, and has been lost."

The twins stared at the man talking to their uncle. He was more than twenty years Waldorf's junior but spoke as an equal. For their uncle to call him his oldest friend was incredulous. Their uncle had boyhood friends which he had known all his life that still popped in on social calls.

"I have brought you a new science," the man said, leaning in conspiratorially and glancing at Spencer and Trudy with a mysterious smile, "though I don't know if this is the time or place to discuss it."

Uncle Waldorf looked at his niece and nephew. Trudy looked offended and Spencer sat up straight, pulled his shoulders back in almost a fighting stance, and moved to the edge of his seat. Waldorf reached for the cigars and cut the tips from the end, covering his smile with one hand and issuing a polite cough.

"Trudy, be a good hostess for our esteemed company, Mister Tucker, and pour us some tea, no cream or sugar please. Some for you and your brother also; you will remain to hear this. You see Jack," Waldorf said, turning to their guest, "they shall both be working with me. Yes, they shall continue their studies, but I am a professor and have arranged for them to gain their degree under my tutelage. Their internship shall be with me."

"Oh Uncle!" Trudy exclaimed, spilling tea on Spencer's leg in her excitement.

"Honestly?" Spencer said, standing in his enthusiasm, not recognizing what his sister had done. He sat down as he realized the childlike response. Adding in a formal tone, "That sounds just fine. Thank you, dear uncle."

Rising from his seat, Waldorf went to the mantle and drew a fag from the tinder pot and lit it from the smoking lamp. He placed it against the tip of his cigar, and puffed. When done, he passed it to Jack to light his own. The children watched as it flared ten centimeters high. Smoke curled lazily above the two men and wafted away on the spring breeze.

Taking two cups and saucers from his niece and setting them on the table, Waldorf asked his friend, "Will you take Scamander cream with your tea?" He placed a hand on the brandy decanter to convey his meaning.

"Yes please," the man answered as he drew a sheaf of papers from his inside vest pocket, "and I think you should look at these."

Waldorf poured a spot of brandy into each of the cups, and took the papers as he sipped the tea. After a moment he set the cup down with an absent movement and picked up his cigar, still reading the papers. Minutes passed in silence. Trudy watched her uncle's face, as Spencer picked at the wet stain on his pant leg. She knew that look, Uncle was fascinated. When Waldorf finished, the ash on his cigar was almost five centimeters long. Jack Tucker sat back in his chair, relaxed, and enjoyed his tea and smoke with an ease that was almost inappropriate. The twins had sipped at the tea and eaten four biscuits each while waiting.

"Do you really think this is possible?" Waldorf asked, holding the papers towards his friend.

"Keep them, they are for your use." Jack waved the papers away as he sipped at the tea. "I know it is possible. I have seen proof, though I am not sure if a machine is the best or only way to make this happen. I will give you caution; be wary and guarded, for this does not come without price. Dark things hide in corners of the universe, and some people seek to release them upon this world."

"Of course, I am always careful!"

"Waldorf," the stranger said, placing a hand on his friend's arm, "I am serious, this is not an adventure without risk of danger. You are not to take this lightly or treat it as a folly. Remember your journey to… Do you understand?"

The men met eyes, and held each other's gaze for a long moment. Waldorf nodded, and his mustaches waggled as he did. "Oh, I understand perfectly, my friend, and I shall take every precaution," he said with intensity. Jack seemed satisfied, and released his arm. Waldorf turned to his niece and nephew, his mood light again. "Spencer. Trudy. Prepare the laboratory; we are changing our focus to a new project!"

In a dark part of town, cultists chanted. They called for the birth of things - which had been lost in antiquity – they called for things to awaken from the miasma of the æther, to return to the place that had once been home to their unnatural forms and lives. Kneeling in their brown robes the acolytes formed a circle, each facing towards the center, and supplicated themselves in prayer.

A large man with a scarred face towered above the worshipers and guarded the only exit from the underground temple. Arms folded across his naked chest, his upper body showed gears and brass where muscle and flesh should have been. He was slack-jawed and his eyes were glazed over as he stared past the scene in front of him. He was there as an honor guard, and in case any of the people within came to their senses and attempted to flee.

A tall, thin man whose bald head gleamed in the flickering light of the braziers led the prayer, surrounded by symbols carved into the stones of the unused sewer. He was bare-chested and wiry muscled, chiseled in a way that spoke of strenuous diet and harsh labors. His skin was covered with puckered brands that had been burned into his flesh. The angry red symbols on his body and the nearby stone glowed in the fervor of the ritual.

The priest held a long, thin blade that had a deformed squid-like pommel bent perpendicular to the shaft of the ceremonial weapon. The tip was pressed to the naked flesh of the young virgin who was held down by four cultists. As he had done on each new moon for almost four years now, he led the unholy hymn as the crouched figures around him swayed.

He could feel the veil growing thinner, and knew that soon it would be pierced, and his glorious master and its servants would once again walk the realm of man, and claim what was rightfully theirs before they were banished eons ago. He had personally stopped the only man that could change that, three decades ago in the Dark Land - a man named Tridington.

A warehouse had been converted into a workshop when the old laboratory was found to be too small. Both children had graduated with degrees and lofty titles just a month before. People mocked them as eccentrics and excluded them from most social events because of their curious and secret work. Spencer kept a social schedule, as courting Ms. Brewer would not be appropriate otherwise. Trudy did have a suitor, Mister Emery Vance, though she had no interest in him.

"Three years, seven months, sixteen days, and eighteen hours later, here we stand," Uncle Waldorf proclaimed to the twins, "and tonight we shall see the fruits of our labors of this project we have toiled upon."

They went to work, shoveling coal into the furnace and ramping up the machines to a fine head of steam. A storm raged outside. Lightning and thunder played their song and electrifal conductors were raised to attract the energy. The yellowed windows above rattled with each crack of nature's power. Though steam set the machine into motion, the lightning would actually open the portal to the Æther. The room hummed and their hair stood on end with the static that filled the warehouse.

Uncle Waldorf was like a child at a fair. He ran back and forth to each device, checking dials as if he had never seen them before, his eyes full of excitement and wonder. His hair was standing straight out and his white laboratory coat flapped wildly around him.

"Spencer, Trudy, prepare the circuits." The twins had already done this, but Uncle Waldorf always enjoyed a bit of theatrics. "We shall test this beast and take it for a ride tonight!"

The air rippled and a chill wind swept through the room. Black whispers were lost on the breeze, as dusky things waited beyond the veil for their opportunity to enter the world, unbeknownst to the trio.

"Remember when that man came to the house with the papers Spencer?" Trudy asked.

"Hm?" Spencer was distracted. He had given up a social engagement to be there. He had confided in his sister that Abigail had allowed him to kiss her last week. It was scandalous. No one had seen, and he had only told his sister, but if anyone were to find out, his betrothed would be ruined.

"You are thinking of her again, aren't you?"

"What? No, I am not," he denied, "I am just hungry." He paused for a moment, head tilted. He was immaculate as usual. He had taken to wearing his collar buttoned and a cravat at all times now. He was a picture of a gentleman, sans the overcoat and top hat. He had also grown a full head taller than his sister. "Actually, I am ravenous!"

"Yes my dear brother, as am I. I hypothesized this may happen. The machine is drawing energy from wherever it can, including our bodies. I expect we will be exhausted when this is over. You see, we exude an electrical current and the device is drawing all that to itself."

"I know, I did help design and build it, if you recall."

"Children," the professor shouted over the din. They hated being called that, but said nothing. "We are almost ready. I will strap myself in now, and when I signal you, throw the switches."

The switches were actually modified brake levers for trains. Moving them would take all of their strength. Uncle Waldorf climbed into the machine. It was a puzzle of brass and wires with a plush crimson chair bolted in the center. The theory was that the electrical field would create a centralized energy field that would interact with the bio-electrical system of the professor's brain, allowing him to become the navigational equipment that would guide the device to transport him where he desired to go. Or more precisely, 'when' he desired to go.

There had been many heated discussions about this, because it seemed there would be no way to return. Uncle Waldorf argued he could build a new machine when he arrived and return here. Trudy pointed out that would only be possible if he was not labeled a madman, could gather the resources, find assistants, and was not disintegrated in the process tonight. Spencer also pointed out that they had no way of knowing what collateral damage would ensue at the arrival point. This much energy being pushed through time and space could create anything from a low pressure system, to an electrical storm at the arrival point, to a permanent doorway that would draw all energy and matter through it from one world to the other, entirely destroying both. As a compromise, Uncle Waldorf agreed he would target a point in time and space that would be less likely to create an issue. He would attempt to travel to Drungia where his father had disappeared thirty years ago. He would send a telegraph to himself and present it to the twins moments after the test was complete, in person. Spencer pointed out that he would then be thirty years older and living in the same world as himself for all those years. As a second compromise, they all agreed instead he would target a field near the country house at which the family normally took holiday in Southern Gallia, one week previous to the time they were currently living in, and still the telegraph message. Six days previous, they had received just such a telegram, and the other uncle Waldorf was due to arrive via train tomorrow morning.

Their Uncle's shout brought them back from their joint reverie. They exchanged knowing smiles and put their back into throwing the switches. That is when the world shattered. The blue electric arcs shot in bands outward from the Prime Machine where Uncle Waldorf sat and an explosion rocked them, throwing them backwards in opposite directions.

Ten minutes later they stood talking together in the ruined laboratory and surveyed the damage. They both knew it should not have happened. A crashing was heard on the other side of the warehouse, and the crunching of footsteps on glass. Two men came into view, walking towards them with a purpose. Trudy puffed up and moved towards them. Spencer had seen these two before though, and he put a hand on his sister to stop her.

Three days previous Trudy and Spencer had been in a local pub. Having finished her meal, Trudy left her brother behind to tend to his social duties. He sat in a dark corner booth, not actually interested in having to deal with social niceties that night. The high back benches gave him privacy and solitude. It had been a busy week and the preparations of the machine were almost complete. Earlier, the twins had discussed it in detail over blood sausage and a drink. Spencer's dark stout was almost finished, but Trudy had barely touched her wine, saying it was too bitter.

Emery Vance had been by to call upon Trudy earlier, ignoring Spencer except for a fleeting acknowledgement; and courted her in the manner that a peacock cross bred with a bull would woo a potential mate. He strutted around, boasting and speaking more to the crowd that was his audience, than to her. After a quarter hour of posturing (Spencer had timed it on his pocket watch), Emery made a grand exit, taking Trudy's chin in his hand and giving a wink and a promise to return soon. Trudy was relieved when he departed, and left soon after so she would not have to see him again that night.

As a son of landed gentry with a large inheritance and a career in the jewel trade, Emery was a much sought after bachelor. He would take over the business soon. He had recently returned from a long visit to the family diamond enterprise in Drungia. He was a tall man with broad shoulders and smile that showed too many teeth, giving him an aggressive appearance. He always wore a diamond pin the size of a pigeon egg in his necktie and shirts that were too tight, and he made sure to remove his jacket and strut around in his waistcoat to show off his massive physique.

Emery did return. Women flocked around him, making noises like hens. He drew them close to him in a bear hug, and proceeded to ignore them after, ordering a tankard of ale and asking his chums about Trudy. Did she look forlorn when he left? Did she talk about him? Did she watch him as he walked out the door? Gimber Smith, his most devout flunky, proceeded to tell him the details, fawning over the larger man.

"How could she not be sad when you left?" the short, greasy man asked. "She threw herself on the table, and tried to talk about anything else except you so she wouldn't chase you out the door and down the street!"

"Of course," Vance replied, "I will have her as my wife. What woman wouldn't want me? And my family name is much better than her ridiculous name. Who would want to be saddled with the name Tridington? And once we are married, I will have the rarest of gems in my possession. Then she can begin to give me many sons! She will welcome the escape from her horrid little life with that crazy old man with his stupid little machines."

The men did not notice Spencer, but two men had noticed Emery. A tall, thin, bald man, dressed in black from head to toe stood and a small glass holding an amber liquid in his hand turned towards the bragging man. The thin man drew a monocle from his breast pocket and put it to his eye. He leaned on a polished silver walking stick, the handle of which was a grotesque - though finely wrought - octopus creature. He looked at Emery Vance much as a mantis looks at a smaller insect, head tilted. A thick man dressed in fine, but plain, clothes stood behind and to one side of the older man. The second man had a horrible disfigurement of the face, as if it had been partially melted. He moved with jerking, almost mechanical motions. His hand was in his pocket, as if readying a weapon. At that moment Spencer thought of the nickname 'The Hideous Man' for him.

"Is this the ward of Professor Tridington of which you speak?" the older man asked, rubbing at a brand on his left wrist. Everyone turned to look at the stranger.

Emery turned and looked at the stranger and his companion, sizing them up through the haze of pipe smoke, trying to decide if he could pummel them and how much effort it would take.

"Yes, she is the same," Emery answered, annoyed to have attention taken from him. "Why do you inquire?"

"Well, because that would make it so much easier for someone of your obvious charm, power, and standing to entice her from such a dull and tedious life," the newcomer said in a voice like oil over a brick. "I am a Doctor and a contemporary of Professor Tridington. I am curious, what sort of work is she being forced into doing?"

"Oh, crazy stuff!" Gimber interjected, coming to his friend's aid. "I heard her speaking of a breakthrough. Said her uncle would travel through time!"

The pub broke out in raucous laughter, encouraging the chubby sycophant. Puffing up under the attention, he was about to go on until Emery pushed him to the side and stepped forward.

"Yes, it is insane. I can tell you all about it," Vance said.

From his vantage point Spencer could see the marking on the thin man's wrist. It was a symbol he has seen once before in an ancient tome his uncle had in the library. The young man found it by accident when looking for calibration notes for the machine. The text had writhed on the page, making the young man nauseous when he tried to focus on it. Waldorf had caught him flipping through the pages in a daze, and slammed the book shut, waking his nephew from his stupor. It was one of the few times he had seen his uncle angry. The older man insisted that he do a full examination of his charge that evening, and nightmares haunted the young man for over a week after.

Spencer felt that retreat was the better part of valor and slipped out the door before anyone could notice him,

Doctor Terrible and the Hideous Man in particular. The nightmares returned to the young man that night, whispering to him in his restless sleep.

The same two men came towards them now. The Doctor had an armful of schematics rolled up under one arm, his walking stick in the other. His lackey was coming towards them with an uneven mechanical gait. Everything slowed down for Spencer. The world became a ballet in his mind. The men were dangerous, that was obvious. After stopping his sister, he turned gracefully and stepped away from them in long strides, until he felt Trudy's arm slide out of his grasp. Turning to look, he saw her face was beet red with fury and she marched towards the men with fists clenched. This created an odd and surrealistic stutter in the slow motion reality Spencer was experiencing. It didn't make sense. It reminded him of when he had the dreams about running through molasses. It normally woke him up, but in this case it didn't. He paused in his own mind, listening for the tinny tinkle of a music box he normally heard when dreaming.

When he was a child, his mother used to play such a music box to help him sleep. It would play Piano Concerto No. 32 in C major by Jobeart. She would hear him having a nightmare, come into their room, wind it up, and sit and stroke his hair and forehead until he calmed enough to sleep. Trudy was never bothered by nightmares. She slept like a stone. She was a hard one. Spencer realized that she had grown into a determined woman. She wasn't afraid of anything, whereas he was anxious about many things. She was his strength, and at that moment, his pillar of strength, his rock, was taking a swing at the Hideous Man.

Things of nightmares crept closer, hungry for the flesh and screams of the creatures that fought in front of them. They could feel the presence of the agent of their master, and waited for him to complete the ritual to free the Great One so they may feast.

Spencer paused, waiting for everything to rubber band back into full speed. It didn't. It was too comical. He didn't feel the panic he expected. Instead it seemed to take on the feel of a dance that was a bit faster, but fun. Like the ones at social mixers where the women flung their skirts to show ankles, and the men twirled around them in shoes that clicked on the floor with each step, and everyone was red faced and sweating, but smiling, when the dance was finished.

Trudy connected with The Hideous Man's jaw with a square punch. The man didn't flinch, though his face contorted like a desert gelatin that had been smacked. His hand moved with determination and easily clutched the throat of his attacker. Trudy's face lost its look of anger and transformed into surprise as her air was cut off. Spencer heard the click of the music box winding. Wondering at it for a moment, he realized it was coming from The Hideous Man. The whir of gears and clicks of mechanized movement came from the arm that held Trudy.

Lumbering forms lurched closer in the smoke and fog, watching and waiting. Their disfigured faces boasted tentacle appendages that quivered in anticipation of the coming meal. They yearned for the taste of flesh and blood, and chitinous hands clutched the machines, bending the soft metal. Eyes which glowed a dull green watched the tall man, and waited for him to begin the final ritual.

Spencer glided across the space which separated him from the man. He noticed Doctor Terrible had a syringe at ready and was looking for an opening to use it on Trudy. Without slowing, though everything still felt unnaturally slow like practicing a choreographed dance, the younger man came in low between his sister and her attacker, and stood up swiftly, his curled fist connecting with the underside of the Hideous Man's jaw. The mechanical man's head snapped back and his hand went into the same pocket Spencer had observed him dipping into three nights ago, the one that held a weapon by the younger man's guess.

Spencer now stood between the two, and slammed his forearm against the man's elbow, knocking his grip from Trudy's throat. She stumbled backwards, gasping. Spencer crouched again, punching once with each fist into the man's midsection. It was like punching one of the machines in the room, solid metal. Spencer felt something in his right fist break. A gun was clutched in the man's dirty hand. Spencer sighed as the muzzle flashed. He later swore he saw the bullet and watched as it twisted into his shoulder.

The music in his head now became more like the steam organ music of the calliope at a carnival. The force of the bullet turned him around and threw him backwards. As he hit the ground he saw his sister pirouette above him with a broken switch, and a meter of iron connected with The Hideous Man's jaw. The man's scarred head wrenched to the side and he whirled into the shadows and crumpled to the ground. Dark things slithered to the fallen form and began feasting.

Trudy focused on the second man. The Doctor shrunk back, clutching the stolen research he had gathered before encountering the twins as she stepped forward. The thin man turned and fled, coat tails billowing behind him, leaving his companion to his fate. Trudy began to give pursuit, but the pained moan of her little brother stopped her. She knew she had to see to her brother before chasing down the villain. She returned to her sibling, dragging him out a side door and into the morning light as he gibbered about shadows with teeth that crept from his mind and dreams to devour them all.

Dark things rose in the shadows of the now quiet laboratory. They gathered around the fallen man and began their first meal of many to come.

The next day found them at the train station. Spencer's left arm had been cleaned, bandaged and set in a sling. His right hand was also bandaged. Abigail was all aflutter when she heard the news of him being shot, and hung on his good arm, insisting she would not leave the side of her hero. When Spencer had tried to explain what had happened last night, of Trudy's heroics, how she had beaten both men back, and the nightmares that had given him no rest, his sister had pressed into his wound, stopping him as he squealed in pain. Trudy explained how Spencer had fought the men and after taking the bullet to save her, scared the man away. Though Doctor Terrible had not been found, pieces of the Hideous Man had been discovered. He had been mauled and devoured by beasts.

As the conductor unloaded the passengers from the train the twins craned their necks, searching the crowd for their uncle. The platform smelled of coal and diesel smoke. Warm steam misted across the feet of the bustling crowd. It was difficult to hold a conversation with the person next to you, and calling out for their uncle would have been an exercise in futility. The sea of parasols and top hats made it impossible to see the shock of white hair that would reveal the patriarch of their family.

"Greetings Miss Trudy and Master Spencer," said a voice behind them. They turned to greet their uncle, only to see the stranger that had sat in their parlor four years ago. He was dressed exactly as they had seen him then, from the dust on his boots, to his vest, long leather coat, and his low brimmed hat. "Jack Tucker, at your service. This must be Miss Abigail Brewer, Wally has told me all about you!" Abigail tittered, raising a white lace glove to her painted lips.

"Where is Uncle Waldorf?" the twins asked in unison.

"He missed the train. Follow me, and I will explain."

Thirty minutes later they sat in the same parlor in which they had first met. This time was very different though. Uncle Waldorf was gone, Abigail was present, and Spencer and Trudy were no longer children. Both men had a brandy without the pretext of tea. Abigail had looked shocked at first at the gentleman she adored being so bold. Her eyes became thoughtful and a smoldering smirk crossed her features as she considered the implications of Spencer being a bit of a bad boy. First the bullet, now the brandy, she had to wonder if he would soon begin smoking a pipe.

"Dark and evil things have been released into this world. I tried to warn your uncle of this, but had no way of knowing of the men and their part in this conspiracy. The two you saw here last night were part of an expedition to Drungia with your Great-Uncle. I doubt the constable will be able to find the man you so boldly confronted," he said, meeting Trudy's eyes knowingly. "We will not be safe here. You must gather your remaining notes and research and we must return to your uncle."

"Why didn't Uncle Waldorf come with you from Southern Gallia?" asked Spencer.

"Your uncle did not make it to Southern Gallia," the stranger began, "Most recently; I met him nearly thirty years ago. I was on expedition in Drungia seeking a huge magnetic flux that may be a natural portal through time and space, reality if you will, with his father, your Great Uncle. It seems Waldorf's father did not disappear into the wilds of the Dark Land, but into something much larger."

"What do you mean? Who sent the telegraph last week?" Trudy said as she stood, knocking Spencer's brandy onto his white trousers.

"I sent it, and you have inherited more than your Uncle's fortune with his disappearance; you have also gained the shadowy legacy that began three generations ago. They need your help. We must lay things to rest, specifically the horrors that came with the opening of the portal last night, as well as stop anything that may be waiting to enter our world. I will explain on the train leaving this evening. You must get packed, and pack light. What has happened leading up to this was a mere prologue to your story, and now the true adventure begins." He stopped to take a sip of brandy as they stood in stunned silence. "Oh, and Trudy? I think it would be best if you left your bustle behind, and brought breeches. And Spencer, I believe a mustache may look good on you now. You have earned it."

Trudy and Spencer smiled at each other.

Faith Be Damned

My traveling companions and I stood in the smoldering ruins of the village. Fires still burned in the corners of charred husks of buildings. We had gone to the castle before this, and it had been burned also. No one knows which fire started first. I found a series of parchments in the castle, a journal of the one who lorded over the people in this valley. It answered some questions, but not all. Searching through the rubble of the inn, a lone traveler's diary was found. Amarilly Belladonna Nicolai is, or was, the name of the owner. No one is sure if she is alive or dead. I am hoping her diary will help fill in the blanks of the information I found in the journal from the keep.

The few surviving villagers say Amarilly arrived here almost a month ago. She told them that she was sent by our mutual friend, Elizabeth, who had helped the village four years ago. Elizabeth and her two traveling companions, Suykimo and Zachary, had discovered the previous lord of the valley was actually a werewolf, and slayed him. But six months ago Elizabeth received a letter from the village, telling her that something darker had taken the place of the dispatched evil. She and her friends were unable to make the journey, so she sent word to her school mate from Bolton in Gallix asking her to investigate, as the paranormal was a bit of a specialty for Amarilly.

I have known Elizabeth and her companions for many years now, and this is also an area of my expertise. Elizabeth had sent me a letter two weeks ago asking me to check on her friend on my way through this area to Drungia. It was not too far out of the way, so I agreed, and convinced my companions to accompany me. I am traveling with Trudy and Spencer; they are twins. We are on an excursion to find their missing uncle. They are also scientists and had assisted their uncle, my longtime friend Waldorf, with many of his studies and experiments. Trudy is a true genius, and her brother has a knack for noticing hidden details. As they search the remnants of the village for clues, I pore over these two texts, hoping to put together enough facts to know the whole of the situation.

Journal Entry - Harton 9th

I have controlled this valley for well over four decades. I have lived for more than ten times that. I am the ultimate predator. I have seen others of my kind come and go; the young are destroyed by ego, the elders by apathy. I have found the secret to eternity, it is in passion. Passion for whatever you choose, but your choices are limited. Some choose the sensual route; sex, love, emotion, art, and other things that delight the senses. The issue is after too much sensation, as in hundreds of years, you become jaded, bitter, and numb. For proof, simply look to the critics that review plays and symphonies. After a mere decade there is little that can please them.

I have seen younger beings of my kind rise in a blaze that draws the attentions of people from kilometers around. They are full of desire and feel indestructible because of their abilities. They challenge the world, and the afterlife. They are simpletons with little vision, and soon enough their ashes that remain behind are testimony to that. I have seen elders of my kind rise to power, build empires, and later fall to loneliness and lethargy. They seek more, the next level of love, sensation, appetite, or any tactile endeavor. They latch onto the living, or the newly created, and feed off them, not in blood, but in emotion. Some would call these beings psychic feeders, but I do not give them that much credit. They are merely leeches, passively feeding and falling off when sated. They are not active. You must have a reason to rise from your rest. They do not.

I rely on the game. It is cerebral. It is the mental challenge set only by myself. No one else controls the rules; they are merely my pawns in the game I create. I adore these little trials, though most soon grow trivial and dull. Though in the past decade I have found a reason to rise. This valley was ruled by a man-beast that had fallen to a curse of science and magic. Lycanthropy is a mixture of the both. I do not care to seek out more answers than that, because they are not important. That is another lesson I have learned through the centuries: to consolidate, do not horde. Do not keep unneeded people, commitments, items, lands, money, or anything else. They only weigh you down and give you a false sense of identity. They are not important. My identity is within myself, and of course in what others empower me with.

As I noted previously noted in my journals, when I first came to this valley it was an easy conquest. Then the miller's son became infected with his disease. I watched him, and guided him, until he was Lord of the region. He claimed to be a protector, but was in earnest, their ruin. I engineered his demise as much as I engineered his success.

Now, the very humans which I drew into the web of my designs, to finish that which I had started, have resurfaced of their own accord. This is such a rare treat, and fascinates me, a snag that I did not put in on my own. Though it is not the Trio themselves, rather some young she-bitch that has been sent here by the Trio. I do not think she will do very much to disturb my plans, but it will amuse me.

I have not decided whether to ignore her and feed on her frustration, if I should manipulate the villagers into destroying her, or if I should confront her myself. Though that is rare for me, I did it with the Trio of Travelers, appearing as a witch of local legend. I do not know how I shall prepare this next delightful dish; I merely know I shall find the intrigue it creates delicious.

Amarilly Belladonna Nicolai Diary - Harton 10th

The train trip had been uneventful except for the insipid man in the top hat and monocle that insisted that a lady should not travel alone. I insisted that I was not a lady, but he still would not go on his way and leave me to mine. So, after two days of explaining I did not want company, I had to show him. I am sure his man-parts will heal fine with the ice the steward brought him. Though it was nice to not see him emerge from his private cabin to trouble me for the rest of the trip, I do not wish him any lasting pain.

The carriage ride from the station to this quaint village was even less eventful. Bumpy, but nothing more. It is dull and steely grey outside, and a chill in the air. There is not much to see in the mountains either. Autumn is upon this region, and I hope to finish my investigation quickly; I do not want to be stranded here in this provincial town for the winter. It is not like my birth country in southwestern Teurone. I lived on the plains there, with my gypsy family. It was cold in the autumn, but the sky was often blue and the air crisp. Here it is oppressive and heavy, and I can feel the thick miasma of more than the weather hanging all around me.

I was greeted with suspicion in the village when I arrived. I expected nothing less. I am used to such reactions. When I was a gypsy no one would trust me. Not even when I was a little girl and went into town with actual coin to buy bread, instead of going with my family to stealthily rob the small towns while they went about their daily lives or slept at night. When Elizabeth's mentor, Suykimo, found me and sent me to the fine University of Bolton with Elizabeth, the people there also viewed me with distrust. I was short and dark haired with the olive skin of the southern folk, not fair and brown haired like the people of the isles, or blonde like the northern peoples. I have trained to spot people's reactions before they know what they themselves feel.

I have learned the way of the blade if they react badly. It is amazing, the training of my old family seemed so detailed and thorough: how to hide the knives, how to throw them, or how to slip them out and use them without someone standing next to me knowing I did anything. It is the art of misdirection. All these things are a matter of looking somewhere else and gasp at someone moving fast, and all around you follow your eyes while you cut a purse, or pierce a side. But I have learned better ways now, refined my skills with knives as I refined my words in school. Elizabeth's friend, Zachary, taught me how to do so much more. Now I hide blades under my lace sleeves, or in the boning of my corset.

I digress, but I do miss the days when I always knew what was next. Though I must say the life I live now is much more exciting, it is also much more tiring. Today was no different. It did not take much to bring the villagers to ease, but afterwards they were full of questions and it was difficult to bring them to the topic of which I needed information without arousing suspicion. Instead of asking elders, I made friends with one of the young girls of the town. Her name is Dariya and she was eager to talk. Her betrothed was killed four years ago, just before my schoolmate Elizabeth had visited here. Dariya is a woman of seventeen now, and refuses to take a husband, instead following the teachings of the local wise woman.

She is very helpful to my investigation. I have to decipher what she means sometimes; not the words, but the actual intent behind the words. She practices 'magic' much like my own people: herbs, rituals, chants, candles, smoke, and spells. The rest of the village are devout worshipers of The Changing Wheel though, but they also practice rituals and use herbs, chants, candles, and smoke, but instead call their spells 'prayer'. I do not believe in a higher power, but instead understand that the science of belief creates results. It is a matter of the electric in the human body and mind, and it influencing the world around you.

Dariya told me about what has happened over the past four years since the lord of the valley was found dead on the slopes near his castle. There had been many killings before his death, and they stopped when he died. The villagers found proof of his being a werewolf at the castle, and I believe that. Now, I may have to defend my belief in this, because of what I said about the higher powers. But I think there are many things in this world we can explain with natural scientific causes if we just look beyond superstition, including ghosts, monsters, and magic.

The people thought their troubles had ended with his death on that night of the blue moon. But they had not. Sixteen months later, in the middle of winter, the killings began again. These were even more horrific than before. Whole families were killed, leaving only one person alive. The first was a father and husband, his wife and six children all slaughtered in the middle of the night. He woke the next morning to the screaming of his wife's mother, who had come to bring the family fresh baked bread. He was hung that day by his own parents, siblings, friends, and neighbors.

The next horror came eight months later, as spring was just beginning to bloom. This time it was a wife and her sister found in the barn in the morning covered in gore - their parents had been vivisected and nailed to the beams and rafters in a spider web of entrails. The women were buried to the neck and stoned to death.

This pattern continued, as someone was killed every couple of months, and the person responsible being found nearby and the evidence overwhelming, so they were put to death. I think the most disturbing thing Dariya she told me about in hushed whispers is when the mayor's whole family was found stabbed and drained of all fluids, except for his five children. The missing liquids were found in a wash tub, and the children bathing in the still warm visceral juices. The children were given proper exorcisms, but when their caretaker was found dead and missing all bodily fluids also, they were burned at the stake.

Now, I am here. And I will find out what is going on. Is it a demon, a disease, or something else altogether?

Journal Entry - Harton 16th

This new girl has been in town for less than a week and has already totally changed the dynamic of my years of manipulation. I can see the fear leaving the villagers, when I watch them from the rafters at night. They dance and sing again, rather than crouching in the circle of candlelight, clutching prayer beads. But that also works in my favor in some ways.

This girl has no faith. She does not pray to any god or carry any trappings of religion. And due to my sensitivity to such things, her not having those habits or items shall make this easier. As her influence over the villagers grows, they shall rely on such tools less also. I shall drive them back to their knees using fear and terror.

I will plan another massacre, and have this Amarilly Nicolai at the center. These ignorant country waifs will string her up and disembowel her without a second thought, and rid me of my opposition. I will delight, watching the frustration and confusion on this girl's face as she is vivisected for the entire town to see, by the very people she sought to protect.

Amarilly Belladonna Nicolai Diary - Harton 19th

I have been sleeping in shifts, making sure I am awake for breakfast, and again for dinner. But I am sleeping more in the day, and looking around the town at night. I do this in secrecy, not wanting the superstitious villagers to suspect me of illicit activities. In the nine days since I first arrived I had not seen anything that would make me suspect something was amiss. Until last night. All my skills and gifts were tested.

I supped with the crowd in the inn, and excused myself for the evening to retire to my room. I had a brief nap and woke an hour before midnight. I freshened up, and donned my night clothes, but not the nightclothes most wore. I put on dark clothes, and in men's fashions. Black trousers, with a dark blue blouse, and my corset over it. I also wore knee boots, gloves, and a scarf around my face. I completed my preparations by braiding my hair and dropping it down my back. I didn't want to be seen on my nightly rounds. I also added a stiletto to each boot, one of silver and one of iron, another of each on my hips, and my corset held a brace of throwing knives. I have trained with each of these for years, and kept them all in fine condition, cleaning and checking them weekly.

Over the past nine days, I have established a search pattern inside the village. I leave by my window, move along the rooftop of the porch, and drop to the ground. I return that way later, shimmying up the post to the roof. I circle around the village, and check the outside perimeter. It is odd doing this to protect a town. I had done it before with my people, as we checked a settlement for quick routes to get away in case something happened, or in the few times they planned an actual robbery. But now I was using these same skills to watch for intruders.

I pay particular attention to the smithy, town hall, and inn, because those are often the gathering place for people. If these crimes were being done by a person, it is likely they would be there at some point. If it is not a person, then my next stop should be useful. I check the well, church, and graveyard. I do these rounds ever two hours or so. After doing my circuit I climb to the highest point I can find, and watch over the village. In this village, as it is in most, that is the church bell tower.

It was just after midnight when I saw movement. Something was making its way along the side of a building. I watched a huge creature on all fours leap up on the roof of the porch of the inn, and it stopped and sniffed at my window. This beast had the look of a jackal of some sort, though much larger. Its hind legs were shorter than its front legs, and the head was box shaped with a squat snout and no ears. It raised itself to stand on its rear legs, as a man would, and I could see it sniffing the air. I couldn't help but wonder if it smelled my trail leading away from my bedroom window and was searching for me.

It dropped to the ground, sniffed about, and appeared to shrug. It loped off to the rear of the building. I slid to the ground using the downspout of the church gutter and followed as quietly as I could. When I leaned around the corner of the inn, I saw it standing on its hind legs again, and prying a window open with clawed fingers.

I have heard of and dealt with many things in my time. Lamassu, ghosts, undead, werewolves, (such as what Elizabeth, Zachary, and Suykimo had dealt with four years previously), and more, just to name a few. Often something in one country is called something different in another, and I can cross reference research to discover what I am dealing with. Many times, it is just a man playing at being a monster. People are most often the true monsters. But this, I had never encountered, or even heard tales of this creature.

The window slid up, and I thought it would be best to confront this thing before it entered the chamber. I drew three throwing knives from my corset and threw them in quick succession. My aim was true, and thrice I struck it in the barrel of its chest. The beast screamed and turned towards me. I dropped into a crouch, drawing my iron and silver stilettos from my boot sheaths. The monster's eyes narrowed, and it pulled the knives from its ribs and licked each one in turn, staring at me as it did.

A woman's scream came from within the room with the open window, followed by shouts of a man. The creature looked inside, leaning towards the sounds of frightened prey, its hunter's instinct taking over. I charged. I came in low, slashing at its legs and belly, staying in a crouch to make myself a smaller target, and ready to spring into a roll or dodge if it lashed out. It was taken by surprise and stumbled backwards. It dropped my knives, and turned to run. I leapt at its back, slashing again.

It moved away at an incredible speed, and as it did so, its body contorted. Changing shape as it moved, it became smaller, sprouted wings, and took to the air, now appearing as some misshapen, giant crow. Within moments it faded from view, but not because of distance or gaining the cover of a building or trees. It just disappeared.

I watched for it, slowing my breathing so I could hear better. Light flared within the room, and angry voices shouted, coming closer. I sheathed the stilettos, scooped up my throwing knives, and ran to the front of the building. I tossed the weapons to the roof, not wanting to put them into the place on my corset, and climbed to the roof. After gathering my knives, I reentered my room through the window.

Within ten minutes half the village had gathered within the inn below. I changed my clothes and joined the villagers. I listened to their wild tales, accusations, and fears. I asked a few questions, though not too many. They know I am here to help, but small town people still never trust an outsider, even if my friends did save them years ago. They seem to think it is a vampire, and I didn't tell them they were wrong. But, it is not. I am not sure what it is.

I telegraphed my friends, the very same people that were here a few years ago, as well as some others, and am trying to learn what I am dealing with. I have pored over my books for hours, and I only have a guess. I will have to wait for more information.

Journal Entry - Harton 20th

The bitch attacked me! There was no fear in her. She does not know who, or what, she is dealing with. I will enjoy eating her, bit by bit. I will take her apart, and devour her fingers while she watches, then her feet, hands, and choice slivers of her body, all while she sits helpless and screams!

I don't think she knows of the manor house I use. I will show her how to find it, bring her here, and toy with her. She shall be the mouse to my cat, and I will delight in breaking her spirit, as I break her mind and body. She will be looking for me now, and it should be easy to lead her here. Tonight, I will kill every woodcutter left in the forest after sundown, leave a trail, and she will know where to go. Or I think I shall make her a map, of their entrails. She can't ignore that!

Amarilly Belladonna Nicolai Diary - Harton 22nd

This beast has struck again. Eight villagers, including three boys, were found dead in the woods after not returning home. Their heads had been removed and placed in a circle, at the compass points. The ground was painted with their blood. The men were laid out, using their broken bones, to resemble a macabre diorama of the village. The boys were in the shape of a castle, the bodies torn and mutilated to form towers and walls. Every hand, all sixteen of them, was made into a compass needle pointing to a very specific place.

When I asked the villagers where it pointed, and what was there, they told me about the lord's manor which had stood empty since my friends were last here, though recently the wood cutters had seen lights in the windows. I couldn't believe they hadn't told me about this sooner. They just made the sign of the evil eye, and spat upon the ground when I told them so. How could they not think this was important? Stupid people and their irrational beliefs!

I went up there during the day. I brought my whole arsenal, even wearing the leather pieces of armor to protect my chest, belly, arms, and legs. It took almost two hours to find it, though it was huge and could be seen from the valley below. The way was blocked by fallen trees and other natural obstacles. The villagers had done that years ago to stop anything else from coming to their precious homes.

When I arrived, I saw more of their handiwork. The manor had been burnt sometime in the past few years. Windows were smashed, and torches had been thrown inside. I pushed open the doors, and left them standing wide. Always leave your escape route open. I did a quick survey of the upstairs, and worked my way down. I tapped walls, checked for hidden passages. I found a few, but they hadn't been used in years. On the main floor, there wasn't much to find. It appeared the good people of the hamlet had also decided to take everything they could sell or use. I bet they didn't do it when others were around though. That would have brought more signs to ward off the evil from the others.

I finally came to the conclusion that I must descend into the basement. It was dark and I brought out my electric torch. It lit the way well enough, though dust rose from my footsteps and clouded the air. This passage was unused, as was every other hall and room I had investigated. The wooden stairs, squeaking and groaning, would alert anything below to my approach, and I didn't bother to try and hide my presence. The lower level was a maze of grey stone walls. Shadows shifted with my light, bouncing and looming as I moved it.

A room opened up before me, wide and tall, with rough stone columns lining the sides. Alcoves with statues showed between each set of pillars. At the far end I could see a throne-like chair with a female figure sitting in it. She sat with her legs crossed and dripped with gold and silver bracelets, rings, and necklaces, and very little else. I thought for a moment to hide but it was too late, she knew I was here. I walked forward as if I were expected, which I think I was.

She greeted me as I came closer, her voice somewhere between a purr and growl. I don't believe she was speaking her native tongue, as her speech was heavily accented. Torches in sconces on each pillar flared to life at a gesture of her hand. The room sparkled with gems embedded in the walls which I hadn't seen before that moment. With another motion I heard the sound of a distant door slamming, and another, and another, each sounding closer until the door behind me completed her show of magic.

I looked behind me, checking to see if I was actually trapped. The door shimmered in my electric torchlight, and I realized something important. Turning back to her, I told her she should leave or be destroyed. She shouted at me, promising tortures and other unpleasant things. She told me she would devour my soul and that my god could not protect me, I would be her plaything forever and unable to gain my ultimate reward in the afterlife.

I stared at her. The sight of her beauty was wavering also. I concentrated harder, willing myself to see what was beyond the glamour. I saw glimpses of tusks, folds of brown skin, huge eyes and nostrils. She was a charlatan and not showing her true form.

I announced that I am godless, do not believe in a soul, and that I could see through her tricks and deceptions. I stepped forward, drawing a knife from my hip, a long curving kris blade. I showed no anxiety, told her that fear also was a trick of the mind, and she wasn't fooling me with her illusions. Most ghosts and demons don't do well when approached this way.

In my research I believe I found what sort of creature she was, a rakshasa, a demon that uses trickery to cause fear and overcome their prey. They were known in the Far East, on the continent of Aeifa. I didn't know why she was here, and I didn't care. I would send her back or destroy her.

She screamed, and flung a ball of flame from her hand. It burst across my chest and for a moment I reached up to slap at the flames. I stopped myself. Breathing deep, I sighed, and lowered my hands. She was furious that I was unaffected. I was a bit surprised as the flames disappeared as quickly as they had come, but it proved what I had suspected. She shrieked again, and became dust. Swirling in a cloud, she swept behind her throne. The room had been dimming as I realized the torches were illusion, as were the gems in the walls and ceiling, and her guise. I could see her hunched form, running away in the fabrication of the haze she was hidden within.

I pursued her, but came up to a solid wall. Upon inspection I realized it was a hidden door, and she had locked it from the other side. I searched a bit more, and when I was sure I could not find a way to the other side I returned here to my room in the inn. I don't think this is over though. I will return there tomorrow and finish this beast.

Journal Entry - Harton 23rd

I am hungry. That human woman has no faith, no belief, and no fear. I could not make her cringe and cower as I had so many others. I have faced countless of her race: wizards, priests, vampires, werewolves, and each bowed under my onslaught as I controlled their terrors, making a hell in their minds!

In the village below I have made fathers kill their wives and children, children tear apart their parents, and everything in between. But this one woman cannot be touched. I cannot control her mind. I will return to the village, and have the people do my work for me. She will die at their hands. Tonight.

Journal of Jack Tucker - Harton 25th

That was the last entry I found in either diary. I can only guess what happened. I hope Amarilly is safe and has traveled on.

Travis I. Sivart

The Foundation of Compelling Curiosities: A Croaker Norge Case File

"How did we get here?" Phoebus asked.

"The storm somehow brought us here," Croaker answered in his gravel voice and tamped the tobacco in his pipe.

"The storm?" the younger man asked.

"Yes," Croaker said, taking a swig of whiskey from his dented flask. He wiped his stubbled chin with the back of his hand, and replaced the pipe between his teeth. "Remember, when we were in that carnival looking for the murderous clown? It was a dark and stormy night…"

"Oh yes," Phoebus interrupted, taking out his own flask. Filled with gin, it hadh his family crest and name, Buckroe, engraved on it. He took a delicate sip, pinky in the air, and screwed the cap on again. He opened the other side of the divided container and took out a cigar. Lighting it from an electric cuff link, he puffed a cloud of smoke and looked at the shorter man. "Nothing good ever starts that way. How

145

do you know we are in a place called New Tartan?"

"Just look around." Croaker said as he waved his arms, causing his brown duster to flap.

Phoebus Buckroe turned in a circle, holding his silk top hat in place and staring at the brick buildings around them. Each building was different from the next. Three story plaster buildings with dark wood trim and crossbeams dominated this area. Striped cloth awnings jutted out over the sidewalk and banners, signs, and flags hung from the buildings, identifying each establishment. In other parts of town they had seen glass arboretums, zeppelin landing pads, brass cranes moving huge gears and pulleys, and a dozen other varieties of architecture.

"Alright Norge, you're the detective, not me. I am just dashing, good looking, and charming. I don't see what you meant for me to see."

"Either your starched collar is too tight," Croaker said and heaved a sigh, "or you're too busy polishing your baubles and jewelry to open your eyes. I didn't mean look around here, I meant to look around in general and you will see things you never knew were there. For example, this town is a mish-mosh of architecture and style. Every block is different. That shows it is run by creative people with a lot of time on their hands. Do you know what that means?"

"Yes, I do. I am not an idiot. It means they have lots of money, and we can turn a profit here."

"No," the older man said as he glared at his companion.

"They don't have money? It looks like it to me, now that you pointed it out."

"I didn't point it out, and yes they have money, but that is not what I meant. I meant they won't have a standard government. Also, they don't have that much money, I've seen urchins roaming the streets and the poor wandering about. I think it is more of a commune sort of government, and they take care of their own rather than having strict class divisions."

"Ah," Phoebus said as he rolled his eyes and yawned.

"How very fascinating. What does this mean to us? And you still haven't told me how you knew the city is named New Tartan."

"I knew because it was on the notice board we passed when we arrived two days ago. And it means that they find work for anyone who wants it, so there may be work for us."

"They have money to pay us is what you mean."

"You have a one track mind. Come along, we're going to find the Mayor who posted the notice about something strange in town."

"Couldn't we go back to Clausen Hall and get a drink from that nice chap, James Dieselton, before we start working?"

The sun set early in the autumn and the two men moved along the foggy streets. Croaker watched the alleys and shadows, and Phoebus looked at the misty rings around the full moon and flickering gas street lights. They were as different from one another as two men could be. Phoebus Buckroe stood tall and strolled along as if he were leaning back, his silver topped walking stick clicking on the cobblestones with each step. His top hat added even more height to his already imposing size and the cut of his tailored dove grey jacket and matching waistcoat showed off his broad shoulders and trim waist. The black trousers he wore had a perfect crease right down to his gaiters and polished shoes. Puffing on his cigar, across with a sparkling smile and a tip of his hat, the young man greeted the few people they came.

Croaker Norge was hunched as he inspected everything around them, his head moving left and right as his hands fidgeted with the leather tool case and contraptions on his belt. His duster was stained and his shirt was wrinkled. He ignored most people after a quick glance to make sure they weren't a threat, though sometimes he would give a small nod or wave his pipe at them when they passed.

They arrived at the Town Hall with the help of a talkative street urchin. The lad ran off once Phoebus handed him a coin at Croaker's insistence. The building was a huge clock tower with public offices on the ground floor. The double doors opened into a lavish foyer with an expensive patterned carpet. Maps of New Tartan adorned the walls, accompanied by portraits of citizens, civil and historic events, as well as various persons of importance.

"We're closing," a soft voice said from behind them. Turning they saw a short man with a dark goatee, sideburns, and a handlebar mustache, his long hair pulled back with a leather cord. Goggles sat on his head, and soot made rings around his eyes. He wore an open jacket of olive green and nothing underneath except tattoos. "Can I help you?"

"Yes, I'm Croaker Norge, Personal Investigation Officer of New Sylians. I saw the Mayor's bulletin on the town notice board, sir. This is my assistant, Phoebus Buckroe. He runs errands and whatnot for me, as well as providing brute force when needed."

"I'm not an assistant," Phoebus said with indignation. "I am Norge's balancing point, and complement and support him in areas he falls short. I'm the part of the team that handles all financial matters. You can deal with me when we discuss pay. I also specialize in strategy and tactics: military, political, or social. I am the quintessential diplomat."

"I'm sure," the man said in a husky voice, so quiet they leaned in to hear him. "I'm Mayor Kravnel, you've found the right man. Follow me to the office, and we'll get the right forms filled out."

The short man led them past a wooden spiral staircase with a brass railing and into a hall beyond. Turning the corner, he opened a door and gestured them inside.

"I'll be right back," Kravnel said, "I need to get some documents from my office. Won't be a minute. But make yourselves comfortable, just in case."

When he had left, Phoebus turned to Croaker, who was inspecting the room.

"Is he a rokairn?" Phoebus asked as he took a cigar from a humidor on the desk. Sniffing it and smiling, he clipped the end off and lit it from a silver lighter. "Don't look at me like that; he did say to make ourselves comfortable. He's so short. And what is with his voice? 'I am the Mayor, do you feel lucky punk?' I mean, speak up little guy, don't be shy!"

"Don't be disrespectful," Croaker scolded, as he poured a drink from a crystal decanter in the corner, following his friend's example. "He is who he is, and that's that. Sometimes it's best to take things at face value and not look any deeper. I've never heard of New Tartan, not in North Mirron, perhaps in Teurone. I think that storm did more than bring us across the land."

"What? Are you going to go on about cultists and strange monsters from the sea or something? How could he have brought us here?"

"I didn't say 'he' brought us here. And hush," Croaker pointed at a vent, "you never know who could be listening."

"I'm not crouched at some vent," Mayor Kravnel said as he came into the office, a sheaf of papers in hand, "but I could hear you pretty clear from down the hall. You guys should learn to speak softer, make people lean in to hear you. It works for me."

"Forgive us, your honor," Croaker said, bowing his head.

"Don't do that, we don't stand on ceremony here," Kravnel said wrinkling his nose. "Let's just get this started so we can get it done. We don't need to worry about niceties or customs and have tea or something, do we? You gentlemen are men of action, right?"

"Just so," Phoebus said as he stood and held a finger in the air. "We're known for our daring and resourcefulness. Never out of ideas or overcome by adversity, we never…"

"Stop talking?" Kravnel asked in his throaty whisper. "How about this Mister Buckroe, you sit down and think about how great you are, and I'll talk with the adult in the room. Sound acceptable?"

"Mister Kravnel," Croaker said with a smirk and a sideways glance at his friend, who had sat down with his mouth agape, "forgive my assistant. He's eager and means well. Please, go on with what you have to show us. How can we help you?"

"Thank you, Mister Norge. I'll make this brief and to the point. Two days ago, we had a new building appear. Anyone going inside has disappeared and strange noises have been heard around it. We need someone to go in and either find out what it is, or how to neutralize it."

"A building appeared?" Croaker asked. "Does this happen a lot?"

"More often than you might think, but it is not a regular occurrence. Will you do it?"

"Yes, we will."

"Wait," Phoebus interrupted, "what do we get paid?"

"It's right here in the contract, Mister Buckroe," Kravnel said, pointing at a clause. Phoebus leaned forward to inspect the document.

"No," he said without hesitation, "we will need part of the money up front."

"No, you don't." Kravnel said in a flat voice that brooked no argument. "If you go in, and don't come out, I don't see the need to have our town's hard earned money disappearing with you. It's a more than generous offer and if, I mean, when you return, you will be more than compensated for your troubles. That's if you figure out what this is and how to handle it, or completely neutralize it while inside."

"I don't think," Phoebus began.

"Good, then we all agree," Croaker interrupted, enjoying someone that could put his partner on his heels with such ease. "We'll go into this place tonight. Please hold our rooms at Clausen Hall and have Mister Dieselton keep the beer and whiskey ready."

"Are you sure about this?" Phoebus asked.

"Yep," Croaker answered, pointing at a weathered brass plaque with symbols around the edge and a spidery script in the center, "it says right there, 'The Foundation of Compelling Curiosities'. This is the right place."

"No," Phoebus interjected.

"Yes," Croaker interrupted in return, "it is. Look, right there!"

"No, are you sure we should be doing this? I mean, we've seen some weird things, but this is a building that appeared from nowhere and anyone going into it never comes back out."

"Yes, but I have my gizmos."

"Why doesn't that comfort me?" Phoebus said to the air as Croaker approached the double doors.

The building was peculiar compared to the other buildings around it. It was square with no buttresses, crenulations, or extravagant décor on the outside. It was a plain stucco and stone building, though the doors were decorated with stained glass windows in the upper half and ornate brass pulls in the center. Light streamed through the windows from inside, adding to the dull glow of the two electric lights outside the doors. Croaker reached for the handle to open the door, and Phoebus laid a hand on his to stop him.

"Why do we have to go in at night though?" Phoebus asked, looking around as if he expected something to charge at them.

"Are you afraid, Phoebus?" Croaker said, raising an eyebrow as the corner of his mouth twitched.

"No, I just don't want you to have a fright. At your age the heart can be tricky. I'm just looking out for you."

"And I'm sure I'll be just fine," Croaker said and opened the door. It swung outward with ease, flinging itself open.

The two men entered, Croaker pulling out a compass, and stepped to one side as he began to walk the perimeter of the room. The entryway was a huge two story affair with marble floors, pillars, and benches. Crystal chandeliers hung from the ceiling, lit by electric bulbs. Six large doorways were evenly spaced along the walls, two to the left, two to the right, and two on the opposite. A kiosk with no entrance stood in the center of the room with a crystal dome covering it. A man in a blue uniform stood inside, smiling as he watched them.

"How may I help you?" the man asked in melodic tones as Phoebus approached.

"What is this place?" Phoebus asked. He circled the desk, watching as the man turned without moving.

"It is the Foundation of Compelling Curiosities, a museum of oddities and artifacts from all over. We specialize in sharing history and culture as no other institution can. Each visitor is treated to a personalized experience to delight and amaze them. I would recommend you each choose a different door to maximize your enjoyment and education."

"Split up?" Croaker asked as he stopped on the opposite side of the counter from where Phoebus stood. "I don't think we will be doing that. Compasses are great to find magnetic or electrical interference. My compass is going wild. It can't find a point. Why is that?"

"The exhibitions within sometimes interfere with magnetic and electrical fields," the figure said in a sing-song voice. "Many devices may have difficulties. I would suggest you turn any such items off until such time as you choose to leave."

"So we can leave whenever we want?" Phoebus asked, turning to the doors they had come in only to find they had been replaced with doorways matching the ones on the other walls. "Hey, where did they go?"

The man inside the crystal dome was not there when Phoebus turned back to the kiosk.

"Where did he go?" the younger man asked.

"Through a door inside the booth, from what I could see," Croaker answered.

"But there is no door. I can see you clearly. Nothing else is there."

"I agree, I see you too. But I turned to look at the doors and when I turned back he had disappeared."

"Is he a ghost? Is this place haunted?"

"Nothing is haunted, just not understood. Yet."

"Oh heavens," Phoebus said, clicking his walking stick on the marble floor. "How do we get out?"

"Getting out is not our goal, getting to the bottom of this is what we're here to do. We may as well begin exploring."

"Should we each choose a door?"

"No, because that man said we should split up, we'll stay together."

Croaker turned in a circle, looking at each door. With a shrug, he headed for the closest one, stopping to wait for Phoebus to catch up. Before entering he looked inside, but could only see an arm's length into the room because no lights were on the other side. The older man drew an electric torch from his belt, unwinding the metal conduit which held the wires that led to the power pack on his belt. Flipping a switch on the contraption a beam of yellow light shone forth and he stepped into the room.

The light from his gadget blinked and went out as the room lit up from above. Glass globes hung from copper tubes, casting a soft white glow across the new room. It was a long gallery and pictures showing scenes from the past hung along the walls behind silver posts with red velvet ropes. Each work of art was detailed and lifelike, showing scenes of primitive tribes farming, fishing, hunting, feasting, or dancing. Some wore grass skirts, others wore hides, and others were naked except for body paints.

"Wait," Phoebus said and Croaker turned. The younger man pointed at one painting of a man with a bow standing over a slain stag. "A moment ago he was pointing the bow, now it shows the stag dead."

"Pictures don't change Phoebus," Croaker said, patting his friend's shoulder. "You must have imagined it. Nerves."

"No, it changed. I know what I saw."

Both men stared at the painting, but nothing happened.

"Let's keep going, we can come back later and see if he laid out a picnic," Croaker deadpanned.

They headed for the far end of the room, both eyeing the portraits as they did. Kings, queens, nobles, and other important figures watched them as they passed. Three doorways waited for them, one on each wall. The one on the left was a brick framed archway; the center was mud and straw; and the right was made of sticks and twine. Croaker hesitated for a moment, then chose the one in front of them and ducked under the low overhang and went into the next room.

The light in the room behind them went out and the room they had just entered lit up. The chandeliers were antlers with stones on the end and a small flame danced on top. The walls were close and made of unfinished stone, making it the feel like a cave. Every few paces there were glass panes and behind each was a scene with primitive men in untanned skins and furs. They stopped in front of one and looked at a family in a cave sitting around a fire. The flames danced in the scene, casting shadows across the faces of the mannequins and giving them a lifelike appearance. The night sky could be seen from the opening at the far end of their makeshift abode.

"Wow," Phoebus said with sincere awe, "they look so real. I almost wish they were alive."

The largest man beside the fire turned his head, staring in their direction, his sloped brow furrowed. Phoebus leapt back with a cry.

"What?" Croaker growled. "What happened? Did a spider land on you?"

"He moved!" Phoebus said, pointing. "You saw him, didn't you? He looked at me!"

Croaker squinted at the scene. "Something weird is going on here."

"Oh, thank goodness you're a detective and can figure these things out with your incredible powers of observation," the younger man said with sarcasm.

"Do it again," Croaker said in a soft voice.

"What?"

"Whatever you did that made him move."

"I just said that I almost wished they were alive."

As Phoebus said the words, five more of the cavemen turned towards the sound of his voice, rising up on their haunches. Phoebus back pedaled, until he was pressed against the far wall. The brutes crept forward; heads tilted and hands out as they approached the glass.

"We should go," Croaker growled.

For once, Phoebus didn't argue and followed the older man, never taking his eyes off the figures. They passed another dozen displays of primitive people, each engaged in daily tasks of bathing, cooking, harvesting berries, and other survival necessities. At the end of the hall there stood two doorways. One was made of fitted sandstone and the other was of metallic blocks. Croaker chose the one on the left and entered into bright light.

They stood in a gallery of beige stone blocks that went up more than four stories and showed the open afternoon sky above them. Windows were set at regular intervals, though they could not yet see what lay behind them. Brightly painted statues of men and women dressed in cloth wraps with heads in the shape of bulls, falcons, cats, and jackals stood between each window and were the height of the room.

The two moved forward, looking around in awe as they did. The first window left no doubt that the people inside were moving. Hundreds of men labored under the sun, chiseling rocks the size of wagons. Flocks of birds could be seen flying overhead and green grasses swayed in front of a scintillating river in the distance. The next window showed a temple scene. Men in white robes chanted as others in sarongs prepared a body for some unknown ritual. Ornate jars waited beside a corpse laid out on a marble slab. Each window had another scene with men and woman moving around doing daily activities, unaware of being observed.

Two doors waited at the end of the hall. The left one was framed in burnt timbers, and the one leading to the right looked like the braided roots of a banyan tree. Croaker led them right. This room was brightly lit also and as they stepped inside, their feet crunched on grass and pebbles. The air was alive with the sound of insects and the sun beat down on them. They stood in an open field, and grasslands were beyond the glass on each side of them. In the distance they could see two exits within a small copse of trees.

"Each room gets weirder than the last," Phoebus murmured. "How can they do this?"

"I don't know," was the only thing Croaker said as he stepped towards the glass, staring at a dozen odd creatures moving towards them. The beasts were huge feathered reptiles with duck-like bills and walking on their hind legs. They stopped to graze on the low hanging leaves of a tree.

"Dinosaurs?" Phoebus asked as he joined his friend. "How do they do this?"

Croaker only shook his head as they watched the foraging of creatures that shouldn't exist, let alone be inside a building. One of the herd looked up and turned its head to look around. Letting out a throaty croak, it bolted. The others followed, straight towards the two men. Four predators appeared, heads popping up above the tall grass. Smaller than the leaf eaters, these also ran on two legs and closed the distance between themselves and their prey with alarming ease.

Phoebus grabbed Croaker, pulling him to the ground as the monsters swarmed towards the glass. Instead of colliding with it, they appeared on the other side of the hall and continued to run. Phoebus stood up as the last of the herbivores passed them and the predators came towards them.

"They can't get us," the dandy said with a smile as he reached out to touch the glass.

"No!" was all Croaker could say before his friend's hand touched the surface of the barrier. The glass shimmered and popped like a soap bubble. The heat of the sun and the noise of the approaching carnivores doubled.

"Run!" Croaker shouted, grabbed Phoebus, and looked at

the doors in the distance. Judging they would never make it that far, he pulled the younger man back the way they came. The doorway had changed, but they had no time to consider that as they ran. The swift and hungry dinosaurs closed the distance between them. The screech of the lead hunter alerted the rest of the pack to easier prey and they all turned towards the fleeing men.

Phoebus felt moist breath on his back as he leapt through the doorway. Silence enveloped them and they slowed to a stop. They were in a room lit by recessed lighting, rather than the overhead sun that should have been in the room. Slick chrome and steel lined the walls, and no glass stood between them and the scene. A single doorway stood in the opposite wall, but no special mantle surrounded it, unlike every other room in which they had been.

"You broke it," Croaker said, his voice rough.

"I didn't know!" Phoebus said, looking around on the floor. "Oh damn, I dropped my walking stick back there. It was my favorite sword cane."

"You can go back and get it. I am sure if you explained to them that you just want your bauble, they will let you get it."

"Where are we now?" Phoebus asked, ignoring the sarcasm.

A round dais with symbols on it stood in front of a circular stone archway. Each stone of the arch had a matching symbol, and a liquid curtain shimmered in the center.

"I don't know, but I have an idea. We need to get to the bottom of this, so we should start doing that. At least we know what happened to the others that came in here."

"They were eaten by hungry monsters?"

"Maybe, but maybe not. I think they went into whatever realm in which they touched the glass, or protective field, and are now stuck there."

"How did we get out of there then?"

"My guess is because we were right by the door and still focused on it."

"What are these?" Phoebus asked and moved towards stone and steel tables covered with odd artifacts that resembled the plasma pistols he had seen Croaker design.

"Nothing, pay attention." Croaker snapped. "Don't touch anything else. Focus, and think of whatever controls this place."

"Alright, and what exactly controls this place?"

"I don't know, but it wanted us to separate. So I think we can't be absorbed into a world we see as easily as we would be if we were alone, because we stuck together."

Croaker inspected the runes on the stone podium as Phoebus fidgeted behind him. He pressed one and it lit up, and the matching symbol on the archway also lit up.

"What are you doing?" Phoebus asked.

"The sign outside, when we came in, had a series of symbols around the edge. This thing has the same symbols. I am trying to reset our 'experience' and start over, or take us to whoever controls this place."

Guttural voices sounded from the doorway and shuffling steps could be heard coming towards them.

"Um, Croaker," Phoebus tapped the older man on the shoulder, "something is coming. You should hurry."

"Oh, thank goodness you are here to tell me these things!" Croaker said, wiping his hand through his greasy salt and pepper hair. "I have to remember the symbols and the sequence."

Humanoid figures entered the room. They were reptilian with faceted eyes and were dressed in animal skins. Hissing at the two men, one pointed and the others lurched forward.

"Oh, to hell with it," Phoebus shouted and pressed the last two symbols. The liquid curtain shimmered and burst outward, then reversed and shot into the circular arch. The younger man sprung over the console and ran into the portal, Croaker following.

They stumbled into a circular room. The walls were black slate and countless copper plates with oval protuberances covered them, along with copper pipes. One section of the wall had brass plates from floor to ceiling; cogs and gears whirred and turned beside them. The ceiling had elegant brass beams bisecting it. The floor was polished black marble and reflected the white light from domes on the ceiling. The center of the room was dominated by a platform with four steps leading to a brass machine, which was six times the height of a man, and had a clear glass globe atop. Electricity arced from the sphere to four brass towers set around the stairs.

A small desk was beside them, and the humanoid upper half of mechanical automaton made of brass turned to them, gears whirring as it did. The machine was more of a metal skeleton embedded in a block of copper than a person. Its head was a smooth oval with indents where eyes would be, and a molded mouth and nose. A small electrical coil atop the head sparked with energy as its spindly arms and fingers clicked on a flat typewriter.

"Greetings," the apparatus said in a melodic voice, "we do hope your experience has been a pleasurable one."

"We were almost killed, twice!" Phoebus said to the machine.

"Yes," the automaton answered, its tone cheerful, "the curious nature of humans compel them and can lead to dire consequences and circumstances at times."

"I think it just called you stupid," Croaker snickered. He continued before his friend could react. Speaking to the machine he asked, "Contraption, what is this place?"

"This is the Foundation of Compelling Curiosities, and center for learning while experiencing. We are a fully automated ætheric elemental portal education system."

"Does that voice sound familiar to you?" Phoebus asked as he walked around behind the automaton.

"Yes, it is the same chipper voice of the security guard, information desk guy," Croaker said as he rubbed the stubble on his chin. "Machine, let me rephrase my question, why does this place do these things? What is its purpose for existing?"

"To allow humans to learn while experiencing," the mechanism answered.

"I see you aren't going to make getting my answer an easy task, you grandiose gadget. The halls were too large to fit in the building, and you had animals and people that no longer exist. How does the Foundation function? How does this machine work?"

"All things exist. It is a matter of being able to interact with them on the wavelength and frequency of their existence. Do you see? I made a science pun when I said matter." The machine huffed for a moment in imitation of a laugh. "It is funny because matter is merely energy. So when I said 'a matter of being' it was a reference to the interaction of said energy on a physical level."

"Yes," Croaker murmured, "very clever. But how did we see the things we saw, and what happened when we touched the glass?"

"You saw the civilizations through a portal which allowed one way viewing by stabilizing their frequency to yours. There was not any glass. What you thought of as glass was actually the generated field to allow you to perceive the realities of the beings beyond your normal human ability to sense. When you touched that barrier it synchronized your frequency with the wavelength of the observed reality."

"These were time travel doors?"

"Incorrect. All things exist simultaneously. Time is merely a human measurement to allow your species to interact with and understand your reality."

"I don't understand any of what this thing is babbling about. I just want to know, how do we get home?" Phoebus interjected.

"The Foundation would realign your frequency to that of the manifestation from which you originated. It is a simple process," the machine answered.

"Can you send us anywhere we want to go?" Croaker asked as excitement filled his voice. "Can you make us younger, or is that unethical?"

"Ethics is another human concept of measurement. The Foundation is not constrained by such measurements. Yes, we can do all the things you ask."

"Why did you choose to appear in New Tartan?" Phoebus asked, crossing his arms. "I mean, you can go anywhere, anytime, and you chose a run down, smoke and fog filled city run by a Rokairn?"

"The Foundation appears in many realities," the device said, its body spinning to face Phoebus. "Each is chosen for a specific series of criteria. The City-State of New Tartan was chosen for its diversity, creativity, and curiosity. It is a wondrous example of what the human mind can create at this stage in its development."

"Why did the people that went inside disappear?" Croaker asked, pulling out a notepad and scribbling as he spoke. "Why can't they go home?"

"When you perceive a doorway and the space beyond it," the mechanism's spindly arms gestured in a human-like manner, "it is drawn from your mind. Any visitor can return to their specific reality at any time, but most do not choose to see a door that would return them to their familiar reality."

"I don't think people are ready for this," Phoebus mumbled.

"I think you are right," Croaker agreed. "Machine, who made you?"

"The Foundation was not made," the device said. "It is. To put in terms you may understand more clearly, it has always been and will always be."

"But who built it? Who designed this device in the center of the room and how is it powered?"

"What you perceive is what your mind dictates," whirred the automaton. "Your limited capacity of understanding has designed what your mind thinks it sees. It is the same as the reality in which you choose to exist."

Croaker was scribbling in his notebook and Phoebus was pacing the room, looking at the device in the center. Neither were sure what to do or ask next.

"Are you a god?" Croaker asked.

"No." Another huff signified the machine laughing. "A divine being is another human notion, though many species have similar notions. It allows an explanation for the unexplainable."

"So gods do not exist?" Phoebus asked, confused.

"Incorrect," the device said. "But also correct. When a species believes a god exists, then their reality conforms to that, allowing them to exist on their current frequency. When such notions are no longer needed the species often, but not always, shifts its wavelength. The variations are infinite, as are the realities which are merely frequencies."

"It transcends?" Croaker asked.

"That would be a fitting description as your current level of experience and knowledge allows."

"So can we create our own world?" Phoebus asked. "Make up whatever we want and go there, and be a god if we wanted to do that?"

"Yes," the machine spun to face the younger man, "but with your limited understanding it would be a limited world. And the probability of it collapsing is great. Your current ability to conceive is not expansive enough at this point in your development. Also, your race requires a random variety of the unknown and unknowable to exist. It requires challenges to learn. If all things were as you desired, you would grow stagnant and collapse into yourself, or self-destruct. The safeguards built into the Foundation would not allow you to attune to such a frequency."

"How did we get to New Tartan?" Croaker asked.

"That was an anomaly which happened when we translocated from your reality to this one," the device answered. "You were brought with the Foundation as it reattuned to this frequency."

"So you made a mistake!" Phoebus said.

"Incorrect," the apparatus said with its happy voice, "there are no mistakes."

"Then why did we come here?" Croaker asked.

"Simply put, you wanted to come here," was the answer the mechanism gave. "Your thoughts when the Foundation shifted were inquisitive about what you felt was 'odd lightning' and 'I wonder what made it', and your companion merely follows where you go, so you were both transported."

"I don't follow where he goes," Phoebus mumbled.

"Well, we are being paid to stop the people from disappearing from New Tartan. Can you change it so they don't and instead go back to the city when they are done looking around?"

"Yes," the automaton answered, "but that would change the reality of the Foundation and no longer allow the beings which enter with free will to choose where they go."

"Can you set up a backup so once they enter a reality," Croaker inquired, rubbing his chin, "they can go back home when they want to do so?"

"Yes," the machine's hands clicked on the flat typewriter in front of it. "The requested parameters have been entered. The beings will return to their origin frequency if they so desire. Though after returning, it is probable they will not accept that the other realties existed."

"You mean," Phoebus asked, "they will think it was all a dream?"

"Correct." The machine turned to face the dandy. "That would be an acceptable comparison."

"Good," Croaker said, "then we have done our job here. I am ready to go home. But I want to remember this place and everything that went on here."

"Me too," Phoebus agreed.

The two men blinked and looked around. The machine and the room were gone. They were standing in the rain, as lightning lit the dilapidated ruins of a carnival around them. The mud sucked at their shoes as they turned in a circle, getting their bearings. Looking at each other and smiling, they wandered towards the lights of New Sylians in the distance, Croaker stopping to look at a mirror outside of the fun house.

"You have your walking stick," Croaker said, pointing at the cane in Phoebus's hand. "And what is that?"

"This?" Phoebus asked, holding up a large carpet bag in his other hand. "It's payment for our work. I thought it would be nice to have a few precious gems."

"Sheesh," Croaker said, "always thinking of money."

"Of course," Phoebus replied with indignation, "if I left it to you we would never make any money. And speaking of being paid, we never did get our fee from Mayor Kravnel."

Croaker smiled and sighed as he looked at his reflection and his smooth features, free of wrinkles around his eyes and mouth.

"Let's go find a tavern," Croaker said as he turned towards town. "You can buy the drinks tonight."

Saving Souls

Jethro stared up at the marvel of stone and glass architecture that was the church. The grey bricks were the size of hay bales and drank in the light of the setting sun. The stained glass windows did not shine with hope, but rather with a deeper and more sinister emotion. He had been born and raised in humid swamps around New Sylians. Every church he had ever seen had been made of wood and white washed boards.

He was being chased by a group of men that shouted with course Southern Gallix accents. He did not know what he did, but he knew they would not explain what it was before they hurt him. He had seen mobs like this, even been a part of them. Dressed in his clean white robes, he had chased Rokairn down like dogs. But they had deserved it; they were not real men. They were dirty animals that sought to be a part of something they had no right to be. They had to die so others may live pure lives, The Changing Wheel demanded it.

Jethro ran up the broad steps to the double oaken doors, and pounded on them with both fists. Sweeping his greasy brown hair out of his eyes, he scanned behind him. He could see the torchlight glancing off the buildings of this quaint town. It was oddly beautiful, but so was a coiled snake before it struck. He could hear the voices echoing off the wooden walls and cobblestones of the street. He turned back to the door and pounded again.

He looked up at the looming stone wheel above the door and said a quick prayer to the Changing Wheel. He jumped, startled, as the door creaked open with a sudden movement. The mob had turned the corner and slowed their approach as they saw the hooded figure in brown robes.

"Sanctuary," Jethro croaked, his throat dry from running and panting, "Please, tre' ne sha." He knew a bit of the language from the Southern Gallix immigrants that lived around his home town. He prayed it was enough.

The monk looked past him at the men he had known all his life and nodded to the crowd, and then looked the foreigner up and down. "Ya my sir, come inside. We will shelter you from the danger that is behind you. We can save you and your immortal soul," the holy man said with a heavy accent.

Head bowed, he stepped aside for Jethro to enter the ancient building. Shadowy laughter could be heard from the crowd outside. It was dark inside compared to the light of the setting sun. Dusky wooden pews were shadows in the guttering light of the candles that lined the walls in small alcoves. It smelled of incense and sweat. Two more robed figures approached, one holding a bowl of liquid. He offered it to the refugee. When Jethro hesitated, the monk raised it to his own lips to show it was meant to be drunk. The North Mirron took it and sipped at it. It was a bitter wine, and burned his cracked throat and tongue. When he tried to lower it, the monk pushed the brass vessel back to his lips, and Jethro drank. As he finished the drink, he noticed how the liquid was thicker than the wine he was used to and clung to the metal.

A hollow booming sound came from behind him as the double doors closed and were barred, startling him again. The first monk took him by the arm and began to lead

Jethro down the aisle, towards the altar and towering wheel at the end. When the foreigner resisted, the monk paused.

"Tre' ne sha, come with us. You should be cleaned, and prepared." Noticing his guest's hesitation, he added, "Maybe my language is not the perfect. You have upset and fears, you are dirty and very scared. Maybe you rest and soon you see the light of the Wheel's mercy?"

Jethro nodded and allowed the brother to lead him forward. It felt surreal. The light from the sun, low on the horizon outside, lit the stained glass on one side of the chapel, showing the scenes of demons with their pitchforks herding and tormenting sinners, but did not touch the holy saints with looks of pity and sadness on the opposite side.

When they reached the end of the aisle Jethro stumbled and fell to his knees in front of the pulpit and before the tortured figures of the Saints, like a petitioner. The two monks that had come afterwards reached for him, hooking their hands under his arms and helping him stand. Their guest's head lolled as he was in part dragged and in part stumbled towards an open door leading out of the main chapel.

"The Wheel will guide us to save your soul, my sir," were the last words he heard before the darkness overtook him.

Jethro came to awareness with slow deliberation. The smell of incense was stronger and he could hear chanting in an ancient language. His head felt like it was full of the cotton that he raised on his farm. Lying still, he could feel a sheet atop his body, and the air was chill. Something wet touched his forehead and he opened his eyes with effort. The neutral face of the monk at the door was above him, framed by the light of the burning braziers in the room.

"He has awoken, it is time to begin," the monk said in a solemn tone. Jethro only understood the last word.

As the man moved out of view, Jethro tried to sit up. He could not. His wrists were tied above his head and his feet were also bound in a spread eagle manner. Panic tickled the edges of his awareness. Something was not right. Looking above him, Jethro could see the carving of a demonic visage on the ceiling above him, with a slaughtered sheep secured in its open, toothy maw, and liquid dropped down onto his forehead.

The chanting rose to a song, and lifting his head as much as he could, Jethro saw a naked man, with carvings in his flesh of symbols and pentagrams that healed into raised scars, coming towards him with arched iron scythes. It became clear to him what was about to happen as his head cleared.

"Wait, you said I was safe!" he shouted.

"No, we said we would save your soul, and so we shall. The Changing Wheel requires its sacrifice so we may live in the peace and glory of its cycles. What you do is for good and holy purpose. We thank you for your gift. Your soul shall save our souls."

Jethro screamed as the dark curved blades cut into his chest and dragged along his flesh to his belly. He could feel his life blood spill over his sides. The chanting voices of the choir rose in an unholy fervor, as the monks shed their robes and began to partake of this glorious feast.

The Big Picture

Jonathan, Jasper, and Jake crouched in the alley and stared up at the dirigible. Their bulky rocket packs whistled steam as they warmed up and readied for the assent that would make the three brothers rich men. Jasper had designed and built the machines. It had taken the past few months, over three hundred Imperial writs, and dozens of specialty parts. Jonathan had the job of finding the rare items. The other two brothers never learned where the oldest brother had procured the equipment for the flying contraptions, but didn't care as long as they were able to pull off their caper.

The tall, lanky brother, Jonathan, never spoke. He had stopped after his thirteenth birthday and the death of their father. The Sherriff couldn't get any information from the only witness, Jonathan. The blood on the hands of their father, the viscous spray on the sand, and the spatter on Jonathan had pointed to the wound being self-inflicted. One person had witnessed it, had been there, and held the hand of the man he idolized as the blood drained from his slit throat. The slaying had been some sort of ritual, and the constable found signs of dozens of people at the site. No one had ever found out why it happened or who had attended. Though before that time Jonathan would go off on his own, he now just did what he was told. He leaned against the wall, feeling the steam from his pack tickling his neck as the pressure valve released the buildup.

Jake had just gone over the plan again. He rubbed his hands together as he looked at the rough sketch in the dirt between Jasper and himself. Jasper glared at his own feet, not daring to show irritation to his youngest brother. It had been Jasper that had come up with the plan. It was daring and risky, but worth it all when it is done. Nearly a hundred thousand Imperial writs in gold and tens of thousand writs in good ol' cash would cover a lot of things. A daytime heist meant a high profile job, but Jake liked the idea of being seen and becoming infamous outlaws. Jasper didn't, and like everything else, Jonathan was silent on the matter.

Jasper remembered the days after their father's death when his brothers would listen to him. In the beginning, the middle brother would come up with plans to raid the other kids' forts – stealing the best tidbits and a few writs - and later how to rob the old widow McCredie of her savings jar. Jake would tag along and rush out before he was supposed to, or go brag to all the neighbor kids the next day. Things changed as they got older. Jasper couldn't intellectually bully Jake into behaving. Quite the opposite. Jake would listen to the plan, then make a few small changes and say it was his own. He'd even threaten Jasper anymore, saying that he would turn his brother into the law if he didn't do it his way. Or worse, he would leave the middle brother out altogether.

"Ya ready, lil brother?" Jake slapped Jasper on the shoulder as he stood.

Jasper gritted his teeth, as much from the sting of the words as his younger brother's hand. He hated that he was called the little brother when he was the older of the two, but he had a plan for that too.

Jasper smiled as he stood, "Course Jake, our plan is perfect."

"My plan, ya mean. Now, fire up your rockets, while I

check to make sure the street is clear."

Jasper could see most of the block from the stack of crates they hid behind. Jake stepped into the street of the small, dusty town. It was nearly high noon, and he cast a small puddle of a shadow around his feet. Striking a pose, he hooked his thumbs into his gun belt. No one was close enough to notice the trio. The two brothers in the alley began their pre-flight check list, flipping switches and toggling controls. Jake looked up and down the street, his copper and leather rocket pack gleaming in the heat.

"Good people of this dirt clod town," Jake drawled in a loud voice, "ya'll are about to witness history as Jailbreak Jake, the man the law couldn't hold, does something no man has ever done before! Look away ya'll, cause if I see ya lookin', I'll shoot ya between the eyes from three hundred meters up, while flying at a two hundred kilometers per hour!"

People were torn between staring at the man or heading into the closest building, hesitating long enough to get a glimpse before running for cover. Heads poked out of stores, alleys, and from behind wagons and stacks of crates. Jasper rolled his eyes. Gripping the hand controls, he nodded to Jonathan. They launched into the air, gaining speed and hurtling towards the airship that was gliding past the western portion of the town. Jake pulled out one gun and fired rounds into the air with a laugh, and then holstered it as he took off with a whoop and spun in a tight circles as he ascended, creating a corkscrew vapor trail.

Jonathan closed on the vessel as the others followed him. Turning with expert ease, he came around the side of the cupola and let off his thrusters as he neared the door. Reaching out with his long arm, he grabbed the handle outside of the main cabin and spun the wheel that secured the door. As his brothers were arriving, the door swung open, and Jake flew straight in, crashing into the startled steward in his way. Jasper followed with less grace, ricocheting off the doorway.

The cabin was split into three sections with the cockpit in the front, the cargo hold behind a locked door in the rear, and where the brothers landed in the personnel area in between. It was less than six paces wide and had wooden benches large bolted to the floor. Along the back wall was canvas mesh stopping crates and extra cargo from shifting during the flight. A few crates had been moved to the middle of the floor as seats and a table to allow the guards to play a game of draughts. The front wall held a pantry and cupboard.

They surprised the five armed guards. Jake whooped, drew his pistol, and shot two of the guards as Jonathan climbed in the doorway, and Jasper gained his feet. The remaining three guards leapt up and scrambled for their rifles. Before they could bring them to bear, three shots rang out as one, and they crumpled to the floor of the airship. Each brother stood with a pistol drawn, smoke curling from the barrel.

"Easy as pie!" Jake exclaimed with a grin that showed a golden tooth with a diamond in it. The cockpit door flew open, and the brothers turned in unison, pistols cocked and arms extended towards the surprised young man staring at them. Jake said, "Wanna live, pard'ner?"

The boy nodded.

"Then lay down on the floor and you just might make it home."

The startled boy, barely out of school, stared at them with wide blue eyes. His complexion was made paler by the blonde hair that was almost white and his wispy mustache. He dropped to his knees and laid face down, centimeters from the expanding pool of blood of the men that had been his friends and teased him about the adventure of the airship gold delivery. Jasper darted past him to secure the pilot, stopping in the door.

"Jonathan," he shouted, turning back to his older brother, "he flew!" The quiet man stepped to the door and looked outside. Seeing a parachute opening, he took careful aim, and three gunshots were followed by a long scream. The boy on the floor shuddered, understanding what happened. The oldest brother turned back and nodded at Jasper, before looking at Jake.

Jake grinned and pushed open the cargo hold. Waiting in the tight wooden hallway were three padlocked compartments on each side. Turning to the last crew member, Jake said, "Ok boy, gimmie that key, or ya get to walk home starting now."

"I can't. I don-don-don't have it," the boy stuttered. "I'm just an apprentice pilot, and they got the key at the tower we're headed to."

Jake was like a cat with a mouse and liked to play games with the people he robbed. They knew the key would not be on board. Jonathan stared with no expression as Jasper let out a sigh. There was no telling if Jake would let the boy live to spread the word of their deeds or kill him just for kicks.

Jasper didn't mind this so much, but in addition to the marks, rubes, and cons, Jake had been doing it with him also. In their childhood, Jake had followed Jasper around, idolizing him. After their father's death though - when Jonathan had become silent and withdrawn and would disappear for days - Jake became wild. Like the dam had broken and he was free of any moral constraints. The youngest brother began doing outrageous things. He'd get into scraps with other boys, kiss girls behind the church, and even flirt with grown women, including their own mother's friends.

By the time Jake turned thirteen and Jasper was sixteen, Jake had taken charge of the gang of boys they had put together. The youngest brother would turn the other boys against his older brother if he objected, and Jasper had no choice but to go along with his schemes.

Jonathan's silence didn't give either brother support. He'd watch and go wherever the group went. He'd been that way since witnessing their father's suicide. It was an embarrassment to the community. Their father had been a well-known man of means and often away for weeks to grand cities. He owned a hotel and casino, three cattle ranches, and had shares in the railroad and the new railplane line. After his death, all his holdings were disbursed or absorbed by various partners and interests. His wife and children were left with the hotel and a modest stipend paid quarterly. Within two years, their mother sold the hotel and bought a large house that she turned into a boarding house. She told them the hotel was too much work for her, but One night Jasper snuck out onto the veranda and to her window, and in that sweltering summer night and had seen the male visitors go to her room.

There was a constant parade of surly and dusty characters in the boarding house. Jake took to listening to the yarns spun by the snake-oil salesmen, cowboys, and other malcontents. A man who claimed to be a bounty hunter stayed in the house for almost six weeks. He told the boys tales of hunts and captures. Jonathan always stood in the doorway, as if afraid to come closer to the man while listening to the accounts of his deeds. Jasper was fascinated and followed the man all over town. When the leathered tracker left for a few days, Jasper would sit at the edge of town and wait for him to return.

Jake teased the middle brother without mercy and called Jasper a puppy and compared him to a swooning woman. Jasper ignored him until the day Jake came around the corner with his gang, and pointing at him, yelled to his cronies, "There he is boys, let's get our bounty for this bastard!"

Jasper was beaten by his friends that day. The youngest brother stood over the tussle and watched as the boys pinned his older brother and one time idol. They hit and kicked him in the face, ribs, and stomach. The gang dragged Jasper to an apple tree after the beatings and produced a noose. Jake proceeded to string him up. Jasper wept and begged as the other boys stood him up on a barrel, threw the rope over a branch, and tied it off on a root. Jake proclaimed his crime and sentence and then kicked the barrel out from under his own brother. For a moment Jasper swung, just like the man the old bounty hunter had brought in less than a week ago. The slip knot around the root broke loose, and he crashed to the dusty ground. His vision popped with black spots and colored sparks as he gasped and tore at the rope around his throat. He felt his younger brother's dank breath on the side of his face. It smelled of licorice.

"Ya went too far, and this is family," Jake's voice growled into Jasper's ear. "Blood is thicker than water. That's the only reason I didn't have them kill ya. That man ain't our daddy, and ya ain't going to treat him like he is no more. I'll be making sure of that. Remember what I said the next time ya see a swinging rope." The younger boy stood up, "Ya crapped yourself, like a little baby. You're pathetic."

It was a week later that Jasper saw a swinging rope with the bounty hunter at the end. The hired gun returned to town from a successful hunt the previous night. That same night the banker, Mr. Johnson, was shot in his own back yard.

The banker's wife Millie, a young beauty that always smiled, told the sheriff that there was a knock at the back door and her husband answered it. He'd greeted someone in a friendly and familiar manner, and stepped outside. As she continued with her needlepoint, she heard a gunshot. She ran to the kitchen but was afraid to open the door. As she stood, terrified, it opened, and a hand holding a gun slid into view. It was a polished silver six-shooter with ornate scrollwork on the stock and ivory inlay on the handle, and her family name in calligraphy along the barrel. The pistol had been given to her husband as a wedding gift from her father. It was to protect Millie during their marriage. She heard a voice yell, "I got another bounty, time to go sleep now!" She said it was deep and mean.

The sheriff went to the only bounty hunter in town. The stranger was in such a deep sleep that he didn't wake when they knocked, or when they kicked the door in, or when they dragged him from his bed after finding the Johnson's pistol on his bedside table. He woke when they were cuffing him in the dirt outside the house, but could barely walk and was dragged to the jail house.

A lynch mob showed up at the courthouse the next day. Jasper watched as Jake's gang kept the crowd riled up, shouting for the killer's blood, forcing the judge to have a trial on the spot. At sundown, Jasper watched the man swing by his neck until dead. Jake smirked as he sauntered close to his brother and patted him on the shoulder. "Welcome back to the family Jasper. I don't recommend ya leave again."

Three months later, Jake began to woo the Widow Johnson shortly after he turned fourteen years old. She thought it was sweet. He told her not to let the men take the bank from her, that women can run a business as well as any man. In time, she spurned his advances. On his fifteenth birthday, he went to visit the Widow Johnson. He told his brothers it was for his birthday celebration. When he home came well past midnight, he had scratches down the side of his face and a bloody lip. When they asked what happened, he smiled his crooked smile and said every bounty has a chase and a fight. The Widow Johnson didn't come out of her house for ten days. During that time, she sold her rights to the bank. The sale was to take place before the end of the month. A week before the contract was finalized Jake told Jasper to figure out how to rob that bank, claiming that the Johnsons owed him something for catching the man who killed Mr. Johnson.

With a sour taste in his mouth, Jasper planned the robbery. It was easy when Jake provided him the keys that the Widow Johnson had 'given' him. Jasper recognized this was more punishment for him from Jake. Three days before the sale contract was finalized, the bank was robbed. The investors backed out, and the Widow Johnson was financially ruined. The three brothers left town with bags of cash that day, and Jake sent the Widow Johnson a thank you letter. Jasper left a note for their mother. And Jonathan was seen by Jasper coming out of the post office with ink stains on his fingertips. So their life of crime began four years ago when Jasper was eighteen, and Jake was fifteen. They were famous by Jake's next birthday.

Jasper refocused on his youngest brother, who cocked his six-shooter and pressed against the temple of the young co-pilot. Glancing at Jonathan, he saw the oldest brother watching the scene with no emotion. Jasper sighed and headed down the narrow hallway to open the locks as Jake played with his quarry. Setting small explosives - which he'd designed and built - on the iron padlocks, Jasper uncoiled the wire and detonated the devices and destroyed the last obstacle between them and their goal. Doors swung open to reveal stacks of gold bars and canvas mail bags full of cash. He grabbed a sack.

A blast from the main cabin rocked the zeppelin, and the air detonated with a resounding pop, like the sound of a heavy rock hitting still water. Jasper was thrown headfirst to the end of the hallway. Though dazed, he realized steam was leaking from a tear in his jetpack's brass air tanks. He slid along the floor towards the central room and could tell the nose of the ship was pointing towards the ground. Shrugging off his pack, he stood and drew his pistol with his right hand. He slung the canvas bag over his shoulder and went back to the main room. Aided by the angle of descent as the airship continued its dive, as he balanced himself with a hand on the wall.

He saw the young co-pilot unconscious across the controls through the door to the cockpit. The altitude levers were pressed forward, causing the downward plunge that would kill them when they hit the cliff or ground. The main cabin showed no damage from the explosion. Jake was unconscious among the dead men, and Jonathan was nowhere to be seen. He may have been thrown out the door by the same explosion that had thrown Jasper backwards four meters.

Through the door, he saw the ground getting closer, and

he formed his plan. Jasper jammed his gun into its holster and ran to Jake. Dropping the bag of money, he unbuckled his younger brother's jetpack and began strapping it onto his own back. Slinging the duffel across his shoulders again, he secured the strap to his harness, leapt out, and fired the jetpack's rockets at the same time.

Jonathan watched from the ground Jasper shot out of the zeppelin, wobbling under the weight and drag of the rucksack that was strapped to his back. His brother didn't have a clue where to go. He came close to the cliff wall and circled back out over the scrub plains, wasting fuel as he tried to figure out his next move. That was the problem with Jasper's plans - they fell short on the closing. Jake always had a getaway but was always fuzzy with the details in the beginning. He would find a great score and plan a dramatic entrance and a daring escape, but have little else considered.

Jonathan watched as a silhouette rose in the cockpit of the airship. The nose of the vessel began to raise and turn it away from the collision with the cliff. He held a large box in both hands. Raising it over his head, the oldest brother toggled the switches and turned a dial. The thick iron antenna sparked and hummed as electric flowed through it. Jasper looked in Jonathan's direction, his attention caught by the movement and flashes.

Jonathan watched without expression as his brother's course was corrected and headed towards him. Continuing his manipulations of the control box, he fingered the slide bar into position and pushed down on the small plunger. The dirigible exploded. The air boomed and the concussive force of the explosion slammed into Jasper midair, turning and tumbling him head over heels. Hot wind washed over Jonathan, blowing his stringy hair back from his gaunt face. Jasper slammed into the ground thirty meters from where his brother stood and slid fifteen meters closer as his rocket pack went out of control. He came to a stop, but the pack still issued forth steam and a high pitched whistle.

Jasper screamed and scrambled to unstrap his harness and remove the contraption as the steam scalded his legs. Debris from the government aircraft rained down around the brothers as Jonathan watched his younger sibling. The remaining structure of the ship slammed into the bluff, causing a series of smaller explosions. The large pieces fell in the distance, but smaller fragments flew in a wide circle.

"Aren't you going to help me?" Jasper yelled as he pushed upright, trying to free the tangled rucksack from the machine before it exploded also. He tore the money bag from the twisted wreckage. Standing, he yanked his braces over his shoulder and shoved his trousers down, revealing the blistered skin on his legs, already raw and peeling. He tried to remain standing as he pulled the dungarees over his boots, falling over again, bursting the blisters, and causing sand to grind into his fresh wounds.

Swearing, Jasper stood again. He spun towards his older brother, his mouth open to yell. He stopped and noticed the scene around them. A dozen men on horses rode out of a sheltered overhang towards the wreckage followed by three wagons. A woman stood beside Jonathan. She watched Jasper, head cocked as the older brother surveyed the scene in the distance.

"The Prophet will not speak," she said. "I will speak for him." She was a head shorter than Jonathan, which made her tall for a woman. She wore men's clothing, a simple brown leather vest over a sweat stained shirt with the sleeves rolled up, and miner's dungarees. Her black hair was pulled back in a tight ponytail, and she wasn't wearing a hat, which made her icy blue eyes squint in the bright sun. It was her scars that stood out. Her face was disfigured, showing where she had been cut many times, and her arms showed puckered flesh, telling a tale of severe burns. The red tint of her skin spoke of her heritage as one of the dasism people native to this land.

"Who the hell are you?"

"I am Genesee. I am the Speaker for the Prophet. I was born into the tribes to join them and do this task. I knew the Prophet's father and served him, and now I serve the Prophet. He says you have a good head on your shoulders, but you are driven by emotion," she said, sizing him up. "We will help guide that."

Jasper looked down and realized his state of undress. He covered himself with his hands and limped to his trousers, pulling them in front of him. "Look, I got the money!"

"No, you got one bag of money. The Prophet will have the whole cargo of gold." She pointed in the distance at the men closing on the wreckage. "He also said you limited vision. His vision encompasses all."

"He talks to you?"

"The Prophet speaks to the pure, and you can see I have been purified." She held out her puckered and scarred arms for inspection.

Jasper stammered, and Jonathan stopped him with a snap of his fingers that sounded as loud as thunder in the rocky ravine in which they stood.

The middle brother looked up. "You killed Jake," he said, "and I would have died too, if I hadn't thought to take Jake's jetpack."

"Yes, a sacrifice was necessary to make this happen," Genesee replied with a calm that irritated Jasper.

"But I was on that ship too. I would have been killed also!"

Genesee looked to Jonathan for guidance. Unspoken communication flowed between them, and Jonathan nodded. Genesee spoke again, "But you weren't. You found your way off, so it is fate that you will continue to assist the Prophet in His great plan. Since His father passed this burden down to Him, He has worked tirelessly, against your and Jake's squabbling, to bring His plan to fruition."

She spoke with an educated tone, and Jasper shook his head. Everything was surreal, and the world spun for a moment. He began to fall. Jonathan was there, catching, supporting, and helping him to shade. The middle brother's mind was in a whirl. This was his older brother's plan? Jasper has designed and built the gear needed to make it happen. How could Jonathan claim it was his own plan? And what was that thing about their father handing down something to his oldest brother?

Genesee held a canteen to Jasper's lips. He took it and drank. She looked at Jonathan, who only nodded. "The Prophet has decided you may know more. His father had great knowledge and plans. A dream of creating an army, a force, of men and machines blended together and using these to overthrow the tyranny that rules this land. The Prophet is no criminal; He is not a thief. He is a man of vision, with powerful allies.

"His father groomed Him to be a leader of men, just as you were groomed to be blindly loyal and an inventive genius, meant to build the tools He would need to craft the creations that would change the face of this torn nation. We will call upon the spirits of the land, the wind and weather, lightning and rock. We will enhance men with the gifts of the earth and make them more than they would ever be without it. This is the will of the Prophet, guided by the spirit of His father."

A rider rode hard towards them. Genesee gripped her hand into a fist, a small hiss and grinding squeak sounding from her forearm. The man reined in his horse four paces from the trio. "There is one survivor. We think it is your brother, Prophet," he panted, glancing at Jasper. "Your other brother."

Genesee smiled. "The Prophet said Jake is strong of body. His survival is also a sign. Jasper, it looks as if we have our first volunteer to become a machine warrior of the New Order. He will be perfect once we have removed his spirit and replaced it with steel and steam. Let it begin."

As Jasper was led away he couldn't help but feel excitement for things to come.

Looming Shadows

The architecture stared down. No, it glared at me during those dark years. It was a constant rain. When it wasn't the rain it was a dark, oppressive gloom and haze from smoke and fire. Everything was gray and life seeped from it. Stone and aged wood loomed over everything and men were lost in the labyrinth of muddy alleys and cobblestone streets.

I recall how the people in the lanes always had their shoulders bent, walking the boulevards in a hurry, while at the same time shuffling in a monotonous and broken manner. It is an odd gait once you recognize it. Even the rich and powerful showed this. Though ramrod straight they still moved with a certain pace that showed their heavy burden rather than a free person. Even aristocrats were constrained by the societal prison of their own design and construct. The clothes were stark and colors were not welcome. The few that insisted on wearing bright and garish clothing were foreigners and outcasts.

I became the monster I am during this time. I was the class in between the two other classes. I traveled, but not in luxury. I worked, but did not toil. I had a chance of earning a fortune and could choose to live on the fringes of either society, but was not accepted as part of either. I was a man of numbers and figures, money and innovation, and I led the industrial revolution and helped bring the world into the modern age. My plans started as shipwrights, and then moved into steel and rails. Trains and steamships were to be the legacy of my children if I had time for the urge for such things. I never made time for that though. It would have meant dividing my attentions and falling to the predators that lurked. These beasts in the form of men were waiting for me to look away long enough for them to steal what I had built. I would guess this is why I fell so naturally into the dark world that embraced me one night, and made me into a cold, unfeeling creature.

You went through your infancy, childhood, adolescence, and into adulthood… but it doesn't end there. Everything has these phases, even countries, concepts, and eras in time. But we have phases in our adult lives also. People do not see these as clearly. Rarely does anything creative survive to full maturity before it is over taken by something younger and more aggressive, because with maturity comes either fear or complacency. I have beaten that certainty though. I have entered phases beyond adult, into an eternal state. I have renewal without losing what I was before. I have creativity through longevity, rather than being remade every decade of my life, like others.

As I grew in my new role and abilities, I no longer merely fed on the sweat of others, but on their very blood and more importantly, their souls. I became the ultimate predator. People trusted me from naiveté or greed. Either way it allowed me to feed from their weakness and grow in my own strength. I had the time and resources to plan further into the future than any person or government would dream. I robbed whole regions of their sons so they may do my work. I bought barren fields and found oil. I tore the very earth asunder for its precious offerings. I planned and succeeded in giving people dreams, dreams that I would steal away at the last moment, taking them for my own uses. I crushed hundreds of others that would threaten my plans, and trampled thousands underfoot without even noticing they were more than the dirt upon which I walked.

I took on protégés and students, even brought them into my personal fold and gave them every gift and advantage I could. One by one, or sometimes in pairs or groups, they would turn away from what I offered for a fleeting personal interaction. It did not surprise me so much as disappoint me. It did allow me to take back what was mine, which was everything they had worked for and created. I left them crumpled in the gutter, drained and alone.

If you recognize how people become bitter and jaded as time goes on, how our elderly are bent and twisted not from age but from experience, then you can imagine how one that does not age can change over a century and a half. I am now ready to change again. In my years I had the wisdom to save, plan, and set very specific designs into motion. I control the news and who receives what information. I control the transportation and who can go where. I even control the little scavenging insects of mankind that are still bent from toil. I control all these by money, power, and distraction. I keep the masses from forming a mob and gathering pitchforks and torches by making them feel safe at home, and threatened outside their own door. I have even taken the meaning out of their daily tasks. Most work had no redeeming or fulfilling qualities.

I now want to bring back the age of looming and glaring architecture, but with my modern twist. Look at the glass and see the smudges. The grey towers reaching for the dirty skies, incomprehensible art that children cannot even see shapes within, and adults ignore as they rush in their broken shuffle to their daily drudge. The large cities begin to cloud over with poisons on the ground and in the air, just as they did a hundreds of years ago. I no longer need the church to control these people; I now have mass media, and consumerism as their God.

It is not big business you should fear, it is my private business. For I shall consume all in my hunger and thirst for power. No hope means no resistance. I rule from the shadows, and I cannot be challenged when I cannot be seen.

The Unchronicled Peril: A Trio of Travelers Tale

The night air was warm, but the breeze cooled the city as it darted through open windows, bringing smells of cooking and sounds of families to anyone that cared to listen. It had been a day as any other in Bolton, where friends greeted each other, shop-keepers laughed with customers, and men and woman fell in love and built lives together. Children had played in the streets like every other day, giggling and running, making some adults smile at their play and others shout and shake a fist at their antics.

On a small side street, along the proposed route for the underground train that would make travel within the city quicker and easier, the hammers, pickaxes, and chisels rang from inside a hole. Echoes bounced off the stone and wood buildings that held shops and homes, lulling the citizens to sleep. The rhythmic tinks and clanks created a discordant and tinny melody that ground on Professor Walter's nerves. He was a man of science and study, and didn't like the thick night air and fog that had settled around the roped off area which was the entrance to the curious artifact below. The Professor had seen the headlines in the paper a week ago,

'Alien Archway Arrests Advancement, Archeologists Atwitter', and contacted his colleague, Duke Crillington, that day.

The two men had known each other for years and had been as close as any two men could be without a blood relation. The Duke often invited Titalus over for dinner engagements, or called upon the man for his insight into history, social interactions, or any variety of topics. And the Professor often called upon his boyhood friend to share financial opportunities, scientific discoveries, or just a fine wine and cigars.

After the stone doorway with the foreign runes and hieroglyphs had been found in the tunnels that were being dug for the new underground train, the Duke had bought the whole city block for this project upon the Professor's recommendation. Within a week the tunnel dig site had become an archeological dig site. The media and other curious onlookers were kept away by hired thugs, and soon people got bored and stopped asking questions. Tonight would change all that though.

A dull boom sounded and the surrounding buildings shook. Titalus Walters could hear pebbles raining down into the hole in an uneven tattoo. A low hiss of escaping air could be heard in the pit, followed by the screams of the workers below. The foreman stumbled to the surface, his face coated with an odd green jelly which ate away at his flesh. The man clawed at his eyes while babbling about the talons of beasts rising from hell. The professor backed away from the area, and then turned and fled.

A midnight train rumbled across the landscape, chased by the moon. Elizabeth stared out the window, watching the shadow of the train dip and leap between the rolling hills under the light the lunar spectator. A fog had gathered, making the details of the countryside blur and distort.

Tendrils of wisp explored valleys in slow movements. The chill from outside crept through the windows and doors of the car, making the woman draw her shawl closer. Her lace collar and cuffs did little to protect her, but the thick layers of her purple dress insulated her well. Her bustle made it difficult to sit in comfort, unlike Zachary, who even in his rust colored leather jerkin and with a sword on his side slept in the seat across from her. Elizabeth tucked a stray brown curl back into her bun and turned to look at her other traveling companion, Suykimo.

Suykimo sat upright and cross-legged, his almond shaped sea green eyes intense, reading a small book. It was a mystery, she knew because that was his preferred genre when he wasn't engrossed in a tome about politics, psychology, or religion. His midnight blue coat, which resembled a robe with gold needlework, pooled around his legs. He glanced up, and smiled, ran a hand across his shaved head and returned to his story. Suykimo always knew when someone was watching him, which was often due to his exotic appearance and Aeifain heritage.

They traveled to the capital of the island country in which Elizabeth had been born, New Gallia. Bolton was a grand city, and she had attended university there, studying social interactions and excelling. Suykimo had insisted they return here after being contacted about a mysterious archeological dig by Duke Crillington of Shirewood. The man had heard of the trio and their adventures. Suykimo had insisted upon coming, though they had heard of a village they had visited and rid of a werewolf was now experiencing another problem of townsfolk being killed. Elizabeth had contacted her university friend, Amarilly, to investigate the town.

Elizabeth dozed off thinking about her friend and the trouble she may be facing. She woke as the train came to a sudden halt. Sitting up, she blinked and looked around. They had arrived in Bolton. Zachary was awake and gathering their luggage from the overhead racks, passing each of them their bags. The few passengers milled about, doing the same. They filed out into the damp morning air. The sun wouldn't rise for another hour.

A coachman waited for them with a motorized coach. The three were shuffled inside the vehicle and set out for Duke Crillington's estate, Shirewood. They arrived as the dawn broke over the rolling hills to the east. Zachary exited first, looking to each side and glancing at the roof, searching for threats without realizing what he was doing. Suykimo, his long coat immaculate, glided down the step and onto the gravel next, appearing refreshed though he hadn't slept at all. Elizabeth accepted the coachman's hand as she stepped down and stumbled as she did. She patted her hair, which had a dozen stray strands, and smoothed her gown. She didn't know how the men managed to always look ready to go, when she needed time to freshen up.

The household staff stood outside to greet them, headed up by the chief butler. He led the way inside as other servants gathered their few pieces of luggage. The servant left after showing them to the library, a large two story room with books from floor to ceiling, various settees, divans, chairs on one side, and a large oak desk on the other. The curtains had been drawn back, the shutters opened, and a small fire set in the fireplace to take the chill from the air.

The Duke swept into the room, his chubby cheeks rosy, and his clothes pressed and starched. He smelled of roses Elizabeth noted - unusual for a gentleman - as he shook each of their hands. A footman entered and served tea as they settled into seats, though Zachary remained standing.

"Thank you for coming," Duke Crillington began, "I am not sure if you have heard about Professor Walter's recent discovery and excitement here in Bolton."

"Professor of antiquities and sociology, Titalus Walters, of the University of Bolton?" Elizabeth asked.

"Yes, the very one. Do you know him?"

"Yes. Well, no." Elizabeth floundered. "I remember him from my time at the university. Always a gentleman, so kind and smart. And a handsome fellow." She trailed off, blushing.

"I do not know him personally, only what you sent in your letter, Your Grace," Suykimo said, his voice a quiet tenor, "but I am sure you will suitably enlighten us."

"Indeed, good sir, I shall. He is a close, personal friend, and during an undertaking to make an underground railway, it seems we have discovered some sort of ancient tomb that has been buried under the streets of our capital city for hundreds of years. We do not recognize the craftsmanship nor the hieroglyphs that adorn the chamber." The Duke paused, sipping at his tea, giving his listeners a chance to ask questions, and show the appropriate expressions of surprise and wonder. When he received neither, he continued, ruffled.

"When my men began excavating the area there was a mishap. It seems a gas escaped. I have heard of crypts being sealed so tightly that they did this when opened, but we hadn't opened this one yet." The Duke paused again, waiting for some response.

"And what did this gas do?" Suykimo asked, his voice so low that the nobleman had to lean forward to hear him.

"Well sir, it drove the workmen mad! A dozen men are all dead, most slaughtered each other, and the couple that didn't…" Duke Crillington paused again, looking at Elizabeth. "Perhaps the lady would not want to hear this. It may upset her delicate nature."

"Her nature may not be as delicate as you think," Zachary said, his tone brusque. "She has seen things most men have not imagined in their worst nightmares."

"Now Zachary," Elizabeth said with a smile as she rose, "I will excuse myself to freshen up, for his Lordship's comfort if nothing else. If you gentlemen will pardon me."

The men stood with her and a maid appeared to escort her to the powder room. Elizabeth was glad to escape for a few minutes. Her hair was in shambles and her bustle had shifted to the left on the train. As she followed the maid, she thought of the dashing man she remembered from the university, Professor Titalus Walters. He was a bit of a rebel, and encouraged women to speak their mind, and even marched in a women's suffrage protest, helping to bring about the changes in society that had altered the world over the past half dozen years. He was also an adventurer, traveling to exotic places like Aeifa, Drungia, and even North Mirron during their war to help the Dasism negotiate peace between the Federation and Empire. She admired a man that could keep his wits about him in any situation. She had to admit to herself that she once had a bit of a crush on him, and even now felt a bit flustered.

Suykimo sat as Elizabeth departed, but the Duke remained standing, and began pacing as he continued with the tale.

"You see, these men were disturbed. They tore their own flesh from their faces, arms, and anywhere else they could reach. We had to restrain them. Only one survived the night, but even he succumbed to the terrors of his mind soon afterwards. We learned little from him before he passed, but he claimed horrors were rising up." The Duke issued a strangled noise that was a strained laugh. "Of course, this is all nonsense. The chamber wasn't even breached and nothing was down there besides dirt and beetles. Lots of beetles though. Thousands of the little buggers came from all directions. They were like a black carpet inside the hole, covering every surface. They wouldn't leave either."

Duke Crillington fell silent, his eyes distant, and his left cheek twitching. Zachary and Suykimo waited, minutes passing before Suykimo spoke, encouraging the man to continue.

"Oh," the lord said, startled, "my apologies. I must have been lost in my thoughts. We covered the area in oil and burned the beetles, but they were replaced by thousands more. They were eating the corpses of their fallen kin. We burned them also. Bolton must have almost no insects remaining. But I digress; after they were dead we noticed the rats. They also devoured the charred bodies of the beetles. You could hear them. It was horrid. An undertone of soft clicking and crackling like a distant fire. We burned them also. The smell was incredible. Local merchants were complained about it. I am afraid we will have many hungry cats."

"My Lord," Suykimo said, "what can we do to help? Why did you call upon us?"

"Oh, yes!" The Duke was relieved to move on. "The three of you are infamous for dealing with odd occurrences. Professor Walters, who shall be joining us for dinner, recommended you. He spoke highly of your skills and abilities. We need you to find out how we may open this container and learn out what lies within."

"Forgive me for asking, My Lord," Zacchary said, "but why would you want to open it after all the peculiar happenings?"

"Those were just coincidences," the Duke said. "I would bet on it."

"Would you bet your life on it," Zachary asked, "and the lives of the people in the city?"

"Excuse me?" The Duke frowned.

"Did I miss anything important?" Elizabeth asked as she entered the library. Suykimo stood, as all three men acknowledged the presence of the lady. Everyone sat again, except Zachary. After the footman refreshed everyone's tea and left the room, they continued.

"We shall help," Suykimo began before anyone else could speak. "Zachary, I would like you to investigate the site. Elizabeth, please check the University library. You know the people there, and worked with many of them since you left. I will tell you more of what to look for as we return to the city. I shall visit my brethren at the churches and holy temples, and see what I may learn there. Your Grace, if we may use your coach to return to the city?"

They returned from the city to Shirewood estate that evening, and changed to more suitable attire for dining at the table of nobility. The grand hall was a fine example of the upper class with crystal glasses and fine porcelain plates. The walls were a bright yellow that reflected the newly installed electric lights. Two footmen in tux and tails waited at each end of the room to receive the silver serving dishes brought by servants from the kitchen. The trio was joined by the Duke, his wife, his daughter, his uncle, and Professor Walters. The dinner conversation was sparse and strained, as the Duke and the Professor avoided any questions about their current affair. After the fine meal, their host showed the trio and the Professor to a sitting room. The men were offered cigars and brandy, and the lady was offered wine. Once they had settled in Duke Crillington asked what they had learned during their outing earlier in the day.

"I shall begin," Elizabeth said, surprising the Professor and their host. "I spent most of my day in the libraries of the university. I spoke with a few professors also," Professor Walters looked nervous as she mentioned this, "and was able to find a trail of interesting information. Hundreds of years ago, this island was inhabited by a race of giant men, the Gallix, at that time. Some still exist and are mainly used for their strength in hard labor or as bodyguards. Men had not arrived in this land yet, and the Gallix held sway.

"Now, before the dark ages, but after the arrival of the comet called Talisman, there had been an invasion by strange creatures called Troöds. They were not the only things to come with the Talisman though. Huge, mutant insects, sudden revolutions and power struggles that toppled kingdoms, and legend even speaks of the dead walking the land. The Troöds were the largest threat though. They had two distinct races, both of reptilian ancestry. One branch of the species was said to be able to shift their shape, camouflage themselves, were very swift, and were the soldiers. They had a green cast to their skins. The second type was grey in colour, and were said to be the leaders, and dealt in the blackest of magics, summoning demons and controlling the minds of others.

"My research didn't turn up very much about them, because men didn't live here. When humans began to lose their hold on the land to the west, some went to live with the Rokairn, others went north into the frozen wastes, and still others came here to Gallia. The Troöds followed those men here, presumably to enslave or destroy them. No one knows why, but the men were able to overcome their foes with the help of the Gallix. Some hint at the use of arcane arts, and using the Troöd's own powers against them. But it was loose bands of men, and written histories weren't kept until hundreds of years later when civilization bloomed and culture was reborn in the renaissance. I think that this archeological find of yours may have been a prison of some sort."

The Professor shifted in his seat, looking uncomfortable. The Duke threw back his brandy in one swallow and refilled the glass. Suykimo nodded, a small smile on his lips. The bald man looked at Zachary, waiting for him to speak.

"I spent the day in the area of the dig," Zachary began in the slow, methodical way he spoke. "I visited shops, spoke to merchants and workers, and looked into the site. I have been to this city many times before, but there is something different now. The people weren't quite right. They stuttered, or would fall into a daze when speaking, and were often aggressive and angry. One merchant even threatened me with a knife if I didn't buy something. When watching the site itself, I observed more than one person that would stop and stare at the hole, head tilted. They would nod, and whisper to themselves, or something else. Many began laughing or scratching themselves, not seeming to notice their own behavior. No one else seemed to note it either. Is this normal behavior for that part of town?"

"No, it is not." Duke Crillington said, rubbing his thigh.

"None of this means anything," Professors Walters said, anger creeping into his voice. "They are scared and nervous about the weird things going on. This doesn't mean my find is of any danger or has anything unsafe contained within it. Even if it is a tomb, anything within would be long dead. If these creatures of which you speak lived for a thousand years, they would have died of starvation and lack of air!"

"Of course, the Professor is correct," Suykimo said in his quiet manner. His voice stopped all discussion as it drew the other's attention. "But I think we should look into this more. I suggest we all visit the box tomorrow."

"I think we can arrange that," their host said, "and once we put our worries to rest, we can resume the excavation. Oh, Mister Suykimo, did you learn anything when you visited the temples and churches?"

"I did," Suykimo said. "As we all know religion fell into disfavor after the dark ages as society became enlightened, and these places that were once holy are maintained more as monuments to an age gone by, rather than places of worship. But some faithful still remain, and I spoke with them. They all said that their gods condemn that place, and to bury it again and never revisit it."

In the morning, after breaking their fast, they set off in two vehicles. Suykimo insisted they take one horse drawn carriage and one electric motor coach. The Duke humored him. Zachary, Elizabeth, and Professor Walters rode in the open carriage, while Suykimo and Duke Crillington rode in the enclosed coach. The conversations in each were very different.

"Mister Suykimo?" Duke Crillington asked with hesitation in his voice. "Are you some sort of monk? I mean, if it is not too forward."

"Not at all." Suykimo's gentle whisper was amused. "I am a student of philosophy. I study all religions, faiths, spiritual paths, belief systems, and life philosophies."

"I see. And do you find much fulfillment in the pursuit of dead ideas, long proven to be false and empty?"

"Oh, they are not dead, or empty. But like science, they have much to learn. You see, Your Grace, too many people believe they have learned the truth. But truth changes as life and the world changes. If it stayed the same, it would become stagnant, and thus rot, becoming fertilizer for the next thing to grow. Very similar to how things happened after the Talisman."

"So do you believe this discovery of mine to be something from the past?" The Duke was staring out the window, his tone dark. Suykimo watched as he rubbed his forearms through the dinner jacket, as if he were cold.

"Is this your discovery?" Suykimo murmured.

"Yes! It is mine, and no one shall take it from me! Do you understand me, you meddling wizard?"

Suykimo was leaning back as he watched the man, who was glaring at him with teeth bared. The bald man smiled and nodded.

"Of course. I do not want it. I merely answered your call. A plea for help you sent, because you recognized something out of place. Listen to your voice, your words. Look at your hands, they clench your trouser legs and have torn a hole in them. I do not think this is you. I see a man that shares with his wife, which has spurned her and left her outside on this matter. I see a man that trusts his servants, but sends them out of the room when speaking of these things. I see a changed man. Why is that, sir?"

The Duke's face reddened and his fists clenched, as emotions clashed within the man. With a sigh, he fell back in his seat, sweating.

"Yes, you are right. I don't know what has come over me of late. There is such a draw to this thing. A passion as I haven't felt since I was young and… and in love. But this is different. I want to possess it. I cannot help myself. But why am I telling you this? It is not proper. I must apologize, sir."

"No, you must not. Many find me to be a good listener. Please, go on. I think it is important."

The conversation in the carriage was very unlike the one taking place in the motor coach ahead of it. The tension was palpable as Zachary sat with his hand on the blade on his hip, watching the Professor. Elizabeth was fanning herself, and Walters was leaning forward and speaking with passion.

"So you see Elizabeth," Professor Walters was saying. "I remember you at the university always beautiful and lovely; a rose in full blush, blissfully unaware of those that craved just a small gift of your scent. You could join me in this quest of mine. Take up my banner, and my name, and discover new and wondrous worlds at my side!"

"I don't think this is proper, Professor," Elizabeth said with a gasp.

"No, it isn't. Not at all," Zachary added.

"Keep your tongue still, whelp!" Walters sneered at Zachary. "This is between the lady and me. I don't even know why you are here. No one wants you here, especially not my find."

"I want him here," Elizabeth breathed. "He is my friend, and a protector."

"So," the professor growled, "there is something between the two of you? You sir, would take away my greatest discovery and rob me of this woman also?"

"She is not your to be stolen," Zachary said, his tone low and calm, "and I was asked to be here by your friend and confidante, the Duke, to investigate what you found. I do not think you are yourself."

The carriage rolled to a stop, and the coachman came around and opened the door. The three stared at one another until the Duke appeared in the doorway and asked if they would be joining him. The Professor pushed past Zachary and exited.

"He is not himself, Zachary," Elizabeth whispered. "This is not the man I knew years ago."

"I am sure that is so," Zachary answered, his eyes never leaving the man, "but, I will still watch him carefully for that very reason."

The two climbed down from the carriage. A footman held the reins of the horses, which were snorting and stamping, their eyes rolling, froth around the bits in their mouths. A small assembly of people congregated to watch the group gather around the roped off entrance into the tunnel. The Duke passed around electric torches and led the procession down into the darkness, while the servants tried to calm the horses and keep people away from the transports.

The five gathered around the stone box. It was the width of ten men standing abreast and an unknown depth, because the sides remained unearthed. They could see where workers had begun digging to see how far back and how deep down the edifice extended. The whole structure was covered with foreign hieroglyphs showing the story of the mysterious find, but they had yet to be translated. A rectangular doorway stood facing them, the frame of which was adorned with spidery runes of a second lost language.

"I have been thinking about this Professor Walters," the Duke began, "and I have been watching. I have noticed a change in behavior of myself, people around me, the people who live and work close to this thing, and even the animals. I fear this is unnatural and to further tamper with it would only lead to tragedy."

The Duke slumped, as if a weight had been lifted from his shoulders as he spoke.

"I disagree, my Lord," the Professor said, "I think this is a great find, and who knows what knowledge and treasures lie within. I think you are either a coward, or a liar, and you are trying to steal my glory and keep all the wonders for yourself!"

"Professor!" The Duke gasped. "Listen to yourself.

That is not like you at all. We have known each other for decades and worked together for most of that time. I introduced you to your dear departed wife, may she rest in peace, and am like an uncle to your children, as you are to mine."

"Yes, exactly," the Professor said with a wild look in his eyes, shoving his hands into his coat pockets, "which is why your behavior disappoints me so much, and makes this so much harder to do."

As the pull of madness overtook him Walters withdrew a small revolver from his pocket and fired at Elizabeth, who was tackled out of the path of the bullet by Zachary. They tumbled to the ground, tangling in the woman's skirts. The Professor turned and shot Crillington three times in the chest. The Duke flew backwards, smashing into the stone door and crumpling to the earthen floor. Laughing like a maniac and dropping the gun, the Professor pressed his hands into his dying friend's chest and pushed his fingers into the open bullet wounds, covering them with blood. Standing, he began to paint symbols on the door.

Zachary and Elizabeth had managed to extricate themselves and stand, noticing what was happening. Elizabeth gasped and covered her mouth with a petite gloved hand, as Zachary lunged forward to stop the man. A hand stopped him and he turned to see Suykimo shaking his head.

"It is too late," the bald man said, his sea green eyes sad. "This was meant to be, we are just observers. Now, we should go. I fear the worst is yet to come."

As he said the last word, the stone of the edifice cracked. The sound echoed through the disinterred chamber. Suykimo had already turned and was making his way out of the hole, holding the edges of his robe-like coat free of the dirt. Zachary gathered Elizabeth and helped her to the surface. A hissing noise of rushing air came from behind them as a mist ruptured the day and spewed out of the dig site. The oldest of the trio waved his hand towards the cloud and murmured a few words and the wind picked up, moving the foul smelling haze away from the three companions.

Suykimo stepped to the horse drawn carriage, taking the reins of the frightened beasts from the stunned coachman's hand. The horses stamped and whinnied, showing the whites of their eyes. Suykimo whispered to them and stroked their necks. They calmed enough for Zachary and Elizabeth to climb into the surrey.

"Come Suykimo," Zachary shouted, looking around as the cloud descended on the crowd that had gathered. The already anxious people were becoming more agitated, yelling and pushing forward, the ones in the front becoming angry with the ones in the back and turning to confront them.

"No," Suykimo said with a calm voice that could barely be heard over the rising tumult, tucking his hands into the ends of his sleeves. "You two go, I will be along shortly. Prepare our things for our departure."

"They will tear you apart, Suykimo!" Elizabeth shouted.

"No, my child, they will not. You know I am equal to this task. I need to be here to do what I can, or at least witness what comes from the prison, for a prison is what it was, though it is no more. Now go, we have wasted enough time."

With that Suykimo turned to the horses and whispered again, and touched them on the flanks. The beasts bolted down the street, careening wildly, causing Zachary to grab for the reins to bring them under control.

Suykimo looked into the thick smoke-like fog that billowed out of the hole that led to the stone chamber. The breach had become a maw-like thing and man sized shadowy forms darted from it, crawling up walls and disappearing down alleys. Screams could be heard, and as the Aeifain walked the streets, he watched as the people became violent. He tried to help where he could, assisting anyone not affected by the mind altering mist to get free of the area.

A shadowy form coalesced in front of him, a familiar being from his past. The creature was not the person that

Suykimo had known, it was much more. Shadows stroked and embraced it, moving as the being commanded. The dark fog grew, enveloping the surrounding buildings and streets.

Suykimo called upon light to disperse the darkness, only to have it repelled. The blue sparks of mystic energies clashed with the being and became a shower of azure stars that fell across the city in a spectacle that lit the dimming obfuscation.

Suykimo stepped back, falling into a bare handed fighting stance against a being that rejected the physical form as often as naught. The dark struck out, tendrils of deep obsidian solidifying to batter at the sorcerous shields that Suykimo threw up in desperation.

"Won't you talk?" Suykimo shouted into the void.

"Of course," a voice of velvet crooned, "I will trade wind and words with you, if only to delay the removal of a thorn in my side that has troubled me for centuries. You have become the essence of my experience, the sensation of my existence. I wonder if I will miss you and toy with the emptiness you leave, the way a person who loses an infected tooth mourns but celebrates the lose simultaneously."

"Why do you do this?" Suykimo asked, swiveling his head to look as the blackness that surrounded him, prepared to strike.

"What a simple question. I expected much more from you, the one who devised the method of my imprisonment. The one who sent me to the one man that manipulates time and space as if it were a skein of wool and creates patterns at his whim. You disappoint me with such a response that any imbecile could contrive. I do this because I have a plan. Something you do not. You are merely reactive. You respond, but never take the initiative. I do the opposite. What you face is the culmination of a thousand years of well laid plans and plotting. That millennia all done in less than half that time."

"That is impossible," Suykimo said, "you cannot be alive for ten centuries within a handful of the same."

"You are so limited," the voice said, "you think in linear terms. You fall short on every front. Your species may live as long as me, but it is only on one front. I have lived longer than any aeifain, but in half the time. I have lived three lives at the same time. And I am the culmination of this experience and knowledge. You face something that you cannot even conceive of within your limited framework of existence. You are a speck within the infinite. I am bound to eternity."

"But you still fear me," Suykimo said as he watched the darkness become more, drawing into itself to take a form that was recognizable, "Marques Brunbach, you are just a mirage of the man that once had a life. I can overcome you through my connection to this world, and the truth within it."

"I form that truth," Marques said, becoming a silhouette of a man that stood three times the height of the slight form that cowered before him. "I manipulate the world, the minds and fears of all men are my tools, and those tools can be my weapon. You cannot stand against me, you can only fall to me. Even now, I toy with you and your pathetic knowledge and hopes."

"I see you, even though you change form. I feel you, and all that you embody. I can fight you as long as my mind and soul has a purchase within this world."

"Well said, then all I need to do is destroy one of those things and you shall no longer be able to stand against me. Which shall I extinguish? Your body, or your spirit? If I kill our body, I shall be free of you. If I wrack your spirit so it collapses, I shall have you as my slave."

"One can only become a slave once they allow their spirit to collapse, and that is one thing I shall never do."

"Your body it is then," Marques said.

The darkness rushed in, battering at the numinous defenses that Suykimo had raised. The aeifain fell to his knees and bowed his head under the onslaught, tucking his hands into his sleeves and thrusted outward with more than his mind. The small man forced his awareness into the blackness, and sought the core of the being that assaulted him.

Seeking the essence of a man that once hoped and feared, as all men do, the found the seed within the being and thrust light into it. Hope clashed with desire, as Suykimo's body as battered by fear and energies that led to destruction. Physical blows landed, breaking flesh and bone, shattering the form to which Suykimo clung. Lashing out with his fists and feet, the mystic fought as he had never fought before.

The darkness laughed, a bitter sentiment that spoke of ambition without hope.

Hours later Suykimo reappeared to his anxious friends, and when they asked him what had happened, because they could see smoke rising from the city all the way from Shirewood, the Duke's estate, Suykimo told them what he could.

"The mist covered ten square blocks of the city, and fires broke out as the madness spread. By the time the sun had set, buildings had been leveled, and hundreds of people had disappeared or been killed. Something dark had returned to our world, something that has not been seen for hundreds of years. I fear for our future and am ignorant of their intentions, but I doubt it is to the benefit of mankind."

The Event of the Mysterious Promontory Fiend: A Croaker Norge Case File

"Once upon a time, there was a poor country widow," Phoebus Buckroe said in a somber tone.

"Oh, stop that!" Croaker Norge interrupted. "We are not in some fairy tale land, chasing dragons to save the fair maiden."

"Well, it is a quaint village, and we are being treated to tea by an ancient, rickety woman," the younger man said, knocking unseen dust from his top hat with an arrogant air.

"Shush, she will hear you," Croaker said and leaned forward to look through the doorway at the old woman in the kitchen who was preparing a tray. "Just because you dress in fine clothes doesn't make you any better than anyone else, and it definitely does not allow you to treat others as if they were second class citizens."

"But Croaker," Phoebus said, straightening his pristine white gloves, "they are. Even the upper class can't compare to me. I am better looking than most of them, and I am an adventurer who has experienced the world."

"You are an arrogant dandy," Croaker said, trailing off

as the Widow Winkley entered the room, hunched over as she carried the tray and set it on the table.

"What were you boys talking about?" she asked, her smile showing a handful of brown teeth.

"Nothing ma'am," Croaker said, straightening his leather tool pouch and wrinkled brown tweed jacket. "Just the weather and beauty here in this place."

"Oh, you flirt," the old woman cackled, patting her grey hair that was pulled up in a bun, "you say the sweetest things. And you are quite the rugged dish yourself, handsome." She poured a cup for each of them, winking at Croaker as she did. "How do you take it? Sugar, honey, milk, lemon, or perhaps you would like a spot of whiskey in it instead? Yes, I think you like it so it takes your breath away. And sugar and milk for the boy."

Phoebus grinned at Croaker as the older man shifted in his seat. Norge ran his fingers through his greasy salt and pepper hair, and then across his stubbled chin. Accepting the tea cup, he sipped at it and glared at Phoebus. The younger man set his hat aside and removed his gloves, tucking them into his coat pocket, smoothing the silk material down as he did. Flipping his glossy black hair back, he smiled a flawless smile at their host and accepted his cup of brown joy.

"Gentlemen," the widow began, sitting as she did, "I asked you to come because we have a monster preying on travelers and the village, a horrible beast that lives in the mountain pass, in the old deserted keep that once protected us. It devours children, and steals horses and maidens from passing wagon trains. I don't take kindly to anyone taking what belongs to me, and if they don't stop, then I find a way to make them stop. We need a hero to go and rid us of this fowl creature."

Croaker and Phoebus set out in the morning, traveling west to the mountain pass. Phoebus had changed to a light safari outfit, with tight jodhpurs and polished knee high boots. His pith helmet was strapped under his chin and a sidearm was on his hip, and a stout oak walking stick in his hand. Croaker wore his usual fare, but had added a variety of gizmos to his belt beside his leather tool roll.

By noon they had reached the abandoned stronghold. Two massive, square barbicans were joined by a stone archway which the road passed through. A set of rusted portcullis hung down like teeth stained with dried blood. The highway was cracked as weeds poked through it in many places, showing years of disuse.

The duo made their way to one of the towers and entered through the doorway, whose door was nothing more than broken planks on the floor. Norge took a steel rod from his belt with a glass covered funnel at one end and a metal conduit leading from the center of the cylinder to a power pack on his hip. Flipping a switch on the device, it lit up and cast a beam of light into the darkness revealing stairs leading up and down. Dust motes leapt up with each step they took.

They descended the circular steps, taking care as the wooden board groaned under their weight. The stone floor of the lower level was littered with rotting leaves and debris, and rats scurried from their light, squeaking in annoyance at the interruption of their foraging. The tunnel smelled of ammonia and musk. Insects wandered from piles of refuse to cracks in the walls, hiding from the intruders.

A cracking sound issued from underneath their feet, accompanied by the creak of a rope. Phoebus tackled Croaker to the ground as a wooden crossbeam with sharpened stakes jutting from it swung down from behind them. They lay on the ground as the trap slowed and came to a stop above them.

"Looks like we need to watch our step, old man," Phoebus said as he stood and dusted off his now stained jacket.

"I guess we do," Croaker said as he pulled a knife from

his thigh and cut the ropes holding the trap, the wooden beam dropping to the ground with a loud crash.

"Now whoever set that will know we are here. Well done!"

"That is the point. We want whatever it is living here to come to us, so we can do what we came to do."

"But the element of surprise would have been nice."

"Nothing to be done about it now. Shall we go on and find this monster?"

The two continued forward and came to another set of stairs leading up.

"I think we missed something," Croaker mumbled. "These lead up to the other tower. We need to double back."

As they made their way back they inspected the walls. They had almost reached the trap they had set off when Croaker stopped and pointed at the ceiling.

"There," he said, pointing his electric torch at a jagged crevice, "there is an opening. We need to get up there."

"And how do you propose to do that?" Phoebus asked, hands on his hips.

Minutes later, and after a heated discussion of who should go first, Phoebus wiggled his way into the fissure, with Croaker helping boost him up. The older man tossed up a length of rope to his companion and began to climb.

Phoebus squealed, and was yanked backwards. The rope went taut and Norge was pulled up, holding on as best he could. As the older man crested the brink of the hole, the rope went slack, and he grabbed the edge to stop himself from falling to the floor below. Noises of a struggle came from the darkness ahead. Scrambling onto the downward sloping floor in front of him, he snatched his light and shone it into the gloom.

Phoebus was locked in a struggle with a misshapen form. A giant of a man stood over the young man, its hands locked on Buckroe's wrists, the oak walking stick having been knocked aside. Phoebus fell backwards, kicking up with his feet and flipping the large opponent over his head and into the wall of the passage. The young man twisted to his feet and snatched his revolver from its holster, and pointed it at the foe. Croaker got to his feet and searched for a way to help his friend.

The fiend rolled upright and swatted the weapon from Phoebus's hand, away from the fight and further down the roughhewn corridor. The monster was dressed in tattered rags and its nails were dirty and sharpened to points. Its face had a scraggly beard under a jutting nose, and it stood head and shoulders above Phoebus's two meter tall form.

The combatants locked in struggle once again as Croaker turned a dial on the box controlling his electric torch, and turned the metal shaft in his hand around so the butt faced the creature. When Phoebus was knocked to the ground, Croaker pulled the trigger and a dart attached to a thin metal cable shot forward, sticking in the towering terror. Electricity traveled down the wire and brute screamed as the voltage entered its body. Pulling the barbed tip from its flesh, the creature turned and fled.

"Are you alright?" Croaker asked as he reached Phoebus, offering a hand to help his friend to his feet.

"Yes," Phoebus said as he stood, panting. "We should get after him before we lose him."

Recovering his gun and walking stick, Buckroe led the way down the hall. Norge followed behind him with the light, which was now flickering after being used to shock their foe.

They could see the receding form of their enemy in the distance, loping in long strides down the hall. It turned a corner and they gave chase. As they came around the bend in the passage, the floor disappeared from under their feet. They fell, and everything went black.

When the older man woke he could hear the sounds of a fire crackling and smelled cooking meat. Croaker sat up, reaching for his light only to find his belt and all his tools missing. Phoebus lay a meter away, unconscious. The only illumination was a small cooking fire. They were in a small cell, with metal bars which extended from floor to ceiling. A shadowy form was hunched over the flames and turning a spit. Croaker reached for his friend and shook him awake. Phoebus sat up and looked around, confused. Taking in the surroundings, he realized the situation. His hand went to his hip and found his holster empty.

"Your stuff is here," came a voice like gravel from the other side of the bars.

"You talk?" Phoebus asked.

"And you learn quickly," the creature answered.

They sat in silence for a few moments. Croaker stood and paced the cell, investigating as he went, poking into the cracks and crevices. Phoebus moved closer to the bars, staring at their jailor.

"So the hunter became the hunted," Buckroe said.

"The hunter became the prisoner," the figure growled as he turned the spit. The fire hissed as juices dripped into the flames.

"What will become of us?" Croaker asked, leaning against the wall next to the bars and watching the creature.

"You will have a choice between becoming a stew or serving me."

"I am no servant!" Phoebus said.

"Serving you?" Croaker interrupted. "What do you mean?"

"I will require a year of servitude so I know I can trust you enough to release you," their captor said.

"And if you don't trust us at the end of a year?"

"Then you become stew."

"How do we know we can trust you to not do it anyway?"

"Because you will come to know me, as I will come to know you. You won't be the first people with which I have had this deal. Many have come hunting me in the centuries I have been alive. Lately though, it has been more than usual. I find bones of horses and children on my steps, and treasures from wagon trains tossed into the keep."

"The Widow Winkley told us the truth," Phoebus said, "you have been taking children and maidens, and attacking wagons."

"The Widow Winkley? Oh, I think I know who you mean, though I would wager she looks different from when I last saw her. She has hunted me for decades, using her potions and spells to control men and cause them to attack me."

"Wait, what?" Phoebus said, confused. "What do you mean, 'control men'?"

"Oh yes, puts stuff in their tea, beer, or whatever they drink. Makes them mad with desire to please her and kill me. But I am not the one that attacks the people. That is her also, sending those same men into the hills to make it appear that I attacked the village and caravans. But it isn't me, no sir."

"Why would she do that?" Croaker asked, his voice quiet and thoughtful.

The creature looked at Croaker and their eyes met. The prisoner felt his mind swell for a moment, and shook his head to clear it. Phoebus was standing over him, holding him by the shoulders to keep the older man from falling to the ground.

"What are you doing, Phoebus?" Croaker asked, pulling away.

"You were standing there for almost five minutes, staring at that fiend," Phoebus said, concern filling his voice, "then you shook your head and started to collapse. Are you alright?"

"I'm touched that you care for me, but that doesn't mean I don't care that you touched me. I am perfectly fine, and I know why he is hunted." The question in Phoebus's eyes made Croaker continue. "People call him a troll now, but it was not always like that. Once upon a time, to use your words, he was part of a great and proud race whose name is now lost to time. Thousands of years ago, before men rose to power again, his people were the perfect species: smart,

211

strong, wise, agile, and masters of arcane arts. But they wanted more. They had their wizards, sorcerers, and mages seek a way to make them even better.

"They found a way that their children would be stronger, healthier, smarter, and more powerful in the ways of magic. Or so they thought. Instead of combining these things, each child was born with either a stronger mind and a weaker body, or a stronger body and a weaker mind. Their once supreme race began to fall apart as the children were born as either trolls or aeifain. But as the ancient lines began dying off, magic changed and began to spread to other races, no longer contained within just their people. They debated what would happen once their species died off. The elders felt that if all the Lords of Magic were to pass from this world, then magic would disappear or would be able to be rearranged at the will of whoever could harness the power.

"Concerned with this, the remaining Lords poured all their life force and magic into four of their own kind, each who had no magical ability of their own. They told these 'chosen ones' to protect what was given to them for the sake of the world, for if they were all killed, horrible things would happen. So he has been on the lam since that day, and this witch is only the latest in a long line of people that hunt him for his power."

Phoebus stared at Croaker, and then looked at the creature by the fire, who was now nibbling on the roasted rabbit still on the spit. Looking back at his friend, the younger man burst into laughter.

"Magic?" he asked. "Trolls, Aeifain, witches, and other children stories? You expect me to believe all that?"

"Yes, because it is all true!" a female voice screeched from behind their captor. Surprised, all three turned to look. The Widow Winkley was rushing into the cavern, waving a willow rod in one hand and slashing at the air with a wicked, curved blade in the other. The wooden stick's tip glowed and brightened as the knife came down and bit into the troll lord's shoulder.

"It will all be mine!" She stood over the collapsed form of their jailor. "This blade drains the very life from anyone it cuts. And within minutes I will have all of his life essence and magic!"

"No!" Croaker sobbed, falling to the ground and rocking back and forth, holding his legs around the ankles.

Phoebus had never seen his friend behave in such a manner and looked at him in disbelief. Croaker winked at the younger man. Nodding in understanding, Phoebus picked up a rock and threw it at the witch, shouting curses and insults as he did. The woman ducked behind the larger form of the unmoving troll lord.

While Phoebus distracted the woman Croaker drew three brass tubes from his right boot and assembled them into a single long, thin pipe. Reaching into his left boot he withdrew a vial and three needles, a puff of feathers on the end of each. Uncapping the small tube, he dipped each needle into the liquid inside of it, and pushed the first into the tube, then set the brass pipe to his lips. With a puff of breath, it shot between the bars of the cell and flew wide of its target.

"What was that?" the witch screamed, standing up and looking at Croaker. She received a rock to the head from Phoebus for her trouble. She stumbled backwards and the second dart flew past the tip of her nose.

"Stop that," Croaker yelled, "you made me miss!"

"Sorry," Phoebus shouted back, throwing another rock at the witch. It careened off her head, making her spin in a circle. "I am trying to stop her from turning us into toads, roasting us alive, or whatever her magic stick will do if we give her a chance!"

The woman stopped spinning, and turned back to the two men behind bars. "With one word of power, I will enslave both of you!"

She readied the wand and drew back her arm. As she opened her mouth to shout the arcane phrase to set the spell in motion, Croaker puffed the remaining dart out from the blowgun. Seeing it coming in her direction, she weaved away from it. Her head met the rock that Phoebus had just thrown, and it knocked her noggin back into the path of the poisoned projectile. She opened her mouth to scream and the dart flew directly inside. Her lips smacked shut just as the paralyzing agent took effect. The witch froze in place, her eyes darting back and forth between the two men, and then she tumbled sideways to the cavern floor.

"So," Phoebus said with a casual tone, "how long does that poison last?"

"An hour or so," Croaker answered.

"I just hope the troll lord wakes before she does."

"Oh, no need to worry about that. This is a poor cell, and all we need to do is lift the door up, and off the hinge pin. Why don't you do that? I did all the rest of the work."

"What 'rest of the work'?" Phoebus said, outraged.

"The troll's story, the witch's betrayal, the paralyzing dart, and everything else," Croaker said, raising his voice. "What did you do? Throw a few pebbles?"

"It was my 'pebble' that knocked her head back into the path of your lousy aim!" Phoebus shouted, towering over the older man and looking down at him.

"Harrumph," Croaker harrumphed, "alright, I guess it did. Fine, I will help you with the cell door."

Three hours later the two men sat outside the keep, the tied and gagged witch between them. The troll lord had woken to find them free and bandaging his wounds. They promised to keep his secret, and turn the woman over to the townsfolk, explaining that it was her that had been terrorizing the people of this town, and proof of the potions could be found in her home. They waited for dawn before traveling back to the village.

"You know what the moral of this story is, Phoebus?" Croaker asked.

"If you rescue a monster, he gives you treasure?" Phoebus quipped.

"No. Wait, did you get treasure?"

"Oh, you didn't? Well, I may have mentioned a reward when you were tying up your blushing beauty here."

"She isn't my anything. And you are always getting into people's wallets and making them thank you for doing it!"

"It is a gift I have," Phoebus said, licking a thumb and slicking back his eyebrows.

"Never mind that. The moral of this story is, you never truly know who the monster is, and you can't be fooled by looks."

"That's right."

"Just like me and you."

"That's right, too. Wait, what? Are you saying I am a monster?"

The two were still arguing when the sun rose and they began on their way back to the village.

Shadows of Worlds

My name is Captain John Phillips Thompson and I am of two minds. I fought in the Great War and came home, but not all in one piece. My body came back whole, but my mind had issues. I saw things while overseas that men were not meant to see. Some things that were made or done by other men, and some things that could have never been made by man except in nightmares. The doctors say I did not really see these things, but they were real to me as I saw people die by the thousands, even if proof was never found.

I spend my time in the hospital now. My mother sits with me most days, knitting and singing along to hymns on the radio. Sometimes I switch it to blues and jazz, but she gets upset and tells me how it is evil. I know evil though, and that music does not begin to touch it. In the beginning I tried to tell her, but she would only hush me and call a nurse to give me medicine which would spin me into the murky grey depths of quasi sleep. And it is in that state that I can see them moving in the shadows.

They are the size of children, at least for now. They dart across the floor, crouched and skittering on all fours. During the war I saw them reach full grown, but my mind slips when I am awake, and it is like remembering a dream and I

217

cannot hold the vision of what they looked like. I am living in two worlds, one of memory and one of reality. One is made of sleep, and the other one is made of awareness.

The draining effect of the medicine washes over me now. As my mother leaves and closes the door, I can see the creatures scurry closer as my eyes close. And for the briefest moment I see them as they pry my eyelid open to peer inside, before I slip into sweet sleep and that other world where I am a complete man, and not laying broken in a bed.

My name is Captain John Phillips Thompson and I am of two minds. I fought in the Great War and came home, but not all in one piece. My mind came back whole, but my body had issues. I saw things while overseas that men were not meant to see. Some things that were not made or done by other men, and some things that could have never been made by man except in nightmares. My superiors said these things should not exist, but they were real to the people that died by the thousands, and proof was found.

I spend my time in the battlefield now, my technician and brother at my side, tinkering on my mechanical enhancements and whistling marching tunes that the big bands used to play before the war. I sometimes hum jazz and blues, but he shushes me and points out how it draws the evil to us. I know evil though, and it is not drawn to music. It is drawn to its own kind. In the beginning I tried to tell him, but he would only hush me and adjust some valve on my hormone amplifier box, making me unable to talk because I need to focus on the rush as all my senses sharpened.

I watch the horizon and I can see them lumbering in their broken gait. Huge, shambling creatures hidden by the fog and smoke that gathers on a battleground. I first saw them during the death ray testing in the desert. They were the size of cats in the beginning, and I thought they were some beast that had been afflicted by man's latest weapons. I remember those idyllic days of innocence and ignorance when I sleep. I dream of that world, and wish I could still live in it. But I can't. One is memory, and the other is reality. One is made of sleep and dreams; the other is made of alert awareness.

The Empire researched the occult and the Federation could not let them gain an unfair advantage. Each searched for cultural and religious artifacts and explored places of power from ancient civilizations. We did it in the deserts. The plasma testing wasn't to make sure the bombs were safe, but was to pour power into the dark things our government found, things the Dasism had hidden centuries ago after defeating them and driving them back into the black holes out of which they had crawled. We ignored the paintings, the carvings, and all the warnings that were left behind for us to find. Once these things had been released we had to find ways to feed them. It was easy. We had enemies everywhere, and no one noticed or complained when they disappeared. If they did complain, their name was placed on a sympathizer list, which was a secondary record of who else could disappear if we ran out of enemies.

Things became worse as each side began collecting captives in concentration camps and experimented on them. Each had found keys to nature and applied them to the human souls and bodies in the dark, hidden camps and makeshift hospitals. Chemicals and radiation were given to tortured prisoners. It drew out things from places inside of those people. Man has great things hidden within him; seeds of awesome beauty through art, as well as horrifying cruelty through other creative processes. I think if things had been done differently, had been done with gentle love and understanding, something else inside of man as a species would have responded and answered to the call and brought about a very different world. But it doesn't matter. That isn't what happened. We did not nurture anything; rather we brought it forth by blood and force. And it responded in kind.

I shouldn't let myself get distracted with thoughts of the past though, I can see the enemy moving now. They are swarming towards us, and the mists move with them. The other soldiers are already falling to what hides in the fog, some tumbling to the ground untouched, unconscious and overpowered by whatever the haze is made of. Others aren't so lucky. I can hear them screaming as the first wave of assault hits us and things grab them from the grey vapors that are too thick to see through. Unless you are augmented, like me. I can see through them, and I can see what lurks within them. And they can see me. They toss smoking poultices at me, trying to overpower the hormones surging through my system. It usually doesn't work, but this time it did and I fell before I could launch my attack and fight back.

I wake screaming. I have been restrained in my sleep, and I can feel the tight bandages around my arms and ribs, no doubt from the scratches and bite marks of the damned creatures in the dark. The radio is playing and sunlight is streaming in through the window. I can hear the birds singing over the sports game, and smell the blooms of the magnolias outside my room. The nurse is here, calming me. I think she is sweet on me, I will ask her for a journal today so I can begin to write all this down. Someone needs to know the truth, they are coming for us. I have seen them!

My mother is back. She brought corn muffins. She smells like our kitchen and a smear of bacon fat and corn meal is still on her cheek. She has been crying; her eyes are red and puffy, and a handkerchief is tucked into her sleeve. She says that they have a special treat for me if I eat all my dinner. The nurse will bring me a malted and wheel me to the common room so I can watch Syd Bark's Federation Swingtime. I blink in surprise, and I can see one of the larger ones behind the door. It is grey and leaning towards the nurse and my mother. It is dripping on the floor like it has just come out of a lake, and I can smell the rot. I blink again and it is gone. My mother and the nurse are staring at me. My eyes must have been wide and my face showing my terror. I compose myself and smile and nod. I tell them, 'That would be swell'. I guess they buy it because my mother swallows in relief, pats my hand, and turns to leave, walking through the door which the creature had stood behind moments ago. The nurse smiles at me, and I ask her for the journal. She says she will see what she can do.

I have the journal now and am watching the dance show, surrounded by dozens of other soldiers. Some are playing cards or checkers, others are napping, and a few are crying quietly. I wonder if they can also see what I see. I didn't see any more creatures until I looked at the small stage. I don't know why the others can't see them too, but every crooner, singer, and dancing teen is a shambling mockery of a human being. Syd Bark is something else altogether though. Whenever he appears I clench my eyes closed, and it helped in the beginning. But now when he speaks, I can see something else behind my eyelids. Something huge and sleeping. It twitches when he talks, and I think they want to wake it up. I want to scream, but I can't. If I scream they will give me more medicine to make me sleep. Every time I sleep the things get larger when I wake, and bolder. But I can't stop myself. I am going to scream…

I dreamt again, and I am not sure why I woke up thinking about this, but it may be important. The Aeifain were the first to see the Great Ones join the war. A twenty story tall mutant dinosaur answered their call while we were still dabbling in mindless men that would attack anything within reach, their sanity shattered by what we pumped into them. As horrible as the Aeifain weapon could have been, it immediately turned on them, destroying their cities. They called upon others to fight the first beast. It worked, in a sense. They fought. But they still destroyed cities and devoured the population. Soon the Aeifain fled to the mainland, and began sacrificing people to the Great Ones.

The Whitestones went another route and created super soldiers from the ancient things they found in countries they conquered. The monsters could not stand the daylight, but they had the strength of four men and could drain a man of his blood in minutes. That is what they fed on; other men's life force. Some said the soul also, and I think that may be possible because they soon started procreating on their own. Fledgling 'vampires' emerged, as well as flesh eating ghuls that moved faster than any man could hope to move. Half men, mixed with animals were sighted across Teurone. Some say these were the same beings, but I think that someone discovered how to recreate lycanthropy. They had as much control over these horrors as the Aeifain had over theirs, and as much as we had over what we created. First the concentration camps were emptied to feed these things, and afterwards the population of whole cities disappeared.

In the west, we regressed prisoners in our experiments, creating mindless hordes of hungry zombies. They could not be commanded though, and created more of themselves if they did not eat the brain of anyone they bit. We also worked with animals, creating monstrous versions of apes, insects, and even dinosaurs. And we had no more control of them than our enemies had over their creations.

The truth is, we did not create anything. We merely released what was waiting in the shadows that lurked just outside of our reach and understanding. Man is the key to his own destruction. We tried destroying these things with plasma bombs. Tikonama was our first attempt. It did not work. We should have known what would happen because of the tests in our own deserts. This is what gave birth to many of our own monsters.

I am face down in the mud and blood. I think it is daylight, but it is hard to tell with the constant cloud cover and thick walls of mist. I roll onto my back slowly, so I won't attract unwanted attention. My brother lays five paces from me, torn limb from limb. Why? Why would they take him, but leave me? I clutch my chest as the tears begin, because of the pain in my heart. I feel the metal plate and small machine that pumps the hormones and adrenaline into my system when it is needed. Did they feel that I am one of them, that I am already a monster?

Am I? Am I the monster? I was created with the same research that made so many of the things for which I was built and trained to hunt. I have a plasma power core. I don't tire like most men. I am stronger than any man known, except for those few that also were altered like me. No, I am still human. I destroy because I must. It is my mission, my duty, and I was given command of men to defend my country by destroying my enemies. I was told to avoid the monsters in the dark places. But this fog follows me now. I cannot escape it. I wonder if it covers the whole earth, or only where I am.

It doesn't matter. I must get up. I must follow these monsters to where they go, and destroy what waits there. I think they are being called somewhere for a purpose beyond human understanding. So I won't try and understand. I will not think. I will just act. That is what I was made to do. I will make history. I go now, to whatever waits for me.

My brother was here when I woke. I asked him how he got here. He was killed in the war. Torn limb from limb not five meters from where I was at the time. He smiled and said I was confused. I asked where mom was, and he hushed me and said she died and I shouldn't worry about anything. He said the doctors would take care of me. I don't know what he meant. He would not tell me anything more than I would have a surgery that would make me better.

I am only partially restrained, and I am still able to write in this journal. The nurse looked sad when she came in. I asked her what was wrong. She smiled and patted my hand and offered me a corn muffin. These are the muffins my mother made; I can taste the bacon fat. That is the secret of their greatness. That is why they won the county fair blue ribbon three years running. I ate it, and asked her about mother. I told her I was confused, that the medicine plays tricks on my memory. She told me that my mother died three years ago, while my brother and I were in basic training. I cried again, because I know that isn't true. She was here hours ago; she brought me the muffins. I saw her. I know what happened. Why would they lie to me like this?

I asked for a newspaper. I read about the bombing of Tikonama. They think this will end the war, once and for all. Something is wrong though, something is missing. I can't figure out what it is, but I know something isn't right.

They came in and took away my newspaper. They shaved my head and drew lines on it. They say my surgery is in a couple hours and I need to rest. They told me this will make everything better, and make all the monsters go away. But I can't rest. I know others can see these things, like the soldiers in the common room. They are coming back; I need to pretend to be asleep.

I have had the surgery. I am in bed. I can't talk, and I can barely move enough to write. But I can see now. They are everywhere. The doctor that put the blade to my forehead, (yes I was awake for it even though they thought I was asleep), had two shapes. One superimposed over the other. A shadow self, grinning down at me with too many teeth. I could see them each time he took a drag off his cigarette during the operation. He smiled at me, because he knew I could see what he really was. Most of the nurses here are also something more than just human. Not the one sweet nurse though; she is normal, and she doesn't know what danger she is in. I will give her this to read. It has taken me almost an hour just to write this paragraph, and I don't know if she will be able to read my handwriting. Every time I blink, I see two worlds. One on top of the other. And they both have monsters. I must sleep now.

I am here. I can see through the smoke and fog without any effort now. I see the gathering of monsters, huddled below me. They are terrified, and know they will die. My allies and I have circled the whole valley, and we are ready to charge down and give our bodies to destroy their souls. And their souls will be given to our Gods. The Great Ones shall feast tonight, and rise up and devour the world. It will be glorious.

The Tridington Birthright: Dark Land

"It's our curse." Trudy yelled at her brother. "The Tridington family's 'shadow legacy' has brought this terrible thing upon us!"

Spencer stared at Trudy as they stood in the center of the smoking crater where their camp had been minutes before. She brushed at the soot on the men's clothes that she wore, smearing the ash across her beige plaid waistcoat. This had become her preferred style of clothing, more often than not, since taking up the mantle of adventurer with her brother and their guide. Jack Tucker was checking the tree line across the river, looking for the beast that had charged out of the portal that had opened moments before.

"You said that about Mister Tucker's missing friend and the Rakshasa that burned that village to the ground," Spencer answered, straightening his handlebar moustache, "but we had nothing to do with that. We merely received a telegram from a school chum of hers, asking Mister Tucker to check on their mutual friend. You said the same thing about the family curse when your paramour kidnapped my intended. But I tracked him down, and returned Abigail

Brewer to her family, unharmed. And you said that about Uncle's disappearance. You've been blaming everything on that curse that since we left Northern Gallia, and sailed for Drungia."

"Emery Vance was no paramour of mine. And I am right!" Trudy adjusted her walking cap, leaving delicate fingerprints in the powder that coated it. "And this is not the first mysterious hole in the air that has appeared and some monstrous horror has burst forth from within! This is a curse that our Great Uncle brought upon the family."

"I wouldn't go that far," Jack interrupted from the top of the depression, a silhouette in a fedora with the morning sun behind him. "A curse is magic. A legacy is something that is handed down, but can be refused. You two chose to accept this. And just so you know, the beast has fled. Now come out of that hole before it happens again."

The twins climbed to the rim, Spencer assisting Trudy on the steep, slippery parts. The three looked where their camp had been an hour before. The sun had just risen and they had put tea on, when the fire erupted into a flaming circular portal and a creature had burst from it, creating an explosion that destroyed the camp as it did. Spencer had been inside the heavy canvas tent, shaving, and was protected from the flying debris and heat. Jack had been in the brush, answering the morning call of nature. Trudy though, had been a dozen paces away, carrying a bucket of water from the river. The blast had made her dump it over herself, which saved her from being burnt, other than a few, minor places.

"Why are they following us?" Spencer asked, placing his pith helmet on his head and adjusting the goggles above the brim.

"It's a curse," Trudy huffed, squeezing water from her brown pants.

"No," Jack corrected, "it is a temporal spatial beacon, and they are drawn to it."

"You mean the equipment?" Spencer pulled his coat on. He had recovered it from the tent before exiting to investigate the wreckage of the camp. He was very proper that way.

"Yes, I do," Jack answered. "The items I brought back from my last journey,"

"From the past," Trudy interrupted, "because you were the one that brought the time machine plans to our uncle!"

"Yes," Jack answered with patience, "as I said before, I last saw your Uncle Waldorf, nearly thirty years ago. I was on expedition in Drungia seeking a huge magnetic flux that may be a natural portal through time and space. I met him with his father, your Great Uncle. It seems Waldorf's father did not disappear into the wilds of the Dark Continent, Drungia, but into some sort of vortex of energy which I was investigating. It appears when your uncle used the machine, the two things resonated with each other, and Waldorf not only freed his father, but also was reunited with him. This is your 'Shadow Legacy'."

"Why didn't the portals and monsters start thirty years ago then?" Spencer asked.

"I can only guess, my lad," Jack said, "but I would think it has to do with the machine your uncle made. You said there were creatures in the lab, trying to gain the plans, right?" The twins nodded, Spencer standing head and shoulders above his sister. "Waldorf had set it back thirty years, to find his father. And that worked, but created the very vortex here in Drungia that your Great Uncle had been lost within for the past three decades."

"That is impossible." Trudy said, with a superior sniff. "If the portal wasn't first created until our uncle went backwards in time, then it didn't exist until now, and his father would have never been trapped."

"But the villainous Doctor Terrible, and the creatures that came with him had something else, didn't they? They were in tune with the energies. I think that is why they hunt us. They want what we have, and are attracted to it, like a moth to a flame. Besides, that is why they are here in this time, instead of thirty years past when your Great Uncle disappeared. Because it started now. But if they can go back to that time, then they can stop us from doing what we will do."

"What we will do?" Spencer asked, furrowing his brow.

"What will we do," Trudy pressed, "and how do you know? Have you been to the future? You do know how to time travel, don't you?"

"Ah, time enough for that later." Jack smiled at his pun. "We need to collect whatever remains of the camp that is salvageable, and get on the boat."

"You mean, 'The Drungian Queen'? Our glorious vessel!" Trudy said, gesturing with grand motions.

The little boat wasn't much. Less than ten meters from stem to stern, and just over two meters from side to side, it didn't give the three much room. A copper boiler stood in the center of the deck with a tiller just behind it, which led to the pilot sweating quite a bit as the heat drifted off the equipment that powered the propeller. The squared off aft portion had a bench going around the rail, and a canvas tarp above for shade. A small cabin was in the fore of the steamboat, providing some privacy or protection, as required. Crates of supplies were stacked around the crowded deck, giving extra seating or a way to secure a tarp when sleeping on deck.

They loaded the gear they could and set off. The sounds of the savannah rose in their ears. Crickets sounded on the endless sea of grass on either side of the river, and the call of a predator or its prey could be heard on occasion. Jack steered the vessel, smiling and whistling like he was born to the task. He avoided sand bars more by instinct than looking for the telltale ripples on the surface of the water that indicated such dangers. They passed distant cousins of deer, which they knew from their country. These animals had long straight horns that spiraled upward, dark haunches, but ocher bodies. They had seen a dozen different herbivores, each odd and new. Some with stripes, some with spots, some with long necks, and others which were no larger than a housecat. The twins knew a few breeds from the Royal Zoo, but Jack named them out loud as they traveled.

Jack had put his vest and coat away, rolled up his sleeves, and wore breeches with braces and an ecru shirt, in addition to his standard brown fedora. He was not a tall or imposing man, and smile lines could be seen around his eyes and under his goatee. He dressed in the outdated fashions of North Mirron, but the younger companions enjoyed seeing such things from the continent across the Talic Ocean. Trudy had cleaned up and still wore her yellow blouse, vest, and light brown knickerbockers, which came to just below the knee and ended with a snap. Spencer insisted on wearing his full kit, even in the heat of the day, though he paid for his choice in sweat.

They chugged along the sluggish waterway for hours, chatting and fanning themselves in the morning heat. Just after noon, as they watched a herd of gazelle drink from the embankment, Jack spotted a disturbance in the river. Removing his pipe from his mouth, he pointed out the churning area to his young compatriots. A blue ring of light could be seen below the surface, far deeper than the channel should have been. The muddy water turned sea green as foreign currents emerged in front of them. The river suddenly widened and water spilled into the plains, as tentacles rose into sight ahead of the boat.

Spencer rushed to fetch the carbine meant for hunting elephant and other large animals, as a kraken twice the length of the Drungian Queen surfaced, flailing with its eight limbs. Jack pulled the wheel hard to port, aiming for the flooded embankment, confident the flat bottomed steamer wouldn't become beached. Trudy stared, then reached for a pointed pole which was used for catching the shore, and held it like a harpoon. The beast thrashed, falling halfway on the opposite bank. A gigantic reptilian head broke the surface, dwarfing the squid, and captured it in its toothy jaws, gobbling it down in three bites.

The new monster had a spiked turtle-like shell just below

its neck, and webbed flippers supported it, spanning the whole river as it lifted itself from the water. The wake rushed over the low sides of the boat, flooding the deck and bringing up a cloud of hissing steam from the boiler. The beast turned its aquamarine iguana-like head and looked at the vessel with one eye that was wider than a man was tall. It lunged for them.

Jack piloted the boat over the flipper in their way as the wave from the creature's movement washed under them, and Spencer fired his gun into the beast's eye. The maw opened, large enough to snap the tiny boat in half, and Trudy threw the makeshift spear with all her might, diving to the deck afterwards. It flew true and embedded itself in the back of the behemoth's throat. The mouth closed on the canopy, tearing it away, as the leviathan thrashed backwards, the wake of its efforts threatening to capsize or ground the vessel. Jack opened up the throttle, feeding as much steam as he could to the single propeller, struggling to keep the boat in the river.

The monster noticed the fleeing gazelle, and turned to easier prey, snapping up a half dozen of the unfortunate animals in one mouthful. The Drungian Queen steamed past the danger, guided back to the center of the channel by Jack. Trudy sighed in relief.

"The rope!" Spencer shouted, pointing at the coil of hemp attached to the spiked pole that was in the sea beast's gullet. It was unwinding, whining and smoking on the rail as it did. Spencer dropped his weapon and dove for the supplies. Grabbing a hatchet, he leapt to his feet as the boat was yanked broadside, throwing him to the deck again. Scrambling to the railing, he chopped at the rope as Jack threw the engine into reverse to avoid being beached.

The beast's head jerked as the line went taut. It focused on its original quarry once more. The cord separated and the boat was free. But they were still sitting sideways in the waterway. Jack spun the tiller and fired the throttle forward again, attempting to get them back on course and away from the attacker. The sea monster threw itself towards them, landing flat in the water, and creating a wave that threw the boat forward and tipped it sideways at the same time. Crates flew into the water as the crew grabbed for anything to hold to stop from plunging into the water.

The wave carried them forward as the immense head landed a meter from the rear of the boat. Trudy stared into the bloody frothing of its orifice, her eyes wide. The boat righted, found traction, and began to pull away as the beast floundered in the shallow river, before sliding back into the hole from which it had come. The Drungian Queen chugged onward.

They took stock of their remaining supplies as the day wore on. They had lost quite a bit, but were not willing to go back to recover the crates that floated along the river. They would have enough food to get to their destination, but they may need to hunt or fish on the way back.

"Oh no!" Trudy gasped as she took stock. "We have lost the parts we brought to fix the machine. They must have fallen overboard when that creature attacked us!"

"Damnation and bloody hell!" Spencer swore.

"Spencer Theodore Matthew Tridington!" Trudy exclaimed as she stood. She put her hands on her hips, furrowed her brow, and pursed her lips. "Just because Mister Tucker has granted you permission to wear a moustache does not allow you to use such language, especially in front of a lady!"

"I may say what I feel, in front of whomever I please. And there are no ladies here. Ladies wear dresses, not trousers," Spencer said with his chin in the air, but he had been chastised and quieted.

"It'll be fine," Jack said. "I am confident we'll be able to make do with what we have to fix the situation."

"I don't know how you think we will do that," Trudy turned her ire towards their guide. "Do you think we shall just use the old copper boiler and whip it into the delicate equipment we need, and for which we no longer have the plans, since they were stolen by Spencer's arch enemy, Doctor Terrible?"

"No," Jack sighed, "we won't need the plans or the equipment."

"What do you mean? What would we use instead?" Spencer asked, leaning forward. "What are you keeping from us?"

"Well, I haven't been completely forthright with the two of you. But, if I'm correct, then it's you we need to fix this."

"Yes," Trudy grumbled, "we know you need us to fix this, which is why you asked us to join you."

"No, dear sister." Spencer's tone spoke of suspicion and dawning understanding. "I think he means more than merely that. Think for a moment. Mister Tucker could have asked anyone to do this. Experienced safari hunters, military men, or brought a score of hired guns. But he didn't. He brought us, and only us. There is a reason for that, and I think I have figured it out."

"Go on then," Jack said with a crooked smirk when the lad paused, "let's see how keen your deductive skills really are, my friend. And once again, please, call me Jack."

"Wouldn't be proper, would never do, sir. But to go on with my theory, you need us, and specifically us. That would mean there is something special about the two of us. You called this our 'shadow legacy' meaning it is handed down, and tied to the family. So, in conclusion, you never needed any parts, but just need us to end this dastardly plot against the entire civilized world!"

Spencer ended with a triumphant flourish, hand in the air.

"Overly dramatic much, brother of mine?" Trudy said as she rolled her eyes at his theatrics.

"I allow you to use your overly complicated words and prattle on like you were a university professor that had been spliced into an auctioneer, and a town gossip, so you can allow me this."

"Fair enough. But Mister Tucker has not answered yet.

You may yet be wrong."

"He isn't," Jack said.

"Oh, then are you some diabolical fiend," Spencer gasped, "taking us to the scene and planning to carve us up for some ritual?"

"Wouldn't he just have killed us and brought what he needed," Trudy teased her brother, "if that were the case, dear Spence?"

"Not at all," the lad continued, not noticing his sister's tone. "He would need us fresh, maybe even need to drain us of blood, and conjure his demonic cohorts while it is still warm!"

"Spencer, Trudy," Jack said, as patiently as he could, "I assure you, I don't need any body parts, and won't harm you. Well, I may need some blood, but you can draw that for yourself. Or each other, I don't give a fig. The machine was attuned to your uncle and his father, and I think it will be attuned to you two also. But there is no longer a machine. It is gone. However, the portal that was created when it exploded should still be able to recognize the family blood."

"Wait a moment," Spencer interrupted, "you said you saw our uncle, thirty years ago. Now, that explains why he has said you are his oldest friend, but not why he didn't just come along with you."

"Honestly, I am a bit stumped about that too. I am not sure what made the vortex flare up, and trap your uncle and his father."

"Terrible!" Trudy said, leaping to her feet with a smile and clapping excitedly.

"I beg your pardon?" her brother asked. "Why would you be so happy if that is so terrible?"

"No, silly!" Trudy bounced as she spoke. "Doctor Terrible. He stole the plans, and built a new machine, and went back in time and trapped poor Uncle Waldorf and his Papa!"

"Hm," Jack said, "maybe. But more likely, if the two machines were both activated at the same time, they created a feedback loop, being so close to each other."

"But then, why wasn't he trapped also? Or was he?" Spencer asked, twirling his thin moustache.

"No," Jack paused to draw from his pipe and collect his thoughts. After a moment he pointed at them with the stem and said, "I think the things you saw in the workshop, which came through the residual portal from your uncle's passage, helped Doctor Terrible out."

"Why?" Spencer stopped playing with his lip, a concerned look on his face.

"Because they were scouts, and need to open the door for the rest of their army, or something much larger and more dangerous. We must lay things to rest, specifically the horrors that came with the opening of the portals, as well as stop anything that may be waiting to enter our world. But for the moment, we need to discuss where we shall sleep."

The sun was making its way to the horizon, and they debated if they should make camp on shore or on the boat. They couldn't travel on the river at night due to not being able to see places they could run aground, snags mid-river, and other dangers. They could sleep on ship, and that may be wiser than having another portal opening up their camp. They would run the risk of another river gateway and monster, but would be able to avoid any natural predators. All three agreed to sleep onboard, and take shifts to watch for danger. Trudy claimed the cabin for her use, since she was a woman and needed privacy.

After a nervous but uneventful night the journey continued. Another day on the river passed, with Jack deciding they would stop at a village they were passing and try to resupply. As they tied the Drungian Queen to the dock they noticed the small collection of huts were abandoned. Spencer climbed a tree to see if he could see any people or activity. After a few minutes, and finding nothing, the trio left without further discussion or investigation. Minutes after they had launched and turned a bend in the river, a snapping sound of a portal opening came from the village. Staring over the treetops they could see a white electrical rift in the sky.

Three spherical creatures emerged. They resembled jellyfish in that they were pale and milky, but the tentacles that hung below the unnatural animals as they drifted were like the kraken's limbs they had seen the day previous. The bodies looked more like a brain, wrinkled and slightly grey, than the smooth surface of the sea creatures. The airborne monsters drifted, electricity crackling whenever their appendages made contact with each other or any other object. Soon they were out of sight as the boat made its way downriver.

"I think the portals are following the two of you," Jack said, "and I am glad we didn't camp on land."

"But why don't they open on the water when we stop for the night?" Spencer asked.

"I am not sure, but each seems to be attuned to a specific elemental frequency. The first we were on land, and had a fire, which it used to enter the world. The second we were on the river, and in a deep part. This last encounter was right after you climbed a tree, Spencer, and high in the air. I think the reason they don't come when we are tied off for the night, is because we are on two elements, and it can't pinpoint how to send something."

"It is confused by mud?" Trudy asked.

"It's the best theory I have," Jack said with a shrug. "You two should get ready, we will arrive at Lake Rikki-Tikki soon, and that is our destination."

The sky was dark in the distance. Clouds roiled and lightning danced inside them, though no thunder sounded. The whole savannah was quiet, and carried an eerie and expectant feel. An hour later the Drungian Queen chugged from the river delta onto the lake.

"My watch has stopped," Spencer said, tapping at the glass of his pocket timepiece.

"Check your compass," Jack said.

"It is spinning wildly and doesn't point to magnetic south

like normal," Trudy said.

"Yes," Jack said, with small smile, "that is normal here. And I still can't get used to compasses pointing to magnetic south."

"Oh, you're silly," Trudy said with a nervous giggle. "Compasses have pointed that way for thousands of years since the poles switched."

"I know," Jack said, "but I am still getting used to it. The reason I insisted on a steamboat instead of an electric motor is because of this area. I knew any of the new magnetic or electrical engines would probably have issues when we arrived."

The twins fell silent as they stared at the clouds. Jack pointed at an island in the center of the lake, drawing their attention to another portal. This rift was the height of a two story building. It sparked and crackled with red, blue, and white electrical current. The center was murky and they could see immense shadows of figures moving on the other side. Two silhouettes were suspended in the center, and a hand as large as a wagon was attempting to grasp them. In front of it, half buried in the sand, was wreckage of twisted, tarnished brass.

"That's Uncle Waldorf's machine!" Trudy said.

"Who is that?" Spencer asked, pointing at three figures which emerged from the tall grass and brush and stood on the shore.

"Is it Uncle and Great Uncle?" Trudy inquired, excited.

"No," Jack said, "that isn't possible. You will see why in a moment. In the meantime, I suggest you two arm yourselves."

As they approached the water erupted into a froth, dozens of tentacles bursting from the inky murk below. Blue circles of light twinkled under the surface of the lake. The appendages were not close enough to each other to belong to a single creature unless it was the size of the lake itself. Jack pushed the throttle forward, jerking the wheel left and right to avoid the searching protuberances which flailed at the boat as they made clumsy attempts to avoid them. One grasped the keel, turning the vessel to port. Jack corrected their course as the twins fired their weapons into the water, forcing the creature to retreat. By now, hundreds of tentacles had broken the surface, and their speed slowed.

Jack tied off the wheel, set the throttle to full, and joined his younger companions in fighting off the hordes of knobby arms that sought to stop them, slashing at them with a machete in one hand and a hatchet in the other. Wriggling, slimy things thrashed as they were struck or shot, the ones landing on the deck writhing towards the three, still seeking their prey.

The boat hit the shore, throwing the companions forward in a jumble from the sudden stop as the vessel beached itself, the engine whining as the propeller became exposed to air. Jack kicked the throttle back to idle, and closed the boiler valve as the twins stared at the approaching figures.

One man stood back from the others. He was clad in black robes from head to foot, and held a large tome. Beady eyes and a hooked nose could be seen under the hood. The lead companion was a thick man, broad of shoulder and massive of limb, his face a melted distortion of what it had once been. Fine clothes hung in tatters from his metal plated body. One hand was an iron pincer, and the other a tentacle resembling the same ones that flopped on the bottom of the boat. He walked with a broken gait, keeling to one side with each step. The third man was unremarkable in every way, except for his pale skin and surplus of freckles. The only features that stood out was the hunger in his eyes, and his crouched, feral stance, as he licked his lips and crept forward.

"Come to me, bring me the sacrifice the dark ones require," the thin man said, holding his hands above his head. His sleeves fell, exposing an odd symbol on his wrist.

Spencer stared at the tattooed rune, and the world spun. The young man collapsed to the deck, covering his eyes and whimpering. Images of text he had seen years before, in one of the many books in his uncle's library, overwhelmed him. Memories overtook him and flooded his mind: of terrors seen in the dark of night in the lab, and when he last saw two of these three men.

"Leave him," Jack said to Trudy as she turned to help her brother. "I will protect him. Just get to the portal."

"'A blood sacrifice of purity and innocence must stain the sands and altar, the blade driven by the hand of passion and lust for destruction', it is written," the thin man said. The freckled man let out a hyena-like laugh, and slobbered with anticipation.

"Written by whom?" Jack said, "No, don't bother. Your book is just one of many. There are other things that have been written. Such as, 'a sacrifice that is willingly given shall free all, and innocence shall sleep in peace'. Trudy, run! Get to your uncle!"

"Wait," Trudy said, hesitating. "I am that sacrifice, aren't I?"

Jack looked at the girl, his eyes filled with pity. "Does it matter? You must do what is right, before they get to your brother and use him. You must trust me."

Trudy turned and ran.

Spencer lay curled in the fetal position, terror and despair washing over him. He felt fevered and chilled in waves. The dark nightmares returned to him, dark things creeping across the earth, and whole towns devoured by grey things in the night. Children's screams and mothers' weeping filled his ears.

Jack twirled his machete and hatchet, and launched himself at the freckled man who was preparing to pursue the girl. With the first blow from behind, the hatchet buried itself deep into the man's shoulder, passing into the chest cavity. His body flowed around it like jelly, and clear ooze slid up the haft of the weapon, touching Jack's hand. Jack screamed as acid ate into his flesh. The pale man spun. The hatchet didn't move with his body. Instead now it jutted from his chest. Clothes melted away as mouths appeared across the man's body, teeth and lips gibbering and babbling at Jack. The sound tore at his mind and his sanity stretched to its limit.

Trudy sprinted for the portal, unsure what she would do once she got to it. The man with the iron pincer lumbered after her, the tentacle arm stretching over three meters and wrapping itself around her ankle. She fell into the sand, swallowing dirt as she tried to scream. She felt herself being pulled backwards, and kicked at the limb. It was like kicking steel. The sound of the pincer from behind grew closer.

"Why?" Spencer mumbled. Music spun in his head, blocking out the black thoughts and images. His mother's voice sang to him, further separating the fear from his mind. The tinny tinkle of a music box played in his thoughts. Since he was a child, he had nightmares. Not the kind you woke from and hid under the covers, but rather the kind that you woke up to someone shaking and slapping you because your screaming woke everyone in the house except for you. Spencer learned to watch the shadows for things that crept in the places others never dared to look. The only thing that brought light to those horrible moments was the music.

The music played now. The darkness receded. Spencer opened his eyes, and looked up. The sky above was becoming shadowed with clouds, lightning flitting through the churning layers of mottled greys.

"Why?" he asked. His back cramped and his muscles ached from being tensed, caught in a rictus of panic and fright. Breathing deep, he flexed his shoulders and arms. Jack's and Trudy's screams reached his ears. He sat upright, his hand falling on the elephant gun beside him. Standing, gun in hand, he turned to take in the scene before him. The lightning flashed, and the forest of tentacles in the lake swayed to the rhythm of the pulse of unnatural power in the air.

Jack's arm was buried to the elbow in the gelatinous mass of the horror with dozens of mouths, on his knees, hacking uselessly at the bulk with the machete. Trudy was rolling side to side, avoiding the mechanical hand of the monster Spencer had once called the 'Hideous Man'. In the center of it all, Doctor Terrible was laughing manically, arms in the air, book in one hand, a curved kris blade in the other, calling to his masters, the Troöds, to come and accept the sacrifice.

Spencer leveled the gun, squeezed the trigger, and let his shoulder take the kick. The bald man's head exploded. The music box tinkled on in Spencer's mind. He reset his sight on the mechanical Hideous Man, and fired again. Hitting the monstrosity in the buttocks, its legs flew out from under it, pulling its tentacle loose from Spencer's sister. The retort of the firearm bucked the boy's shoulder, and he dropped the gun. Reaching for it, his fingers grasped it, but pain shot up his arm to his shoulder when he tried to lift it.

Hearing his mother's soothing song which she sang when he woke screaming during his childhood nightmares, he reached for the rifle with his left hand. Kneeling he balanced it on the rail of the Drungian Queen and aimed at the amorphous mass that the freckled man had become, pointing at the grey blob in the center of the creature. Pulling the trigger again, he smiled and hummed as he saw the gel explode and Jack fall backwards. Sighing with relief that it was over, he dropped the carbine and slumped to the deck.

Trudy rolled to her back, panting and sobbing in relief. Jack landed in the sand, cradling his hand, which was a red oozing mass of flesh. Lightning struck the sand without a sound, leaving glass craters behind. Three separate forks struck each of their foes. Doctor Terrible shuddered, and his neck burst open as tentacles grew from the bloody cavity to replace his head. The blob of the pale man shimmered and shuddered, then began wobbling back into a mass, congealing and growing. The Hideous Man sat bolt upright, electricity running across his body like a spider web of power.

"Trudy," Jack croaked, "run, finish this!"

Spencer pulled himself up, wondering at the panic in their guide's voice. Seeing the horrors reawakening, he scrambled for the gun again. Setting the gun on the rail, he sighted down the barrel and pulled the trigger to hear an empty click. Jack scrambled backwards from the restored atrocity in front of him. Trudy pulled herself to her feet and limped to the portal. Standing in front of it, she looked around.

"What now, Jack?" she shouted, her voice harsh. "What do I do?"

"I don't know!" Jack answered, his tone bleak. "Try the machine?"

Trudy fumbled at her uncle's broken time machine, pushing knobs and pulling levers. Nothing happened. She turned back to Jack. The man was crawling away from the blob beast, Doctor Terrible was standing upright, his hands held to the sky, blade glinting in the lightning. Spencer was in the boat, trying to reload a large gun with one hand, the stock braced against his chest. The mechanical man was a few yards away, malformed hands reaching for her as he stared at her with dead and melted eyes. She threw herself at the portal. She bounced off of it, wiping her bloody and scraped hands on the surface as she fell.

The lightning flared, and then stopped. The huge shadowy figure clawed at the murky surface for another moment, before fading away. The red, blue, and white electrical arcs that surrounded the portal faded, and disappeared. Doctor Terrible, the Hideous Man, and the blob of mouths collapsed to the ground, motionless.

"That's it?" Trudy asked. "That was a bit anticlimactic." The clouds broke and the sun shone through, lighting up the small island. Trudy looked up. "Oh. Well, that's not much better."

A hand fell on her shoulder, making her jump and spin around. There stood Uncle Waldorf, white moustache and crazy hair waving in the breeze. He smiled.

"Maybe," Uncle Waldorf said, "but the portal is closed

and the nightmares have been sent back from whence they came. Now we have to get home. And, I would like you to meet your great-uncle, and my father, now five years my junior."

The Devil's Triangle: A Trio of Travelers Tale

The Catalyst was built as the fastest and most advanced subnautical machine known to man. The technologies it boasted dwarfed any that a government had on their best naval vessel. Captain Villes was a genius, but that was a close step to madness. He had explored the most daunting of areas around the globe. The polar caps, the deep trenches, underwater volcanos, and so many more places of mystery. He now endeavored to open the one part of the map no man had ever returned from, the Devil's Triangle. Even if it meant the lives of his crew.

Elizabeth had known it had to be done, and she did it. The man had been mad, and he had to die. The Captain lay in a small pool of his own blood. The hair pin, dipped into the concentrated excretions of a lion fish, still jutted from his jugular. A few loose curls hung from the tight wound bun and cascaded around the nape of Elizabeth's neck. The bun was supported by her one remaining hair pin; and its crystal-coated end cast small prism rainbows across the small cabin. They danced as the phosphorous algae in the lantern poured its almost white light across the room.

Elizabeth sighed and sat upon the bunk she had been provided. Zachary would have to be put in control of the vessel. That would not be hard, but first she needed him to come to the cabin and not react to the dead Captain. That would be more difficult. She needed to hide the body until she could explain the situation. All the furniture was bolted down to stop it from shifting as the oceangoing ship was rocked by the currents, so none of it could be used for that task.

She did not have time to debate this with herself; action must be taken. Standing with a determined clench to her jaw, she threw the blanket from the bed over the dead man, shrugged and sighed again. That would have to do. Stepping to the door, she opened it and spoke to the two sailors that stood their post outside.

"Andrew, Charles," she said as she peeked her head out the door, "please fetch Zachary. The Captain is in need of his assistance. Thank you." She smiled as they exchanged a look with each other. Nodding in unison, Andrew turned and left to find the ship's Quartermaster.

Elizabeth closed and latched the door and looked around the small cabin, taking in the polished brass and rich velvets. Sighing again, she sat in one of the two chairs at the table. Women were not normally allowed aboard a sea vessel, but she was the exception to the rule. She always was the exception. The Captain's advisor, Suykimo, had recommended her for her special skills. Little did she think she would be learning the new skill of assassination today. She was a woman of emotion. Not just her own, but of other people also. She had a way of knowing the emotional state of others, and influencing it when she needed to do so. Suykimo and she had met at an auction, where he had somehow noticed her using her talents to win certain items, or with the touch of a hand, a nod, or a soft smile making men spend more than they wanted for a piece she did not want. Suykimo had noticed her gifts and had drawn her aside after the auction, offering her a job as a nanny to a large group of older children. Grown children it seemed - the crew of the Catalyst.

Elizabeth had been a nanny before that time. When she learned of her employer's passion for her, she had abandoned that employment, minutes after the man's wife mysteriously learned of her husband's scandalous past with other nannies. It was not proper for a man to behave in such a manner. Elizabeth made her own way after that. She went to the horse races and other places. She was adept at determining even the spirits of the horses, and quite often won any wager she placed by studying the animals before the race.

Within a minute of sitting, a delicate rapping sounded on the door and broke her reverie. The fan in her hand popped open as if it had a mind of its own and began fluttering, cooling her face as she flushed in nervousness. She crossed the chamber in two steps and unlatched the door and opened it a crack. Suykimo stood outside, his hands tucked in the end of his sleeves and his head bowed in respect. She opened the door wide enough to allow the wizened cartographer and advisor inside. He was shorter than Elizabeth and the light reflected off his shaved head as his sea green almond eyes looked around, taking in everything in the room.

"It is done. Let us hope it is not too late," he said in his quiet, accented voice. "Of course you already sent for Zachary." Suykimo rarely overlooked anything, and the missing sailor outside the door spoke volumes. He stepped to one side of the room, and by the time the he stood in the corner another knock came, this one loud and bold. Suykimo nodded at the woman as she glanced at him before reaching for the door and opening it.

A man in reddish leather armor stepped in, ducking so the handle of his sword on his back would not catch on the low door frame. He kept his weapons well-oiled and cared for, and his armor mended. The brass buckles shone in the light of the phosphorus algae lamp. He slid in with a sidestep, and swept the room with a look, his eyes settling on the covered form as his hand went to the polished wood grip of his pistol. Elizabeth closed and latched the door again.

Zachary was a warrior by nature, and was exceptional at making quick decisions under pressure, reacting with instinct from years of training. He moved with a fluid grace that seemed to be a blend of a dance learned from a snake and a hunting cat. He always looked as if he were about to crouch, never standing his full height and keeping his knees bent, unlike military trained men. His short black hair was combed back and his tanned skin showed that he preferred to be outside. He was not the type anyone would expect to see on a vessel that traveled under the waters.

Suykimo had known the man since Zachary was an orphaned child. The older man had come upon the boy in an alley standing over a pregnant dog and fighting five teens. Suykimo watched as Zachary took a beating which left bruises and cuts. But within minutes the older boys were scattered about the alley, defeated by the younger child. Suykimo had taken the boy to a dojo, after buying him a meal and cleaning him up, and introduced him to the art of swords and hand to hand combat. Over the next decade Zachary became trained in a dozen forms of combat from shooting to archery, from weapons to bare hands, and from solo tactics against groups to military strategy. The boy that had been passionate and angry became calm and collected under the direst of circumstances.

"Zachary," Elizabeth began, his eyes darting to her face to read it as she spoke, his hand never leaving his sidearm, "I shall speak plainly. Pray, listen to what I say. Suykimo revealed the Captain's course to me, though neither had revealed it to the crew. We are bound for the Devil's Triangle." She watched his face for any response but found none. He stayed his hand though, and she took that to heart.

"He planned to penetrate the mists that devour sea ships and airships alike to find what lies beyond. Suykimo already knows what is there, or at least has a singular idea. Death awaits us, not so much from the elements, but from something much more dangerous. He has chosen to not reveal what precisely this is, but assures me it would not be wise to venture there. He advised the Captain to turn aside from this folly, but was reminded of his place."

Zachary looked at the foreigner, narrowing his eyes as if searching the horizon. Suykimo raised his to meet this gaze with a calm look, and nodded once.

"Go on," the warrior said.

Elizabeth continued, her fan cooling her flushed face, the lace of her high collar dancing in the breeze. "Suykimo is certain none of us would survive if we continue this journey. We need you to take charge and return us to safe waters." Letting out her breath in a rush, she waited for the man to reply.

"The First Mate is the one that should take charge, and you should be put in the brig until you can face a tribunal," Zachary said.

Suykimo's whisper of a voice was firm as he spoke. "Sanders is not the man to make strong and quick decisions. You are. And I have this." The small man pulled a rolled document from his sleeve and held it towards Zachary. "It states that if Captain Villes were to no longer be able to command that you would take his title and duties. It is in his hand and bears his signature and seal. The First Mate is aware of these wishes and will not debate your right."

Zachary took the paper, unrolled it, and read it. Elizabeth was relieved to see that the Quartermaster's hand was no longer on his weapon. Nodding, he passed it back to the older man. Kneeling, Zachary gripped the woven rug on the floor and with a sharp movement, popped the brass tacks that held it.

"Get the Captain's feet," he said to Elizabeth as he stepped to lift the dead man's upper body. Together they placed the corpse on the carpet. He rolled the body in the rug. Standing with the dangerous grace that made men move from his path, he looked at Elizabeth. "Take care of this. Do not let the crew see the body; it would not be good for morale. Place it in my quarters and set Andrew and Charles to guard the door. Find me on the bridge. Suykimo, you're with me." The decision made, he moved to the door and opened it. Suykimo in tow, he turned left and glided past the two sailors without looking at them, leaving the door standing wide.

Elizabeth arrived on the bridge of the Catalyst. The thick forward facing glass gave a panoramic view. The murky waters outside danced with jewel tones in greens and turquoise, showing they were near the surface, the light filtered by the heavy seaweed forest which the vessel glided through. The bright lights of the command deck contrasted with the outside. Brass shone, wood gleamed, and glass sparkled, all having been polished to a high sheen. The gentle chug of the steam pistons in the back of the vessel echoed through the hull even this far forward in the massive ship.

"Why haven't we quit this ocean jungle?" Elizabeth asked, ignoring the scowl of a crewman who thought women on board were bad luck, and a woman on the bridge was disastrous.

Zachary directed her attention to the instruments. The compass spun madly and the others seemed confounded also. "It was too late," he said. "We had already entered the seaweed forest. To turn about without any point of reference may be worse than continuing on a present course, considering we have no way of knowing how far we would actually be turning."

Another man glared at the lean acting Captain. With a flick of his eyes, Zachary brought him to bear. "Leftenant Simmons feels he could determine exactly when we reach a complete turnaround, but I am not willing to risk it, or risk the plants binding our propellers."

As he spoke the ship shuddered and the helmsman shifted the gear lever, slowing the propellers and reversing them. The hull calmed as the ship's movement stopped. With careful manipulation of the rudder and propellers, the man freed them from the grasp of the sea plants and the craft continued forward.

A few minutes later the vessel shuddered again as the propellers were once again bound by the plants. Attempts to repeat his last endeavor brought no success or freedom for the ship and crew.

"Electrify the hull," Zachary ordered. The other crewman manned the machinery to charge the battery of conductors. The ship was a modern marvel; no expense was spared in the creation. This was no simple military submersed paddleboat, this was a piece of art that genius created and passion built. The bottom third of the submarine was various engines and power plants. The steam from propulsion was not the by product. That gaseous form of water was created from bringing seawater in through portholes, the water super-heated for steam, leaving behind salt for wide uses on the ship. The steam itself was broken down further, some sent to cooling tanks where it became drinkable water, another portion to power the movement, and another portion delivered to a very particular machine in the tail of the vessel. This device would separate the hydrogen and oxygen from each other and cycle the breathable air into the crew's portion of the ship, and the hydrogen was stored in separate tanks for use as high power propulsion, or as a weapon in the depths of the oceans.

Turbines spun in the bowels of this creation and a steady hum could be heard as the electricity built its charge on the hull. A sudden burst and the lights dimmed and flickered for a moment. The ship jerked as it was freed from the vegetable octopus. Forward movement began again.

"We can't use that charge too often," Suykimo said in his quiet voice. "The ship may have power enough for a few of those, but it slows our movement, and worse… it may attract unwanted attention."

"Get the walkers suited. Get them on the hull with the saw poles. We will do this with men," Zachary told the First Mate without turning.

They continued to move forward at a slow pace as the men prepared to move into position. After donning deep dive suits, they filed into pressure chambers in the four corners of the ship. These were sealed from the rest of the ship and filled with water. An outer door opened and the men lumbered onto the hull. Overweight magnetic boots clung to the shell of the vessel. Each of the men had a polearm strapped to his back, but instead of the medieval weapon sort, it had a eighty centimeter serrated blade at the end of a meter and a half long pole. The men walked with care, using an two meter long steel cable with two carabiners at the end to secure themselves to metal rails that ran the length of the craft, centimeters above the hull. They would walk three meters until the first carabiner caught on the small metal arms that secured the rails to the hull, bend over to attach the second carabiner and remove the first, and continue on their way.

Elizabeth watched with concern as the men found their places. The outer lights had been activated so dangers could be seen, before the dangers saw them. Twelve total, four near the rear propeller and rudder, two for each of the dual midship rudders, two to protect the delicate instruments outside of the looking glass of the bridge, and the remaining two on the nose of the ship. Suykimo gazed into a depth finder, hoping to give the new captain more information to work with, but to no avail. Zachary watched everything, his knees bent and his body moving with the natural bounce of the ocean that you feel even when under the waves.

Elizabeth gasped and pointed as a dark silhouette undulated in the thick sea grass, winding its way towards the ship. The men outside were focused on the task of directing the seaweed away from the hull, or cutting through it before it could entangle the ship, and didn't notice the predator of the deep. The shadow was seven meters long and moved with a deadly grace as it swam a path around the perimeter of the ship, staying just outside of the circle of light. The crew on the bridge stood and stared, trying to make out what sort of creature this was.

"Tap out the warning for the men," Zachary said. A man jumped to fill that order. Grasping a large mallet, he slammed it against what appeared to be a gong. Rather than hanging free, it was embedded in a thick jellylike membrane. A thin sheet of water ran across the surface, keeping it moist. No noise issued in the room, but the men visible through the window stopped, as if listening. The vibration was sent through a series of organic channels in the ship and radiated outward to the hull. This system was made from an odd breed of creature that was something between a jellyfish and a sponge. They grew in huge colonies in dead coral reefs, filling every nook and cranny. They would send out waves of vibration that threw off the equilibrium of predators, and attract beneficial fish that lived in a symbiotic relationship with the colony. Suykimo had helped design the channels throughout the ship, the ciphers that now warned the men about the danger, as well as the countless other codes.

Aware of this new threat, the sailors on the hull looked around, while still dealing with the thick vegetation wall. The first man was still taken by surprise, even as his station companion pointed. The creature snaked out of the weeds with lightning speed, and the eel-like snake grasped the man in a mouth that was larger than any crocodile's. Rows of pointed teeth snatched the man from the ship, his cable snapping taut as the beast attempted to take him. Its mouth went across his midsection, teeth showing on the other side of the man's wide girth. The man's companion rushed forward as fast as the magnetic shoes would allow, his cutting tool at ready. Before he could reach the other man the monster tore his meal free of the restraining cable with a sudden thrashing movement. Blood floated through the ocean water. Thin, wispy trailers, like smoke in the air, dissipated. Then the crew noticed other movements. Dozens of dark sinewy shapes glided just outside of the circle of light, attracted by the scent that their brethren had left in the water. Their movement became more excited.

"Issue the retreat. Get those men inside now," Zachary ordered in crisp tones. The crewmen with the mallet beat out the tattoo that would bring the men back inside. In the slow motion that the sea demands man live in, the men turned and began to move to the doors. The creatures did not wait. The attack was swift and brutal as three and four monsters shot out of the shadows with swift movements. Two would focus on one man, tearing him from the ship and snapping his cable, carrying him away as they fought for mouthfuls of their meal.

The bridge vibrated as the doors in the stern and aft opened to bring the men inside. The beasts followed, tearing the men out of the safety of the interior of the ship. The captain opened the channels on the console in front of him to communicate with the waterlocks, his voice crackling across the speakers, "Shut those doors as soon as the last man is in!"

"Aye sir!" The frantic reply came back. The man held the announcement channel open, stopping two way communications. The bridge could hear the order repeated to the men controlling the outer doors. One man was screaming that some of the monsters had followed the last man inside the chamber. The bridge vibrated again, confirming that the order to close the doors was being followed. Other announcement channels reported that no men had made it back in alive. The terrified man that held the first channel open ordered the inner door opened as soon as the waterlock was drained, and weapons readied to kill the monster.

Zachary tried to use his direction of communication, but was blocked since the other man still had his end open. Realizing the inevitable, Zachary turned to an enlisted man. "No. Ensign, go tell that man not to open that chamber, leave the beast in it. Now!" The young man shot through the door to go pass the command on before the chamber drained and the man let the predator into the ship. They waited and listened as they watched scores of the beasts frenzy outside the window, snatching and tearing at the men they had taken.

The voice of the man crackled across the connection, ordering the door opened. The sound of the lock being spun filled the room from the speakers. A young voice came across the commotion, repeating the order he was sent to deliver. Screams began, showing he was seconds too late. The terror of the man in charge was the last noise before silence filled the room as the channel went dead.

Elizabeth shuddered and forgot to fan herself as she thought about what was going on in that hall. Her attention was torn away as Suykimo spoke. "They go for larger prey. They know the Catalyst holds food, and they are not stupid. They use the seaweed." He did not need to point for the others to see what he meant. The beasts grabbed the tips of the florae and swam in spirals around the vessel, wrapping it in the vegetation. The plants tangled the propellers, stopping their forward movement. The monsters then began wrapping themselves around protrusions in the ship, including the large metal wheels that opened the waterlocks, convulsing and writhing. Suykimo smiled a neutral smile as he realized what was happening.

"These creatures are as smart as a squid or octopus. Look, they open our doors to get at the food inside. Fascinating," the foreign man said. "I would suggest yellow defense again Zachary." He used the familiar term instead of the man's title. No one seemed to notice, showing the unspoken station of the little olive skinned man.

"Charge the batteries and prepare the hull for the Electric Tide," Zachary said into another announcement channel. "Shut all outer portals if able. If unable, then retreat to an inner sanctum and shut the inner watertight portals."

The light by the door began flashing yellow as they

prepared for the dangerous defense. The ship hummed under their feet as the turbines charged the coils of copper wire that spiraled between the two eight centimeter thick layers of metal that created the hull. The vessel shuddered as the electricity erupted throughout the skin of the massive machine. The Catalyst shifted downward in a sudden movement as a thin layer of water around it was vaporized and the vessel dropped. The creatures wound around the extremities of the ship screamed and writhed as they tried to escape the painful death, but their muscles had already locked from the shock, trapping them and condemning them to their doom.

After fifteen seconds the newly promoted captain spoke again into the general announcement channel. "Terminate the Electric Tide and engines full speed ahead for sixty seconds, and then throttle back to exploration speed. Stations for the whole crew, we won't be taken without expectation again."

The crew followed orders flawlessly, acting as one with the craft that any mariner would have given his life to serve on. Many on board had given up lives to be here. Any crew member that signed onto the crew signed off his mortal life for something greater; the journey of exploration that was the Catalyst. Within ten minutes the seaweed forest thinned enough for limited visibility.

"The coral fields around Tector are challenging, but this is as challenging in its own way," Suykimo said.

"I think the beasts that inhabit that depth are far more fearsome than the ones we have encountered here, my friend," Elizabeth replied.

"Perhaps, but I think the inhabitants of the land in the center of this maze are much more dangerous than the great beasts of Tector."

Zachary turned towards Suykimo, gazing at him with careful eyes. "What do you know of what we approach?"

"We approach a nest of the most dangerous game," Suykimo said, as if everyone should know his meaning.

Zachary nodded, because he did understand.

Dark, wide shapes loomed around them as the plants thinned further, the sight of land jutting up from the ocean floor, the tops of mountains creating a massive island chain, an archipelago. The seaweed grew around them still, but not as thick as before. One of the crew members gasped as they saw something. Pointing, he drew the attention of the rest of the bridge.

Lights shone through the dark green waters, not natural light of phosphorus or the glow of the angler fish or some other marine life. Rather it was the yellow glow of man-made light, and not the flickering light of a candle or gas light. Huge rectangles of open space became visible in the side of the underwater sides of the mountains, windows showing people inside, staring at them in amazement.

As they glided close to one, they could see the expressions on the faces of the people inside. One moved to a metal rectangle on the wall and lifted a smaller silver box from it and spoke into it. Though they could not hear what was said, the intensity that showed on the man's face did not belay a feeling of welcome.

"Increase speed," Zachary said to the helmsman. "We need to get through." He was interrupted as the Catalyst shuddered and listed to starboard. Three small vessels sped past the larger ship, odd tentacle-like rudders spiraling behind the one-man ships, propelling them with speed and agility. Two turned in tight, controlled arcs and the third threw itself out of the water and turned in midair, diving back into the water and speeding towards the Catalyst once again.

The ship was equipped with spring and air harpoons, depth charges, the Electric Tide, and a split nose on the front for ramming, but had no weapons that could match the speed and agility of these submersibles. But these new machines were vastly superior to the Catalyst, and the Catalyst was the most advanced any crew member had ever seen, far surpassing anything any government had ever commissioned.

"If these peoples have those ships, they use energy. If they use energy, they have places that generate it and probably use the sea to power them. Find that and initiate the Spire Shift," Suykimo said, his calm unbroken as if he expected this very thing to happen.

"They are just afraid," Elizabeth said, her eyes glazed as she used what she called her female intuition. "They have been hidden in the Devil's Triangle for a long time, and they will protect their anonymity. They will not let us return the way we came."

With a glance Zachary took in both sources of information, and with the same swiftness he acted with in every circumstance he said, "Surface. Use the array to find the strongest power source. Communications you will see if we have any way to tie into that source. Helm, you will steer us towards it at top speed."

The ship lurched as the speed increased and rose in the murky waters. The viewing glass drained of the water as the massive ship broke the surface of the waves. The sky darkened as the clouds rolled in the sky with unnatural speed and purpose.

"They control the very winds," Suykimo observed. "This is why water and air ships alike have disappeared in these waters for as long as legend and myth remembers."

The smaller ships easily kept pace with the Catalyst, peppering it with their weapons. The ship shook but did not take on any substantial damage. Soon the small one man vessels fell back. Zachary warned the crew to be aware and watch for enemies. Within moments they appeared, but not in the sea as expected.

"There!" Elizabeth was the first to see them. She pointed to the air. From the black clouds came ships of similar design to the water vessels that had attacked them. Small wings jutted from the sides and the tentacle-like rudders were shorter. Lightning from the clouds struck these flying vessels and they channeled it as bolts towards the Catalyst.

"Charge the Electric Tide," Zachary barked, "then reverse the turbines to bring the charge in and direct it to the engines."

"Sir," the gunner in charge of the Electric Tide said, "the ship is not designed to do that. With all due respect, it is theoretically possible, but could burn out the engines. We have no way to dissipate the excess energies." The man encountered a hard gaze from the captain. "Aye, aye sir," the seaman said as he relayed the command through his announcement channel to the engineers below.

The ship hummed as it absorbed the charges from the aerial attack. The engines began to growl, the whole ship shaking as it gained speeds it was not accustomed to and the angry waves battered her. The airships had retreated after seeing their weapons had little effect.

"Energy source detected," said the man at the communications array.

"Steer us towards it helmsman," Zachary said quietly.

"Walls sir, dead ahead," the helmsman announced nervously, "they seem to have openings we can pass through, but we may become trapped."

"Do it," said the captain. "Prepare the fore harpoons with depth charges."

"They only use natural sources of energy and weapons," Suykimo noted aloud. Zachary nodded his acknowledgement.

They passed through an opening in a wall, and banked hard to port as an island appeared in front of them. They maneuvered between another opening and another. The waves, winds, and currents pushed them towards the walls and slowed their movement. The next opening that appeared had a gate across it that was just closing.

"Fire the harpoons when in range gunner," Zachary said with calm. He was in his element, and was poised on the balls of his feet, as if in personal combat. The ship had become his body, and he spoke as if it was a thought sent to his limbs.

The harpoons fired, hitting the wall and exploding. The ship rocked with the blast and the wall crumbled. The opening that appeared was not wide enough for the ship though.

"Ram it," the captain said. The Catalyst shuddered as it crashed into the damaged barrier.

"We are within one hundred yards of the power source," said the crewman monitoring the energy source.

"Prepare the Spire Shift and steer for the energy source."

Steel nets appeared in front of them, being drawn taut, creating a more effective barrier than the walls and gates they had passed moments before.

"Bring the Electric Tide to maximum, fire the harpoons, and ram the net."

"Sir," interjected a crewman, "even if we break through, the tatters of those nets will bind our propellers."

"I know," Zachary said.

The ship launched forward, explosive harpoons leading the way. An explosion rocked the Catalyst as she hit the nets moments after the charges.

"Initiate the Spire Shift."

The vessel groaned with speed, its electrified hull and specialty propulsion kicking into action simultaneously. It rocked hard to port and began to turn on its side as the nets turned its nose. A blinding blue flash made the crew avert their eyes and then all was calm.

The storm clouds were gone. It was night and the Catalyst stuttered as an explosion sounded from the aft of the vessel. The engines stopped. The power flickered and the ship went dark as power was lost from the machines on the bridge.

"Get a navigator and sextant topside," Zachary said. "We need our location."

"Sir?" the helmsman asked. "The instruments show, well, nothing is right. Not even the stars. Where are we?"

"A new world, or perhaps an old one. Only time will tell."

The Adventures of Friends on the Road to Manhood

I recall the golden days of my childhood as they float in my memory with the smells of summer and the sounds of locusts in the day, and the warm breezes and crickets at night. How my uncle would sit on the porch whittling a thick piece of cedar as he smoked his cigar. I think it is with him I found my love for the curling smoke and slow, relaxing times I spend in my adulthood enjoying a hearty cigar and whiskey. After he returned from the war, he would pass the days in his rocker, squinting across the field of our grand plantation house. He would sit there for hours. I would look in the direction of his gaze, but never knew at what he stared. Sometimes I would ask him, and he would chew on his stogie for a minute before turning to answer.

"Young'un," he would say in his slow and methodical manner, "a man sees things that a child cannot. But a child sees things that a grown'd up can't. You should enjoy what you see, and always see the world through your own eyes. Appreciate that everyone else has their own eyes, and their own way of seeing things, ya hear? But don't try and see through someone else's eyes in place of your own."

I don't know if I agree with what he told me, but I understand what he meant. He meant for me to be my own man, and not worry about what others think. But I nodded at him then, because when I was young I didn't question my elders when they told me what to do. I'd sit next to him for hours, trying to emulate him with my own pocket knife and a piece of pine. I would carve guns and horses, and he would carve things he had seen while traveling. He never carved things of war though. I think he was tired of guns and fighting, and instead preferred thinking about elk, mountains, clouds, and such things.

Those summers were some of the best times of my life, and I remember them with a fondness of childlike wonder. I had a few friends. There was Tyler, he was the son of the chemist. He was always pale and skinny, and never looked very healthy. His parents made him wear a starched collar and clean his boots. He was afraid to get dirty. He was often in poor health as a boy, and I think his father made him scared of dirt because it made him sick. I also had Randal. Randal was the one that always had an adventure in his head. He smiled all the time, and didn't mind that his one front tooth was a bit crooked. I think it charmed others to see it, a bit of imperfect perfection with no worries or cares. That boy took risks. It was Randal that showed us the old twisted tree we used to climb, and that in which we eventually built our fort.

I recall, with clarity, sitting in that rickety wooden box we had cobbled together from scraps of the church the town had built in the spring and barn raisings from around the county, the rain falling in a downpour for hours. Tyler sat on his coat with his feet dangling over the side and his chin resting on the railing that I had whittled into a snake. It was a rough carving, but I was immensely proud of it. Randal was attacking the rain as it fell with a stick that had become a sword in his mind. I sat whittling a block of wood into a bear and watching them both. I could feel the tree sway and raised my face to the wind, smelling the scents that only a storm brings with it. Thunder boomed.

"You know the ol' cemetery," Randal shouted, making Tyler and I jump, "it's haunted, it is. I know it is because my Memaw done tol' me all 'about it. Said that Crazy Sidney Carter went and kil'd a man up there in a cave right behind the graves."

I was staring at him as he acted out the story with his stick and the trunk of the tree, stabbing it through the place at which it branched. I looked over at Tyler and he was wide eyed and pale, unable to look away from Randal. When I touched his arm he jerked and turned to me, startled.

"It's ok, Tyler," I reassured him, "it's just a story. It ain't true."

"It is so!" Randal insisted.

"Naw, it ain't. Your Memaw just told you that so you don't go up to those caves."

"You callin' my Memaw a liar?" Randal loomed over me, one hand on the hip of his overalls, the other holding his stick beside him.

"Naw, I ain't calling your Memaw nothing! Maybe she had a boyfriend up there and would go play kissy face in the cave and didn't want you following her to see her beau!" I giggled at the outrageous idea. Randal began snickering and soon we were all three laughing, and rolling around holding our sides in exaggerated mirth, the way boys do when they are trying not to be afraid. Soon we settled down and were staring out at the storm which had let up and become a steady drizzle.

"I reckon we should go see," Tyler whispered.

We both looked at him with surprise. He never wanted to do anything scary or dangerous. Tyler was the one that always used common sense to battle Randal's impulsive whims.

"Why are you looking at me like that?" Tyler asked, turning away. "I heard things about those caves too. I heard the man who was killed was a pirate and that he was killed over his treasure."

263

That settled it. We gathered our few things and Tyler put his coat on, and we headed out into the damp day to find our adventure. It took about an hour to walk there and the storm had blown over by that time. The day grew hot and muggy, and the cicadas began their droning song in the tall weeds. Grasshoppers buzzed and flew past us as we walked the seven kilometers to town. As we passed a farm, we saw Old Widow Norge glaring at us from her porch. Her husband had died in the same war that my Uncle fought in, and the woman hadn't smiled since. Her son couldn't take it and headed out years ago, and that hadn't helped her mood any. She watched us until we were out of sight, leaning on her broom the whole time.

We ate lunch as we walked, having packed a knapsack with apples, cheese, and bread before we headed to our fort that morning. Tyler had some candies from his father's store and Randal carried a water skin that his father had bought from a Dasism trader when he was working on the railroad back in '12. When we arrived at the graveyard, Randal told us to wait and ran over to the small shed at the edge of the cemetery. When he returned, he had a pick and two shovels, saying we may need them in the cave to find the treasure. He passed a shovel to each of us and kept the pick for himself, which was only fair since he went and fetched the tools and it was his idea.

We picked our way through the tombstones, stopping at Tyler's Grampa Joe's plot so he could pay his respects. He put a pebble on the top of the marker, because it was part of his religion. Tyler's people were followers of Tarra, Goddess of peace and healing. We didn't talk about it much back then, but his people had a lot of weird ideas and traditions. I remember making fun of him during winter for not having Turning Day presents, until he told us that he got eight days of presents. That shut us up real quick, and I even asked my parents if we could worship Tarra too. I got a switchin' and was made to be the altar boy for a full month at church for asking, including midnight mass for Turning Day.

We followed the winding trail into the shade of the hillside. Back then we called it a mountain, but we were kids and we thought everything was bigger than it really was. That's the delight of being a child. Some things don't matter at all, like when you're walking a fence with your arms out and your head tilted back, not scared of falling, not even for a second, because you don't know you shouldn't be able to do that. But other things, your mind and imagination just snatched up and ran with, like noises at night and stories of treasure.

We headed into the caves single file. Randal took the lead by right of the pick, which was more of a weapon in case we ran into a bear, a rattler snake, or a mountain lion. None of us mentioned the possibility of meeting a ghost or a pirate, or even worse... a pirate ghost. But we were all thinking about it, and you could tell. Poor Tyler was as jumpy as a long tail cat in a room full of rocking chairs, and even Randal was quieter than usual, not boasting and shouting like he usually did.

The caves weren't very big and in about twenty minutes we had gone through them twice, finding nothing. Randal wasn't put off by that though. He found a place that would be a likely spot for a murder and buried treasure and we started digging. Randal swung his pick to break up the hard packed earth and I shoveled the loose dirt out of the way. Less than a half hour later Randal suddenly stopped.

"Where is that weasel?" he asked, his tone angry.

"What?" I looked around and realized that Tyler had gone missing. We shouted his name and headed off to find him. Randal muttered about how the younger boy always tried to get out of the hard labor, and we weren't gonna split the treasure with Tyler if we had to do all the work. We heard our missing friend before we saw him, and the sound of the shovel scraping on rock echoed as we turned a corner. Randal's mouth was open to yell at our absent companion, but he stopped dead in his tracks before anything could be said. I leaned around him to see what had brought him to such a sudden halt.

"It only made sense," Tyler said, pointing at the hole just above head height in the wall. He had scraped stone away and revealed a secret compartment!

"How? How did you know to look there?" Randal stammered.

"Well, everyone always looks down, so hiding anything in the ground is a sure way to get it found. I saw something funny here, and I knew you wouldn't listen if I told you about it, so I just snuck off to check it myself."

"Did you find anything?" I asked, unable to hide my eagerness.

"Yeah, I found something, but I ain't pulled it out yet," Tyler answered. "Thought you guys might want to be here for that part. You want to grab it, Randal?"

"You big chicken!" Randal laughed. "You ain't pullin' the wool over my eyes. You just 'fraid that there's gonna be a scorpion or a spider or something in that hole, that's why you waited!"

Tyler didn't deny it, and shuffled his feet in the dirt a bit. Randal swaggered up and bold as brass just stuck his hand right in there. He smiled at Tyler, who wouldn't meet his gaze, then froze. Randal gasped, then screamed and jerked his hand back, clutching it to his chest. Tyler screamed too. I ran up, grabbing for Randal's hand to see what had happened. The older boy began laughing, and let me have his hand.

"I was just joshing! Ain't nuttin' in that hole that's gonna bite me," he said, still laughing. I punched him in the arm because he had scared us both with his stupid trick. It was pretty funny though, and I had to give him due credit. Even Tyler was smiling by the time Randal reached back up to check for treasure again. He felt around for a few moments, before slowly drawing something out.

"What's this?" he asked. We all gathered around. We could see it was a piece of wood, some sort of broken plank about the size of the cover of the big holy book the preacher used at church - or the cigar box in Tyler's father's pharmacy. Marks and writing were carved into the surface, but it was too dark to read in the dim light inside the cave. We brought our treasure outside into the sunlight where we could better inspect it. It was a fine piece of work. The dyes still showed on the map as soon as the sun touched the wood, though aged and weathered.

"I reckon it must be a hundred years old," said an awestruck Randal.

"It's a treasure map, look!" I pointed as I spoke, showing my friends the lines that were clearly a path to adventure. We began plotting how to find this prize. We drew maps in the dirt, and then headed back home with a plan. We would each go home and tell our parents that we were going to camp out with the other boys, and then we would make our way to the river and head south, towards where the map showed our treasure to be.

It didn't quite work out that way though. Randal and I made it there without anyone suspecting a thing. Well, without my parents suspecting anything. I don't think Randal's Pa much cared where his boy went, and his Ma had left to take care of her sick sister back east last spring. It hadn't been an easy year on Randal. His Pa worked down at the stables, selling horses, and after work spent a good spell in the saloon each night. And when he was home my friend tried to be somewhere else to avoid his father's drunken temper.

My parents did care, and so did Tyler's, which is why we had to fool them. Randal and I were laughing and eating spring carrots when we heard Tyler coming, and he was mighty loud. We turned and my stomach dropped when I saw the chemist and my father. Tyler was being dragged forward by his arm, forcing him to reveal our secret meeting place. I knew he had told them everything.

I got a switchin' that night for trying to run away. I couldn't sit for two days. The rest of the summer I had more chores than any other year I can recall. I still found time to sneak out to the tree fort though. We had adventures still, but it wasn't until three years later that the map showed up again.

It was the summer of '27 and it was a real scorcher. We were about thirteen years old at that time, and Tyler had been back from boarding school for a couple weeks. Randal had almost stopped going to school and instead worked at the mill when he could. I guess my life was the most normal of the three of us. I still lived with both my folks and went to school. That summer would be different though. My parents had gone to visit my cousins and left me home with my uncle. The servants took care of the house and I had freedom like I hadn't seen for years. I could go away for days at a time, and as long as I told my uncle where I was going and when I would be back, he didn't trouble me none.

The three of us - Tyler, Randal and I - were down by the crick. It was right about noon on a Therin, and the middle of the week. The day was as hot as a tea kettle about to whistle. We had been digging for crawdads and what we had caught were now roasting over the fire we had built. Our pants were rolled up as our legs dried. Tyler had snuck some spices from his house and I had dug up some spring onions to cook with them. It smelled like a wonder. We watched them sizzle and pop with our mouths watering. We ate them like we were real river men, juices dripping down our chins and laughing about the things that boys love to laugh about. When we finished, Randal pulled out a corn cob pipe and loaded it with baccy. He leaned back under the tree, trying not to cough while making smoke rings. I was enjoying the last of the peppermints when Tyler spoke.

"Remember that map?" the skinny boy asked. We both knew exactly which map he meant. It had been taken by his father and we thought it had been burnt. We nodded. Tyler reached into his knapsack, the same one that he had since we were kids, and pulled out a plank of wood. I pushed up my straw hat as we gathered around. Randal and I were stunned. Tyler just grinned.

"It's New Sylians. The sewers to be exact," he announced.

"How do you know that?" Randal asked, running his hands across the bright dyes, just as he had years before.

"I did some research. See, I found it in the woodshed during the winter, so I stashed it in my school stuff and brought it with me when I went back after the holiday break. See those numbers?" We nodded. "Them there is longitude and latitude. I looked them up. And flip it over."

We did as we were told. On the back were faint lines with holes drilled straight through to the other side.

"The top is a map of the city, and the holes are sewer entrances. The lines are a map of the sewers." Tyler stood over us, hands in his pockets, rocking back on his heels, proud as a peacock. We all three burst out talking and by sunset we had a plan to get to New Sylians and find our treasure!

Now, this was a plan of boys, so it wasn't very complicated. We would go down to the great Whiting and flag down a passing steamer. You see, in those days the wheelboats had official ports, and unofficial ones. And if you stood on the shore they would sometimes pick you up and for a small fee you get to ride and sleep on deck. For a lot more you could get a cabin if one were available. Randal had some money from his job and he'd pay our way as deck passengers (he didn't have enough for a cabin), I would bring food for us, and Tyler would navigate our way because he had figured out the map.

Two days later we stood on the deck of a steamboat, leaning on the railing and watching the shore sweep past us. It would take a couple days to get to the city. We were more excited than a pup on its first cattle drive. We talked about all the money we would find and what we would do with it. Randal would buy his very own horse and lariat, and practice until he could go on a drive, which is what made me think of the pup thing. I wanted to get my uncle a new whittling knife and one for me too, and maybe a rifle to hunt coon and squirrel. Tyler didn't know what he would do with his, but we had enough ideas that he didn't have to think of anything on his own.

I think we talked too much because, before long, we attracted attention. We were standing at the water barrel, ladling out a drink, when a dark man came up behind us and threw his arms around Tyler and myself. The pale boy jumped and squeaked, and I spun around throwing the man's arm off of our shoulders. The man was tall and unshaven. He grinned at us, showing black, crooked teeth. He smelled sour, and his clothes were stained with sweat and clung to his body.

"Whatcha boys got there?" he asked, as friendly as a snake.

"Nothing. It ain't none of your business what we got!" Randal puffed up and stepped in between the man and us. I don't think I had ever seen anything braver than that in my whole life. The man cuffed him with the back of his hand, and sent my friend sprawling on the deck.

"Then you won't mind if I take a look at nothing."

He reached past and shoved me to the side with his elbow, grabbing Tyler by his suspenders. The man pulled him close, and I could see my friend cringe from the smell of fetid breath. The man reached into Tyler's bag and took our map. He grinned, and it reminded me of a wolf stalking a rabbit. Poor Tyler was paler than I had ever seen him, and I could see him trembling.

"I'll just hold onto this, because it belongs to me now," he said with a voice like oil, as a bit of spittle mixed with chewing tobacco dripped down his chin.

We all three started hollering and tried to grab it back. He held it above our heads with one hand, laughing, and used the other hand to shove us away.

"Something wrong here, Dirk?" came a booming voice from behind us.

"Naw, John Jack. Just some kids took something of mine and I had to take it back."

The man he spoke to was huge and carried a hickory stick that I had seen him use on a drunk earlier, dropping the man like a sack of potatoes. The rouster had a shaved head and a big bushy beard. I could just imagine a squirrel building a nest in it.

"That ain't true!" Randal shouted, red in the face. "He took it from us!"

"Aw, John Jack, you know how boys are. Ain't no harm done. You don't need to be throwing them in the river or nuthin'. I'm sure they'll behave from here on out." Dirk said.

Oh, how I hated that man, right then. In my head he became 'Dark Dirk', a river pirate with no ship. I heard Tyler gasping for breath, and when I looked, he was squatting down with his head between his knees. Randal was still trying to face down Dirk. I grabbed my friend's arm.

"Come on, Randy. It ain't gonna matter what you say. The ol' stinkin' liar ain't gonna give it back." We all knew how grown-ups stuck together, and my friend did the smart thing and came over with me to check on our navigator. I looked up as the men were leaving, and saw Dark Dirk smiling his greasy grin back at my glare.

We watched Dirk for the rest of the day as he got drunk. He never let the map out of his grasp. He had tucked it in his rucksack and leaned against it when he wasn't looking at it. Randal said he had a plan though. Tyler told him to forget about it; we couldn't beat the man in a fight without getting hurt, or worse, thrown overboard for causing trouble. Even if we snuck it out of the man's bag, he would only tell John Jack we had stolen it again. Randal just got a sly look in his eyes and said he was going for a walk.

It was a bit after dark when Randal came back, grinning like a jack-o-lantern. When he saw that Dark Dirk was snoring with his head on his bag, his smile got even bigger.

"My Pa sleeps like that. Ain't nuttin' gonna wake that man up till he sleeps off the booze. I think I need another walk."

We watched as he slipped across the deck, and circled the

man. It was crowded and most of the passengers had bunked down for the night, taking up whatever space they could find to sleep. No one paid one boy any mind. He knelt down beside Dirk, and looked back at us, smirking and looking too much like the grown man had looked a few hours before. We shook our heads as he reached into the man's coat that was being using as a blanket. Randal tucked something into the man's pocket, and then reached under the older man's head and into his sack. He pulled out the wood and stood and stretched, walking back to us with a confidence that left us speechless.

"He'll know it was us," I whispered in a harsh tone. Tyler nodded and gulped.

"Don't worry about a thing, I got it all taken care of," was all Randal would say.

About an hour later, John Jack came by with a nervous, fine dressed gentleman who wore a tall black hat. They were discussing something.

"It is pure silver, with a chain to match, and it's inscribed," the rich man said to the tough.

"I know, you told me that about ten times, Mister Jenkins. Don't worry, we'll find out who took it." John Jack assured the man.

"Is it a pocket watch?" Randal asked, his voice cracking. Tyler and I stared at him like he just grew another head. "Because I saw that man looking at one while he was eating some beans earlier." Now, Dirk did eat some beans for dinner, but he didn't have a watch.

"Yes, son," the well-dressed man said, "it is. Mister Jack, I insist you check that man for my watch. He has an unsavory look about him, and just may be the type to do such a heinous deed!"

John Jack sighed and looked at the three of us for a moment, as if trying to figure out something. He turned and clumped over to Dark Dirk, and poked at him with his cudgel. Something glinted in the moonlight and slid from under the coat, and a metallic clink sounded as it hit the deck. The big man bent over to retrieve it, and held a pocket fob up for his companion to inspect.

"Yes. Yes, that is it! You must remove that ruffian from this vessel, at once!" the man in the hat whined, his voice growing shrill.

The bald, bearded man reached down, and lifted the sleeping man by his collar and shook him once. It did nothing to wake Dirk. He shook him harder and the drunk man's head jerked back and forth, drool flying as it did. Dirk began to wake.

"Ok Dirk, I warned you. Now it's time for you to take a swim!" John Jack growled. "The shore ain't far and the gators should be sleeping."

Dirk was fully awake at that and began babbling about not having done nothing wrong, as John Jack reached down to grab the other man's sack and coat, and shoved it into Dirk's arms as he pushed him towards the railing. The other passengers were awake now and watching the show. Moments later a splash sounded and cursing could be heard, as well as threats from Dirk that he would come back and cut every one of 'you boys from gullet to gizzard'. The gentleman chortled and turning, he looked down his long nose at Randal.

"Good lad. Take this for your honesty and help," he said as he slipped some coins into my friend's hand.

"Thank you, sir. Just doin' my civic duty," Randal mumbled.

John Jack gave us a long hard look as he left with the passenger, escorting him back to the main dining room. Randal burst into laughter as soon as they were gone and leaned in close to us, showing the coins in his hand and Dirk's wallet. It was two bites in coins and the wallet yielded six more.

"We made eight bites, gentlemen," Randal said.

"Actually, minus the three bites we paid to ride the boat, and the thirty-two crumbs we paid for the extra jerky, we made four bites and sixty-eight crumbs," Tyler corrected.

"It don't matter none," I chimed in, "we already done made a profit, even with what it would take to get home again."

We all stood grinning like simpletons and split the eight bites, one fifty each for Tyler and me, and the rest for Randal since he paid our fare and thought up the plan. We had learned to keep our mouths shut, and the rest of the trip was spent enjoying the river.

I can still close my eyes, and feel and smell the wind from that trip. Whenever I sit still on a hot summer day it always brings thoughts of that steamboat, the Elsie Delilah, and her wonderful journey downstream. The warm sun on my face, the wind moving no more than a crawl, and the sounds of the frush, frush, frush of the sidepaddle mixing with the constant, distant buzzing of the cicadas.

We docked in small places to take on wood for the boilers, and big places to unload cargo and passengers, and take on more of both. The three of us even made a little bit of money by helping with the tasks. The steamboat mostly traveled during the day and only a couple times at night, because a pilot can't see the snags on the river in the dark. When we did travel by night, it was slowly and only during the full moon. Passengers would crowd to the front when they sent out a smaller boat to do soundings in the shallow or tricky parts of the river. We'd crowd to the side when we passed or were passed by another steamboat, calling and cheering for our boat to take the lead. Once we saw two huge steamboats racing. We pulled to the side of the river to let these beauties pass us. They glittered in the sun with pure white paint and gold highlights. It was a spectacular sight to see.

One man had a cane pole and would sell a fish for a nibble, usually perch or a brim, and a catfish for a ten bit. For another nibble, you could have the kitchen fry it up after dinner was served. It smelled so wonderful, standing outside the door, watching the ladies with parasols and their gentlemen with tall hats promenade past us. The cook, an old rokairn that went by the name Walter, breaded them for us too. I don't think any of us had tasted something that wonderful before. I look back now, and think that it was the taste of adventure and freedom, that not having a care in the world has a certain flavor you only recognize in memories.

We arrived in New Sylians in due time, not soon enough for our youthful excitement, but we were all a bit sad to be back on land. A steamboat is a magnificent thing and brings out the wanderlust in the meekest of people. It's different than traveling by horse or by train, and nothing ever compared to it. We docked close to sunset, and wandered through the big city. Tyler led us to a riverside tavern and we celebrated with a big meal that cost twenty crumbs each, and a five crumb cigar for each of us. Tyler turned green by the second puff and rushed outside to relieve himself of his supper, because no one had told him not to inhale. I only smoked half of mine before letting it go out. Randal smoked his until it burned his fingers, but we could tell he wasn't feeling so well either by the time it was finished.

We watched the men gamble at cards, and the women flirt with them and pair off as the night grew long. One rough shaven man in a long coat sat in a corner and watched everyone as he sipped at a mug of something. We had learned our lesson and kept our conversation to things like coon hunting and riverboats, not wanting to attract anymore unsavory characters. We slept in a room that night, all sharing a bed. It cost us a whole bite and we were almost too excited to sleep, but it was worth every crumb. We went over the plan, and even made a cover story in case anyone saw the tools we brought or asked questions.

We were dressed and downstairs before the sun was fully up, and planned our day over coffee, eggs, and ham. As we left the building the same man that had been watching the crowd last night was on the porch, smoking a pipe.

"Mornin' boys. You're up early," he said with a voice of gravel that spoke of years of smoking and drinking.

"Morning, sir," I replied, "We got business to tend to."

"What sort of business do three boys that stay in a seedy hotel in the dock part of New Sylians have before the sun even peeks over the buildings?"

"Ain't nuthin' much. Just looking to get some tools for the farm we work on. We took a riverboat in to get them, and the overseer gave us only enough to do what needs to get done."

"Well, you boys be careful."

"Oh, yessir. We will!" I replied as Tyler pulled on my sleeve to follow him and Randal.

Setting out into the morning bustle was an adventure of its own. Horses clopped along and wagons rattled behind them, and shop-keepers swept their porches and walkways. The smells of the city were very different than anything we had ever experienced. Smoke hung over the buildings from coal and wood fires, and people everywhere shouted to sell their goods as we passed shops and carts. We kept an eye behind us, making sure no one was following us.

Soon enough Tyler found the entrance he thought was closest to the treasure. It was nothing more than a hole in the ground with a raised steel grating above it. A thick grey trickle of water from the street drained into the alley that housed it. No one paid mind to three boys squatting in a backstreet. We all three had to work together to pull it up, and we lowered ourselves over the side and used slippery metal rungs to climb down. The smell washed over us as we hit the bottom. We put bandanas across our noses and mouths to buffer against the stench. It was worse than a stable that hadn't been mucked for a month. We rushed through, eager to reach our goal because of our excitement, as well as the stink.

I don't know if we became used to the foul air or if it grew fainter as we moved from the wet parts to the less used and just damp portion of the sewers, but it didn't trouble us much after a few minutes. We lit a torch we'd brought with us to help show the way, and traveled along with care, stopping at any noise. Rats scurried about their business, bothered by the light, and water dripped down walls. Our footsteps echoed, making it seem like someone was following us. The shadows shifted and jumped with the flame, and our faces were a peculiar shade as we moved forward.

We came to an arch that had been boarded. Bricks had tumbled down around the single step that led into it. It looked unstable, but without a word we set to work, pulling the few tools we brought from Randal's knapsack. As we pried the boards loose they crumbled under our hands, having rotted through. The way was open within moments. We leaned in to see what was inside. The cul-de-sac was just larger than most horse stalls and stones blocked the only other tunnel out of the small room. In a corner was a crate the size of a steamer trunk.

"There it is, boys," Randal whispered.

We pushed forward and fell to our knees in front of it, Tyler holding the torch high. Randal and I pried the lid open, and we peered in to see what it held. There were books and sheafs of documents that been tied together with twine. We groaned with disappointment and began pulling the stuff out and tossing it aside, looking for something better than some stupid old papers. I hauled out a small wooden strongbox, banded in iron. It was heavy and we heard lots of small metal things sliding around inside.

"You boys find what you lookin' for?" came a graveled voice behind us. We spun to see the man that had spoken to us on the porch. His coat was drawn back and he had a revolver holstered at his hip. We backed away until we hit the wall. He must have saw the fear on our faces, because the look on his became gentle.

"Aw, it's alright. I ain't gonna hurt you." As he took the hand from his hip the coat fell over the gun. "I ain't gonna take what you found either. I just want the papers. My name is Norge, Croaker Norge, and I'm a detective. I work for the law... sometimes, and for other people sometimes. Right now, I think I can use the stuff you don't want, and even pay you for it."

"How much?" I asked, before I could stop myself.

He smiled, and we let out a collective breath we didn't realize we had been holding. A shuffling noise came from behind him and he spun, hand catching on the coat as he reached for his weapon. A wet thud sounded, his head snapped backwards, and he crumpled to the ground. Standing in the shadows of the arch was the last person we would have expected, or wanted, to see: Dark Dirk, and he had an axe in his fist. The end was wet from where he had hit the other man with the handle.

"Ain't no roustabout to help you here, boys," he growled, "and as soon as I take care of this one," he pointed at the prone figure at his feet, "I'm gonna take care of the three of you, permanently."

He took a step towards the fallen man, and raised his axe.

We grow up slow. It takes years to become a full grown adult, but I think you become a man in leaps and bounds. That moment my friends and I took a big step towards being the men we would be one day. It may have been how little sleep we had gotten the night before, or that I just wasn't thinking that day, but I don't think I have ever been so bold as I was that day.

"No sir, you got it wrong," I said. "Ain't one here to help you," I threw the coffer at his head.

He brought the axe down to knock it away, and missed. It only hit him in the chest, but it knocked the wind out of him. The small wooden box fell and busted open. We all saw the glint of gold in the torchlight as the coins bounced and tinkled across the ground. Randal leapt forward and slammed his shoulder into Dirk's midsection, and trapped the man's weapon between the two of them as they fell backwards in a heap. Tyler ran over and began stomping on the man's ankles and feet. But Dark Dirk was stronger than both of them together.

Dirk shoved with the axe and tossed them aside easily. He pushed to his feet and turned towards them. I could hear him chuckling as he kicked Randal in the belly. He turned his back to me, and that was his mistake.

"I'm really gonna enjoy this," he said as he raised the axe and towered over my friends. He never saw me behind him with the crowbar. It only took one swing and he was down again, falling on top of Randal and Tyler, both boys screaming in terror as he did.

He screamed too, but in rage. He rolled to his feet again. Everyone froze when we heard a pistol cock. Croaker Norge was leaning against the wall and holding his bleeding forehead, pistol in hand, with Dirk in his steady sights.

"Move away, boys," the detective said. We moved, Randal clutching his left arm as blood oozed between his fingers, and gathered together in the back of the cul-de-sac. "Now, roll over on your yellow belly, ya bastard."

Minutes later Dark Dirk was sitting with his back against the wall, hands manacled and feet tethered together with rope, so it would only allow him small steps if he tried to walk. Croaker was true to his word. He told us to collect the coins and he would lead us out of the sewers. He knew of Dirk, who was a wanted man with a bounty on his head. The detective told us to go back to the hotel and ask for Margie. She was the cook but had a fair hand with a needle and would see to Randal's arm. Croaker would bring us our reward in a few hours.

When we had made it out, we discussed just leaving, but Randy was bleeding something fierce, and we were afraid to not have it looked at. He played brave, but he was turning really pale. We went to the hotel. Croaker did turn up later, and gave us each ten bites. He said the reward for Dirk was fifty bites and we deserved more than half between the three of us. He also arranged for us to ride in a wagon train back north with a friend of his.

It took more than two weeks to get home, and we made new friends on the trip. The wagon master offered us a job if we ever wanted one, but I know he mostly meant Randal. Randal did more than his share of the work on the way back, even with fifteen stitches and his arm in a sling.

It was odd being back home after that. Some of our innocence was gone, but the small town we lived in was the same as when we had left. We saw it with different eyes though. We knew a little more and could see differences in everyone, even our own families, which a child never sees. It makes me a bit sad as I think back on it. But my uncle was the same. He didn't hide things, or wear a mask like most folks do. He spoke slowly and simply, and said what he meant. I respected him more after that adventure.

When I came walking back up to my house, I gave him a brand new buck knife, and he looked me up and down, and he knew I was different. He never said a word about it though. He just nodded, put a hand on my shoulder as he looked into my eyes, and nodded again. Randal moved out of his father's house by the end of the summer, taking on an apprentice role at the blacksmith, and within a year he began going on cattle drives. He did buy himself a horse, lariat, and a revolver with his share of the money.

Tyler went back to school and I never really knew what he bought. But he was changed too. He walked a bit taller, and looked his father in his eye when he spoke to him, instead of looking down and shuffling his feet.

I put a small bag of the coins under my father's pillow. I knew we had been having problems with money, and didn't know how to tell him that could help. I reckon he was too proud to take help anyway. He never knew where the money came from. He asked all the workers, and the couple of house servants, and even asked my uncle and me. But he never found out. A week or two after that I was sitting on the porch watching the tax man leave after being fully paid and my father going back into the house, not looking quite as tired and bent from the weight of his worries. I smiled a little bit and, as I turned, I saw my uncle leaning on the rail of the porch near the corner of the house.

"You're gonna be a good man," he said with a small smile, then turned and went about his business.

I didn't see as much of Randal and Tyler after that, as we did when we were kids. We had chores, or school, or a job. We got together when we could, during summer or winter breaks, or when a county fair, or a barn raising went on and we were all in town. We were still friends, but life moved on as we left our childhood and headed for adulthood. We would swap stories, but we all lived in different worlds now. I guess we always did, but we didn't know it when we were kids.

It was autumn of '29, and Tyler wore spectacles by then and had finished his schooling. He'd be going away to learn something else in the spring, something about being a pharmacist. Randal was between drives, living on a ranch and working as a hired hand until the next cattle run. I still didn't know what I would do, but I had been hearing the call of the river. My Pa had been sick last winter, though, and I was needed at home. He just couldn't work like he used to do.

Xaco had been a hot month, and the corn had thick husks that year. The squirrels had been extra frantic and gathering nuts early, and lots of them. The wooly worms had been extra slow and their fuzzy coats grew thicker than usual. Everyone knew we were in for a bad winter that year. That's why Tyler wasn't leaving until spring and the cattle drives had dried up early.

Randal, Tyler, and I were all on the porch of the new saloon playing checkers and drinking sarsaparilla. Well, it wasn't exactly new. It was built more than two years ago, but so little changes here that it was thought of as new. The railroad would be coming through soon. They had been laying tracks all year and we saw more strangers in town every day. The Aeifain and Gallix had moved in and built homes as the government gave away land grants, and the other immigrants were just starting to trickle in. It wasn't unusual to see a freed Rokrain, neither. So we didn't pay much mind when a man came clumping up the steps carrying bags, heading for the bar.

"I'll be damned," a voice of gravel said, and we looked towards it. There stood a rough shaven man in a long coat staring at us. "If it ain't the boys I put on a wagon train."

It had been four years, but Croaker Norge hadn't changed a bit, not even his coat. He could have just walked out of the sewer we had met him in, except that his forehead was healed. He didn't smell like a sewer anymore though. He smelled of oil and coal. I could smell it from three paces away, and he had smudges on his neck and on his cheek. He had been working some sort of engine.

"I was hoping to run across you. I have a proposition for you three. Interested? Come on inside and we'll talk. I'll buy you dinner," he said without waiting for us to answer, and turned and went inside. I looked at Randal and Tyler. With a shrug we stood, collected our drinks, and followed him.

We sat around a table that was set for dinner, but later would be used for cards. Croaker had taken off his long coat and we could see the same revolver on his hip. He didn't wear it low slung like a gunfighter; his weapon was a tool rather than the way he made his living. We made idle chit chat for a bit, discussing weather and our lives, catching up on things we had never discussed with the man. He had grown up here and left town soon after his Pa died, upsetting his Ma and leaving her alone. We all remembered Old Widow Norge. She had just died a few weeks back, and that was what brought him back to town. Back in New Sylians, Croaker worked as a private detective with a partner most of the time. The man that had run the wagon train we came back with had been a childhood friend of the Croaker's. He told us stories about his misadventures, filling the time while we ate. Norge was a simple man with a sharp eye for detail.

"You remember the papers in that chest?" he asked after the plates had been cleared, coming around to the point. We nodded and waited as he pulled out a leather tobacco pouch and filled his pipe.

"Well, I kinda cheated you boys. Now, I know you got

what you wanted, but I got much more. There were government bonds in those papers, and more. I spent the bonds, cashed them in and bought what I needed and some extras. But," he leaned in close and so did the three of us, "there was a map too, a map that leads out west to a stash of what appears to be more than just a few coins. I waited this long because I needed enough time to pass so no one else could lay claim to this. I could use some strong lads to help me, be my backup, and split the treasure with me. Interested?"

Four hours later we left, coat collars pulled up against the chill wind of the season, and headed home. We would be leaving at first light in two days. We would ride to the closest town that had a train that went west, which was about a day and a half southwest of us, and take the railway to Kalektat.

I told my family I would be gone about a month. My father gave me his warm coat and advice about traveling, camp fires, and coyotes. I'd heard tell of his time on the trail, but now he showed his experience. My mother fretted over me and didn't want me to go, but never said a word against it in a direct manner. Instead, she packed me tea, cheese and a quilt, and told me to wish on the moon if I grew homesick, because she would look up at it each night and pray for me until I returned home safely. My uncle gave me his service revolver, an antique which he kept in good repair, as he did with everything. He didn't give any advice. We had been camping together enough that he knew I'd be ok, and he hadn't forgotten my last trip. Leaving home went easier than I'd thought it would.

Randal didn't have anyone to ask permission of, or to fret over him. He just told the rancher he would be away for a few weeks and would be back soon. Tyler apparently had it a bit more challenging. His father outright forbade him going, and his mother wept, cried, and even fell to her knees to beg him not to go. He dealt with that for two days. I sometimes think Tyler is the bravest of the three of us. He's so meek most of the time, but he pulls up courage at the times it counts. I don't know if I'd have been able to go if my folks had been like his. As it was, he didn't fight with them or yell. He just told them he was going and let them say what they would. Before he left, though he wouldn't speak to him, his Pa gave him a medical kit and his mother gave him a kerchief full of sweets, and cried the whole time as we said our goodbyes. We could still hear her weeping as we rode out of town.

The trail was easy those first days. The weather was brisk when the sun was up, and the skies stayed clear. We slept under the stars the first night, but in a hotel the second. Croaker insisted on paying for everything, and always made sure we had jerky and hard rolls in our saddle bags. He also had a nice shotgun on his saddle. He bought the train tickets the next morning, and we checked our saddles and just carried our saddle bags into the train. You just feel like it's an adventure when you sling your saddle bags over your shoulder, know what I mean? One hanging in front, the other thumping your rump as you walk. It just makes you swagger.

Oh, and I should mention the hats. Hats are important when you're on the trail. They keep the sun from your eyes and your head warm. Randal always had a hat because of what he'd been doing for work, but Tyler only had a school cap and I usually wore a straw hat when working outside. We had to buy hats for this trip. Tyler went with a wide flat brim, and forgot to get one with a chin strap. That first day he had to chase it a half dozen times. We'd laugh every time and started calling him jackrabbit because of how he would hop after it, sprinting then leaping. That first night Croaker took a knife and some leather cording, and poking holes in the brim, made a strap for Tyler. I had a nice new cowboy hat, and the others kept telling me to curl the sides of the brim, which I did eventually.

We laughed a lot that first week. I smoked a cigar every night after supper, and Croaker and Randal smoked their pipes. Tyler didn't smoke; he never had another cigar, or anything else, after that one in New Sylians. We drank beer with our meals, and I think it was the first time that Tyler had drunk anything with alcohol in it. He was drunk before he finished his first one, and sick as a dog the next day. He spent most of the morning between train cars, sicking up.

When we arrived in the Kalektat territory, Croaker bought some more horses and a small wagon. We saddled up and headed out. It was warmer there in the day than it was back home, but it could get to freezing at night. Kalektat was a wild place back then, having been made a territory about twenty years before, and having been a part of the Federation side in the war. Adoma Dasism lived in the northeast and Whulek in the east of the territory. We were going to ride right in between the two nations. We took a southwest trail directly through a forest of petrified trees. They were hard as stone in some places. The land was dry and beautiful, but rough. Great cracks went across the land, and hills rose up that had bands of color from brown to red. We had never seen things like that before. We even saw the abandoned jade and ivory pueblos of the Dasism, great buildings carved right out of the stone.

We stopped and traded with the Adomas when we crossed their path. It was tense, but not too bad. We were more worried about the Whuleks, and we'd meet them soon enough. We'd been riding for five days when we saw the first scout. We watched him, and he watched us as we rode past. About three hours later we saw a party of a dozen Whulek heading our way. We reined in and waited. Croaker had been prepared for this.

When they arrived, he showed them some furs, and spoke a couple of words in their tongue. They wouldn't smile; mostly they glared. But they settled down and took our gifts, and gave us a bone handled knife in exchange. We knew we'd been cheated, but the safe passage we got in the bargain was more than a fair trade. We spent the night around a campfire with them, and they played wooden flutes and tapped out rhythm on hide drums, as we passed a canteen of whiskey around and ate fresh rabbit. In the morning they were gone.

Tyler was out of sorts because he liked to know what he was getting into, but hadn't been able to research for this trip. Croaker and he spent hours each night going over the notes and maps, while Randal and I played dice on the hard packed earth. It was two days later we saw the small mountains to which the map pointed. It was an abandoned mine that was the first marker. We had to move slow after that. We were looking for a small side camp about a kilometer away that had been abandoned a couple decades ago. We almost missed it, and if it hadn't been for the rotting outhouse, we might have never known we found it. A small creek ran past it and Randal found the cave entrance, which had been dynamited and closed.

We camped that night, preparing everything for the morning. A few hours after sundown, we saw another campfire a few kilometers away and kept ours small, hoping not to be seen. It didn't work. A bit after the sun came up, a dozen men rode into our camp. They looked like military but were a ragtag bunch, their uniforms piecemeal and dingy.

"What are ya'll doing out here?" asked the one in charge, a weasel-like man with a beard that wouldn't grow right. He smiled and you could see his few remaining yellow teeth. A big man was at his side, cradling a double barrel shotgun, and another man on the other side looked like he could be his brother. That one had a mean scar running along his cheek and a twitch that was distracting.

"We got a right to be here," Randal said with a sneer.

"Oh, you do? I don't reckon you do. I think yer a bunch of squatters."

"No sir, we got papers," Croaker said, giving Randal a look as he pulled some documents from his saddlebag. Croaker had thought this may happen, and had told us to get some panning gear out. We had been squatting over the creek when the men arrived, and looked the part. The man took the papers and stared at them for a moment, his brow wrinkling in concentration.

"These ain't got no name on them," he said.

"No sir, they say that whoever holds them has rights to the four square acres that we're on. You see, right here?" Croaker tried to point at the papers, but the man jerked them away.

"I know what they say. Alright, it's fine. You go ahead and dig in the mud, but you ain't allowed to be blasting nuthin'. That's the law in these here parts."

"Yes sir." Croaker took the papers back, and tipped his hat at the man. They stared at each other for a long moment, and then the man looked away. At his command, the soldiers turned their horses and headed out.

"Keep panning boys. We need to give them a couple hours to get far away before we set up the explosives," Croaker said quietly, still watching the retreating men.

It was well past three before we started setting up the explosives to open the cave. I pointed out to the others how it had been blasted from above, so to close the cave, but not collapse it. We set long fuses, and went around the corner before setting off the eight sticks of dynamite around the edges of the rock pile and one barrel in the bottom. The barrel would go off first, loosening it, and then the sticks would go off and open it up enough for us to dig it out.

It worked beautifully. We had an opening large enough to crawl through from that, and the rest would have to be cleared by hand. We worked past sundown, hauling and passing loose stones, and when we settled in for dinner, we could walk into the cave if we bent over. We took a few torches in after we ate and were amazed by what we saw.

This was no mine shaft. The walls were smooth and clean, and Tyler said it had been carved by nature and water, not men and tools. It had the same layers of color that the mountains had and lines that flowed like liquid. It was beautiful. We went in with caution, making sure it was stable and wouldn't collapse. It was damp, but warmer inside. The cave winded around for thirty yards or so before opening up to a chamber. A path of water shone in the torchlight on the far side of the oval room, coming out of one wall and going into the other. The creek outside was fed by this cave.

A half dozen rotting crates were stacked neatly along the wall with Federation markings on them. Croaker smiled, and Randal whooped and ran forward with a crowbar in hand. He pried open the first one and when he lifted the lid, torchlight glittered on blocks of gold stamped with the mark of the army. We set it down and opened the other five. Four of them were identical in contents, but the sixth one held several boxes. Each of the smaller containers held various gems and jewelry. We were rich!

We backed the wagon to the opening and spent the next few hours loading it with the contents of the crates. We had to take the valuable bricks out one at a time, since the containers weren't sturdy enough to lift. The moist air and the years had done their work, and rotted the wood through. Croaker had us divide up the precious stones and hide them on our person. We wrapped them in cloth and hid in our boots, coats, saddle bags, and in small linen pouches that we tied around our neck and dropped down our shirts. We went to sleep giggling like we were small children that had snuck a pie that had been cooling on a window ledge.

When we woke we hitched up the two horses to the wagon and broke camp. Tyler and I went back into the cave to make sure nothing had been overlooked. We hadn't been in there five minutes when we heard a drawling voice yelling. We looked at each other and crept towards the entrance. Peeking around the last bend, we saw that the soldiers had returned, and their guns were drawn and pointed at Croaker and Randal. I could see the twitching man with the scar looking under the canvas tarps we had put over the gold.

"You were warned, but you didn't listen. Now you're under arrest, and you're gonna lose everything. Maybe even your lives!" the man with yellow teeth said with a tone of sadistic glee. I could see Randal trembling, and knew him well enough to know he was considering doing something rash. Croaker put his hand on the younger man.

"Yes sir. You can take us into custody. We ain't gonna give you no trouble," Norge said.

"Where's your other friends? Still in the cave? Well, since you opened it with blasting when you weren't supposed to, and you ain't supposed to even have it open, let's close it the same way."

One of the other men lit a stick of dynamite off his cigar and the short fuse sparked to life. He casually tossed it underhand to a spot above the opening Tyler and I were hidden in. I stood up and ran out with my hands held high, and I could hear Tyler scrambling behind me to do the same. The force of the explosion threw me forward four meters and I ended up face in the dirt. I coughed and sputtered and tasted blood in my mouth. As I blinked the dust out of my eyes, I realized Tyler wasn't beside me.

Randal ran towards the cave, and the men on horses were laughing as they got their mounts back under control. Croaker stood still, but I couldn't tell much else about what was going on, because I was heading back to the cave too. Tyler had almost made it out. He laid face down, rocks piled on his legs. Randal tossed them aside as he tried to uncover our friend.

The men let us continue. Once we had him freed, I began to check him. He woke screaming when I touched his left leg. It looked to be broken, maybe in more than one place.

"This'll need splinted, and he'll have to ride in the wagon," I told them. They didn't argue. They were too busy passing around the gems and trying on the jewelry the twitching man had found in the wagon while we helped our friend.

"We already took your weapons, and don't feel the need to tie your hands. If you run, we'll just shoot ya in the back, and then shoot your friends," the one in charge said.

We went along without a fight. It took a day and a half to get to the town at which the men were stationed. We tended to Tyler as best we could on the road, having him ride in the back of the wagon, and when we arrived we asked for a doctor. We were thrown in a stockade and ignored. Croaker took control, calling out for an officer in charge. He was taken away to speak to whoever ran the place. When he returned he told us not to worry; everything would be fine.

It took another four days before we were set free. When it happened, we were brought to the commanding officer. The older gentleman looked chagrined and stood at military rest with his eyes downcast as a very stern man dressed in a fine suit glared at him. The man in the suit was holding a letter from the Governor, as well as his own credentials as Senator. It seems our friend Croaker Norge knew a Senator, as well as the aunt of the Governor of the Kalektat territory.

With long and drawn out apologies, they returned our gold to us, though some was missing, as well as most of the gems and jewelry. But we still had what we had hidden amongst our own effects. The men hadn't even thought about searching us for more than weapons once they had found the loot in the wagon.

We spent the next two days in a fine hotel as a doctor checked over Tyler, and we left as soon as the man said our friend could travel. The Senator made sure we were given a stagecoach to use that would take us to Bannerstaff - a glorified mining town where everything is expensive and was littered with timber, sheep, and cattle - where we could catch a train back east. Croaker stayed behind, telling us we couldn't travel with that much gold now that it was known what we had. He would work out how to get us our share and send it to us as soon as he could.

We returned home as the first snows came. This adventure was another step in us becoming men. We learned about trust that goes deeper than thought. That gut instinct that steers you even when your head can't think straight. Like trusting Croaker, and him trusting people he had helped in his past. And not trusting every man who did work in the name of the government. When we left with only what money and precious stones we could carry, we learned another lesson: to accept what you get and not mourn what you never had.

My mother died that winter from pneumonia that had settled in her lungs. My father slowed down a bit once she was gone. He tried to throw himself into the work around the plantation, but never moved with the same energy he had before. I think he'd always thought she'd outlive him. Our share of the gold came in on a stagecoach in the spring, true to Croaker's word. He sent a letter with it explaining that he had to pay taxes on it, as well as pay a substantial fee to have it delivered, but it was still more than we'd thought possible. I gave most of it to my father and uncle to use for the farm.

I didn't see much of Randal or Tyler after that. I apprenticed as an engineer and in time became quite well known for my work with engines. I later tried my hand at trains, but it didn't hold the same joy as the river and a steamboat. It didn't have the freedom. You were stuck on two rails and always knew what every day would be like. On a boat, the river was always different. That was my love. There, I met the woman I married, and we lived on the river until our second child. Our first child was a son, and I named him after my uncle, who had died the year before. Our second child was a girl who we named after my mother, and after she was born we went back home and moved into my father's house. Though he adored my son, he loved that little girl more than anything. She was his sunshine.

Randal headed east, and I later heard he had joined the army and went overseas to Teurone. Tyler finished his education, took over his family business and was married before another year passed. Tyler's leg never healed right, and he walked with a cane for the rest of his life. But like the scar on Randal's arm from the axe, this was just another trophy to be displayed with pride. I would write to him and followed his life like a story. He had five kids, two boys and three girls. I went to the river, got on a river boat and thought to never look back. That's how it was, until I had a family of my own. Once I returned I saw Tyler in town, of course. Our children played together when there was an event that the town got together. But the world had changed, and you couldn't let your kids roam like we did when we were boys.

We did see Randal one more time in 6547. He and his wife came to town for Croaker's funeral. He stayed with me and my wife, and we spent a week together. Tyler joined us when he could. Randal married a Gallix burlesque dancer that he had met while in the Foreign Legion. He told us stories about the wars he saw and we were fascinated. We envied him for the constant adventure that he lived. They were headed out to Van Tisvelete after the funeral to open a dance hall where his wife would be the star.

Randal envied us though. He always was on the move, and never settled down. He watched Tyler with his five children and would get a sad look on his face. I think he was afraid he would be too much like his own father, and that is why he never had children. Tyler and Randal agreed I had the best of both worlds.

We parted ways on a gray winter afternoon. After the service for Croaker Norge, we stood around talking. It had been simple funeral. Not many people here knew Croaker, though he had hailed from these parts. He had come back to town about two years before, in 6545, and lived his couple of remaining years sitting on the porch of the saloon, smoking his pipe and grousing about the weather and trade.

The three of us - Randal, Tyler and I - lifelong friends, stood and waited as the small crowd dispersed. We walked back to the cave behind the cemetery, where it all started and wandered through it. We had come full circle, but things were so very different now. It was all so... plain. It wasn't dark or mysterious anymore. Not to our adult minds. The wonder was gone. We laughed and told a few jokes, and recalled the day we had found it. I think we were all a bit sad. Croaker's death hallmarked more than just the end of his life. It closed the final chapter in our great adventure. Randal left the next day, and Tyler and I returned to our separate lives.

I think of these friends and times when I sit alone on my porch with my cigar and whiskey. I stare out across my well-manicured lawn, not at all like the field of wild flowers of my youth, and I think how things have changed. How I see the world through my eyes, the eyes of other men, the eyes of my childhood, and now the eyes of my own son who is finding his own adventure in the world. I see him watch and emulate me, and I only hope he can look back on these days with the fondness and wonder that I had in my youth.

Travis I. Sivart

Appendices

Money Systems

Coins	Empire Writs	Federation Notes	Teurone Weights
One	Citizen	Bite	Royal
Half- 50	Half Writ/Emperor	Half bite	Noble
Quarter - 25	Quad/Senator	4 bit	Lord
Tenth - 10	Judge	10 bit	Master
Twentieth - 05	Officer	Nibble	Journeyman
Hundredth - 01	Century	Crumb	Apprentice

Calendar

The basic calendar is a lunar calendar. There are thirteen months in each year. There are twenty-eight days in each month. There is a new moon on the first day of every month. The first day of spring is on the Equinox.

Seasons	Months		Days
Spring	Loen	1.	Ginof
	Hapok	2.	Bestuf
	Axara	3.	Mida
		4.	Therin
Summer	Surem	5.	Uthr
	Santara	6.	Dunwith
	Xaco	7.	Lasin
Autumn	Harton		
	Thon		
	Ault		
Winter	Witen		
	Maleo		
	Frear		
Thaw	Milwen		

Want a free ebook?

Go to
http://www.TravisISivart.com/FreeBook

About the Author

Travis I Sivart lives in a state of flux between Richmond, VA and Washington, DC with his son and cats. He has written and published poetry and short stories, as well as editorials on manners, pipe smoking, and medieval re-enactment. He can be found at www.TravisISivart.com.

If you enjoyed this book…
Please let others know by reviewing it on Amazon or Goodreads, and let others know your thoughts!

Other books by Travis I. Sivart

Aetheric Elements: The Rise of a Steampunk Reality
Automatons and airships, bustles and beasts, corsets and curses, dandies and dastardly deeds, all await you as you explore the cultures which evolved into a Steampunk industrial civilization. An anthology of nineteen tales of terror, mystery, and adventure.

Steampunk For Simpletons: A Fun Primer For Folks Who Aren't Sure What Steampunk Is All About
A primer followed by a guided tour through the world of steampunk, from the basics such as where to go and what to do, to the aesthetic of the arts within steampunk.

27 Thoughts on Enjoying Life
Twenty seven thoughts on helping create happiness in your personal life, success in your professional life, and even manage depression on a daily basis by suggesting ways to improve and maintain your mental, physical, and emotional well-being.

Journal of a Stranger
The thoughts, ideas, philosophies, and inspirations of a time traveling adventurer. Delving into the psychology of man, life's eternal questions, burning passions, and the quirky pseudo-science of his mind, and more.

The Downfall: Harbinger
The Talisman came again, but this time it didn't leave. The magical emanations of the comet have brought terrors from the bowels of the earth and increased the powers of an insane necromancer. The chaos above brought out others seeking to wrest control of the land. Five people from different walks of life are thrown together by these events with the knowledge that the world as they know it is ending.

Made in the USA
Lexington, KY
23 May 2017